THE COLLAGEN COVEN

ANA PAULA VASQUEZ

Belladu Ltd

Oakwood House, Guildford Road, Bucks Green, Horsham, West Sussex, United Kingdom, RH12 3JJ,

Copyright @ Ana Paula Vasquez 2025.

Ana Paula Vasquez has asserted her right to be identified as the author of this work in accordance with the Copyright, Designs and Patents Act 1998.

Published by Belladu in 2025.

This novel is a work of fiction. The characters, names and incidents depicted in it are the work of the author's imagination. Any resemblance to actual persons, living or dead, events or localities is purely coincidental.

Print book ISBN: 978-1-7394427-4-3

ePub ISBN: 978-1-7394427-5-0

All rights reserved.

No part of this publication may be reproduced in any form or by any means, mechanical, electronic, photocopy or otherwise including information, storage and retrieving systems, without permission from the author.

For Gê, Nina and Bella

Acknowledgements

I am lucky to have been born into the family I was. We stuck together despite all the challenges and adversities; we have been separated by distance; we lacked things, even health at times, but never love and care for each other. I have also been blessed with the friends I've made along the way. Some have been by my side since the beginning, some I've met at high school, university or later at work. Some were friends of friends or amazing neighbours that life brought to live near me at different places, at different times. Love you all, you know who you are.

Thank you to my husband and kids for the unconditional support and everlasting patience during my long hours working on this book after my day-to-day work and many working weekends. Thank you to my brother and my two sisters-in-law for the constant support. Thank you to my grandma, my mother and my daughter for being such strong women and for inspiring me, every day. Thank you, Angela, for the beautiful cover photo. Thank you, Kim Farnell, for the editing and Gabi Moraes for the graphics. It has been a pleasure to work with you.

It takes a village, a community, a coven. It takes a parent, a relative, a friend, a teacher. It takes patience, dedication, respect and most of all, it takes LOVE.

Prologue

'Look at her. Isn't she perfect?' Teresa was mesmerised by the tiny girl in front of her.

The three girls loved looking after baby Karishma. Teresa's father had remarried and his new wife, Purnima, had a baby daughter. Teresa wasn't jealous. On the contrary, she was happy, as she'd always wanted a sister. Since her parent's divorce, five years ago, Teresa had lived in Brazil with her mum, returning to London for four weeks every summer to stay with her dad.

Christina's and Petra's parents were neighbours, and their mums had attended the same antenatal classes. Teresa's father, Robert and her Brazilian mother, Ines, moved to the same cul-de-sac in Islington, north London, when Teresa was one year old. Ellie and her neighbour Margaret had been pregnant with Petra and Christina respectively at the time. The three families became close. When Robert and Ines got a divorce, Teresa moved back to Brazil with her mother. Robert and Ines remained close friends, and every summer Teresa would come to London to spend time with her dad and to see her best friends, Christina and Petra.

July was always her favourite time of the year. Teresa got to enjoy summer twice, every year, both in the northern and southern hemispheres. The three girls would wait impatiently all year to be together. But this time it was even better than usual. Teresa got to see her best friends and meet her new stepmother and stepsister.

'She's gorgeous. I love babies. I want to have a lot of babies when I grow up.' Petra said in between blowing raspberries on Karishma's tummy.

The little girl giggled out loud.

'I'm not sure about many babies; I want to be a mum as well, but I want to travel the world first.' Christina said, whirling around with her arms wide open. 'What about you, Teresa?'

'I'm not sure about babies. I think I want to be a lawyer like my parents, or maybe a rock star?' Teresa started singing a Brazilian bossa nova song, and Petra and Christina covered their ears with their hands.

'Oh, well, you may start learning how to play an instrument. You aren't the best singer.' Petra said acidly.

'OK, then I might marry a rock star. I can't play anything and apparently I can't sing either.' Teresa made a face, pretending to be upset until the two other girls laughed.

'Seriously, if you had magic powers and could be or do anything, what would you do?' Christina asked.

'Teresa would be able to sing,' Petra said.

'Yes, I'd have a great voice, like Tina Turner.' Teresa agreed.

'I'd be the most talented artist, and people all over the world would pay trillions for my art.' Christina said.

'What about you, Petra? Would you be a singer too? We could form a band,' Teresa said.

Petra's expression suddenly changed and she looked sad. 'I'd be a witch. I'd have powers to create magic invisible strings tied up to everyone I love, and make sure they'd always be with me. That they'd never leave.'

Petra's eyes filled with tears and Teresa and Christina grabbed her in a hug. Even Karishma joined in. Petra's mother, Ellie, had left the day before. It wasn't that she didn't love Karishma, but she was a free spirit. She'd left Petra's father to do the hippie trail through Europe and Asia with a group of like-minded friends. Petra wasn't old enough to understand her mother's choices and was convinced that somehow Ellie had left because of her.

'We'll always be with you.' Christina kissed her friend on the cheek.

'Always, forever and ever.' Teresa kissed the other cheek as Karishma looked at them with a smile on her face.

1

Goodbye, Petra

'She wanted it to feel like a life celebration, a party, not a traditional and sad funeral.' Christina explained to Mrs Phillips, the gossip from number four while trying to convince herself it was a good idea to have music, colourful cupcakes and balloons scattered around Petra's parents' house for such an occasion.

'I understand, dear, but isn't it a bit… disrespectful?'

'No, it isn't. This is exactly what she'd have wanted. Petra left explicit directions about her funeral. She even selected the playlist.' Teresa was quick to jump in, noticing Christina's red face and realising her friend was slightly upset by the moaning lady going around complaining at everyone and making snide comments. 'And she didn't want us to call it a funeral, by the way.'

'Well, if she wanted… I guess… it may not be as disrespectful as it looks and sounds.' Mrs Phillips rolled her eyes.

Christina was about to open her mouth and put

an end, a harsh end, to the discussion when Teresa wrapped her arms around her friend and pulled her away, and whispered in Christina's ear, 'Not worth it. Leave it. She's a bored lady, set in her ways; she doesn't mean any harm.'

'She didn't leave a playlist.' Christina had tears in her eyes.

'Nope, she didn't, and she didn't have to. We know all her favourite songs. We're doing it as she wanted, you know that,' Teresa insisted. 'And you're going to get the same when you die — and that won't happen anytime soon. And so will I, and Karishma and all of us in our big, bonkers made-up family.'

'You're right, you're always right.' Christina grabbed a glass of wine. 'Remember that amazing trip to Spain, the four of us girls?'

'Of course I do.' Teresa closed her eyes and pictured the four of them on a lovely afternoon in a bar by the sea at the Costa del Sol. Petra, Karishma, Christina and herself, eating tapas and drinking sangria as a man played an acoustic guitar nearby. She couldn't remember how the conversation had started, but they were all a bit tipsy and had started making their funeral plans.

'*With balloons and good music rather than the old sad vibe of a traditional funeral that makes everyone depressed. That's not me.* I remember Petra's words clearly,' Christina said.

Petra had always been full of wit, always trying to see the positive side of things, and she was always organising parties and events to keep their families united.

'True. She said no matter who left first, those who stayed behind should sing and dance and remember all the amazing things we'd done together. And Petra insisted we should call it a life celebration, not a funeral. I also remember,' said Teresa.

'That was the *collagen coven way!*' Karishma had overheard them and joined in. 'I remember us dancing salsa all night and lip-syncing words we didn't understand.'

The four friends, Petra, Christina, Teresa and Karishma, called themselves the collagen coven — an inside joke they'd come up with after their gap year in Brazil when they were very young.

'Mrs Phillips is mad at us for all the music and balloons.' Karishma pointed at the lady across the room with a grumpy face.

'Oh, God. Ignore her.' Teresa grabbed her friends by their hands and started dancing gently as *Don't stop me now* started to play.

'Mum's favourite!' Marina, Petra's daughter, joined them, wiping away a tear. 'I can't believe she's gone.'

'I know, darling.' Teresa, who like the others, had always been close to Marina, gave her a kiss on the forehead. 'We're all shattered, but you know how your mum would have wanted us to be strong. Especially you.'

'I know, it's just too soon. I always thought she'd

live forever, that nothing could stop her.' There were now too many tears rolling down to be wiped as Marina closed her eyes and kept moving her head and body slowly to her mum's favourite song.

Christina gave Teresa a look as if saying *I've got this,* and patted Marina's arm. 'I know it's not the same, but you have me. I mean, you've got the whole coven, Teresa, Karishma and myself. And you need to be strong for the kids. They'll miss their grandma.'

Out of all her mother's best friends, Marina had a more formal relationship with Christina. Although she was more distant from Marina, she was also the one she admired the most. Maybe because Christina was always the strictest, sometimes even stricter than her own mother. Whenever Marina had done something wrong, Teresa and Karishma would quickly help her cover her tracks, but not Christina. She'd always make Marina come clean, and give her an earful, whenever needed. On the other hand, she was also the one who gave Marina amazing gifts and pep talks before a tough exam at school or before prom night. While it was fun to have people spoil you rotten, it was also good to know there was someone to steer you in the right direction.

When Marina fell pregnant at eighteen, the same age her mother had been when pregnant with her, she told Christina first, even before Petra. Despite being visibly concerned and somewhat sad,

Christina had vowed to support her no matter what she decided, and was by her side when she broke the news to her mother and father.

Petra was jealous that Marina had told Christina first, but she got over it after a while. Marina had kept the baby, and, looking back, she wouldn't have done it any other way. Joe, her first boyfriend and the father of her child, hadn't stuck around for long, but Louisa, her daughter, had brought so much joy to her and to Petra and her best friends that life was unimaginable without her.

Having a baby so young didn't derail her life, mainly because she was lucky enough to have her mother and the collagen coven always there, supporting her, looking after the baby for her to return to her studies and go to college a year after giving birth.

Christina, Teresa and even Karishma, who was still very young at the time, had done the same for Petra when Marina was born. They'd all jumped in and helped raise Marina. They took turns and shared childcare duties between themselves so Petra could go to back to her studies. It takes a coven, they used to say, a *collagen coven*.

'I love that you call yourselves witches. Mum loved that.' Marina's voice was heavy with nostalgia.

'Your mum always said she'd rather be a witch than a fairy. Petra used to say that witches were strong women who weren't afraid to speak their minds or follow their dreams, even if they ended up on a bonfire,' Teresa said. 'And we always promised ourselves that we'd never let the collagen run out. As if we could control that!'

'Not so sure about the collagen, but definitely witches, the good kind.' Karishma laughed. 'Just like your mother's friends in Rio. Ines told me all about it.'

◆ ◆ ◆

Across the room, Mrs Phillips was now haranguing Marcus, Petra's ex-husband and Marina's father. 'Don't you think this *life celebration* is a bit tone-deaf?' she asked. 'I think they've gone too far. They're even dancing.'

'Look Mrs Phillips, no matter what I say, you wouldn't understand. They had something special, a real bond, the four of them. They knew each other so well and would do for each other more than one can imagine, so yes. They have the right to throw a life celebration event as Petra wanted, instead of a funeral, and yes, I believe this is exactly what my ex-wife would have wanted. If you'd excuse me, I must check on the food and drinks.' Marcus politely left the old woman and made his way to the kitchen to check in with the caterers.

Mrs Phillips, a widow who'd lived in the cul-de-sac where the girls grew up since anyone could remember, was shocked and embarrassed by the way her objections had been promptly dismissed by Marcus. She decided to give in and quickly grabbed a glass of prosecco, making her way to the food table. *At least they'd put on a nice spread,* she thought, digging into some canapés.

♦ ♦ ♦

'How are you holding up?' Daniel, Teresa's husband, asked as he approached Marcus. 'You remained close, even after your divorce. I've always admired that.'

'I'm still shocked but coping. It was so unexpected. I honestly thought she was going to make it,' Marcus said. 'We'd always believed we'd die old after a long battle with some nasty disease like dementia. But no, she went on and sped up the game by having a heart attack. Not fair.'

'I know, right? We never expect that, a heart attack. It may be a good death for them but it's hard on the ones who are left behind. No time to process. Not that any death is easy, but it was so, so sudden. Teresa is putting a strong front, as she always does, but I know she's broken inside.'

'I know, mate. The girls were close. I don't remember them without each other, and I've known them forever.' Marcus looked at the four friends gently dancing around his daughter.

'And about this coven thing? It started when you were all in Brazil, right?' Daniel was surprised they'd never talked about it, as the two men had known each other for a long time and were reasonably close.

'I was on the same trip, the gap year in Brazil, but not there at the moment they decided they were a coven, a collagen coven, as they call it.' It was now thirty-six years since Petra, Christina and Teresa had come up with the group's name during a New Year's Eve ritual by the sea. 'Something to do with a Brazilian pagan religion and hot ladies at the beach.'

'Yes, they mentioned something along those lines,' Daniel reminded himself. 'They're a crazy bunch,' he said in an affectionate tone.

Marcus and Petra had been divorced for fifteen years. They'd been good friends since tenth grade, when they'd met. The friendship of Petra, Christina, Teresa and later Karishma was so strong they'd become a big family. A made-up family, as they liked to say. Their children saw their parent's friends as aunties and uncles, because it did feel like they were sisters and part of the same family.

'Hello, everyone.' Teresa spoke loudly, trying to grab everyone's attention.

Marcus and Daniel turned in her direction.

'We promised we wouldn't give a long eulogy, but we want to say a few words.' Teresa looked at Marina and gestured for her to go ahead.

'My mum was full of life,' Marina started. 'She always saw the bright side of everything. For Mum, the glass was always half full. She never liked funerals, and she always said life had to be celebrated, not death.' She wiped a tear. 'Not that me and Mum's best friends have to explain ourselves.' She threw a look in Mrs Phillips's direction as the lady had also approached her earlier regarding the tone of her mum's funeral party. 'But my mother would have wanted you all, her friends and family, to take a moment to remember her life, her happy moments, the way she'd never allow a birthday to go by without a bunch of balloons or cupcakes and how she loved to dance and to listen to her favourite songs. There was always music in her life. She'd dance as she cooked meals for me, always picking my favourite songs, and then for my children and Christina's children. She used to take us to concerts, sometimes wearing glitter boots or whatever the occasion demanded.' She looked at her oldest daughter, Louisa, and at Samantha and Vanessa, Christina's daughters, who were sitting nestled around each other on the floor. They were all close in age.

Everyone laughed. Declan, Petra's eighty-something father and Ellie, her mother, included.

Christina approached Marina; it was her turn to say a few words.

'Petra was my soulmate. We shared a life, we shared sad moments, happy moments, secrets, laughter and tears.' Christina said with her eyes puffy from crying. 'I can't believe she's gone, but I won't be sad. I owe it to her to try to keep strong. And to be cheerful and happy as we remember the moments we had together. We all should.' Christina glanced at Karishma.

'I've known Petra, Christina and Teresa for most of my life,' Karishma said. 'I've always looked up to them and they' always included me in their lives, despite me being a *bit* younger.' Everyone laughed as Karishma was around a decade younger than the rest of them. 'As soon as I was old enough, they let me join their wine Thursdays and have always made me feel part of their team. We'll miss you, my dear, but you'll always be with us in our hearts.'

Teresa started to talk again, her voice filled with emotion. 'My friends here, they've said everything. My life wouldn't have been the same without my dear girls, not even close. And Petra, she was our rock and our glue. I'll do my best to keep living up to that and to be as strong as she was and to keep us united.' She concluded with 'I love you,' quietly looking upwards.

The party continued for a couple more hours with music, food, drinks and dancing, just as planned. Despite it being a sad occasion, the friends managed to bring some happiness and even laughter into it, like Petra would have wanted.

As people started to leave, someone knocked on the door. 'I'll answer it,' said Karishma, already making her way to the door. 'Someone must have forgotten something.'

As she opened the door, a handsome young man, likely in his mid-thirties, was standing there. 'Hi, sorry to barge in. I can see you're having a party. I'm looking for Mrs Margaret Lanyon's daughter,' he said politely.

'It's not a party. I mean, it's a funeral, but it's also a party, in a way. Where do you know Christina from? Have we met?' Karishma was intrigued.

'No, I don't think so. You don't know me. Neither does Christina. I'm the son of one of her father's friends and I wanted to have a word with her. I only had her mum's address and the old lady across the road told me I'd find her here.' He pointed at Mrs Phillips, who'd left the party and was going into her own house. 'But hey, I didn't know it was a funeral. I'm sorry for your loss. I'll come back another day.' The man looked awkward, as if he had something delicate to say to Christina. And whoever had died, a funeral certainly wasn't the right moment for that.

'Christina's here; I can call her for you,' Karishma offered, even though she didn't know who the man was. He could be a thief or a sociopath. She was now sure she'd never seen him before, and he seemed oddly unsettled. But there was something about him that made her feel safe, not threatened.

'Please don't. I don't think this is the best occasion to talk to her. I'll come back another day. It's not urgent. Thank you and sorry again. Sorry for your loss and for turning up at such an inappropriate moment.'

'No worries. Do you want to leave a message for her? Or something? I can take your number; she can give you a call when things are more settled, perhaps?' Karishma said.

'That would be great. Thank you. I'm Theo, by the way.'

'Why don't you send me a text so I can save your

number.' Karishma gave him her phone number and he obliged. 'Got it. Saved. I'll pass it on to Christina.'

An awkward silence followed their contact information exchange. They stared into each other's eyes for a moment, both trying to ignore how uneasy they felt. 'Great! Thank you. Nice to meet you. I mean, nice of you to take the message,' Theo said and he then left.

'Who was that?' Marina approached Karishma.

'Someone looking for Christina. Not sure. I got his number. I'll give it to her later.' Karishma made her way back inside with Marina.

As evening fell, the guests slowly left. Only the caterers, Petra's parents, Christina and her mum, Margaret, stayed behind.

Ellie, Petra's mum, had obviously been crying. Losing a daughter was the most unimaginable pain. 'You can leave now, dear. Go have a rest. Your mother looks tired. Take her home. I'll clean up tomorrow.' Ellie placed her hand on Christina's shoulder.

'I will. Thank you. It's just... I wish this was all a dream, a bad dream. I'm sorry. This must be a hundred times harder on you.'

'It is, darling, it is. Losing a daughter or son alters the natural order of things. It should never happen. But as you all said, she'd have wanted me to be strong. For my granddaughter and my great grandchildren. And my old man there.' Ellie looked tenderly at her husband who was sitting alone in the corner of the living room, staring at a family photo above the fireplace. Declan was almost ten years older than Ellie, and Petra's death had left him devastated.

Ellie was a nickname for Eleftheria, meaning 'free' in Greek. She was of Greek descent from her father's side. Ellie and Petra had shared a troubled relationship for a good period of their lives. Ellie had left Petra's father, Declan, when Petra was a young girl. She'd joined a group of friends, and a Spanish lover, on a long self-discovery trip, only to come back a few years later, when Petra was already a mum, when the Spanish lover had found a new love interest younger than her, and the friends had turned out not to be as friendly as she'd thought. Declan had always been crazy about Ellie and took her back — they never spoke about it again. Petra eventually forgave her mother, but was never as close to her as she was to her father.

Declan had been the one who was always by her side, the one who guided her, who comforted her when she had her heart broken, who looked after her whenever she was sick, the one who shared her hard moments and the one who celebrated all her achievements along the way.

'Goodnight. Be well.' Christina gave Ellie a kiss and grabbed her own mother by the arm. 'Mum, let's go. I'll stay with you tonight. Peter's taken the kids home.'

Later, in her childhood bedroom at her mother's house, Christina reminisced about her friendship with Petra. They'd always been friends. They'd gone to the same schools, shared the same friends, liked the same things. Both had studied art and they had a business together, an art gallery. They even looked like each other, and would sometimes lie that they were sisters. Usually, people would fall for that.

Petra was fair-skinned, of athletic build and had wavy blonde hair. She had beautiful green-blue eyes, just like her mother, Ellie. Petra was the life and soul of the party. Always in a good mood, she loved a good joke and social events with her friends and family.

Like Petra, Christina also had fair skin and wavy hair, but she wasn't blonde, she was more like a golden brunette. In the last few years, she'd let herself go a bit. She'd put on weight and hadn't exercised much. She was a year younger than Teresa and looked younger than her age as well, just not as much as her friend. Christina was harder to decipher. She was polite and intelligent, more reserved than Petra, but no less interesting and joyful.

She knew sleeping wouldn't be easy and even though she wasn't a fan of drugs, she took a mild sedative to help. As the effects started to kick in, she thought about when she was at the hospital holding Petra's hands, trying to reassure her friend, saying she'd recover, even though the doctors had said that the heart attack had been major and she was in a critical state.

'He's back. He came looking for you, but we connected and… I'm sorry. I couldn't help it.'
Petra

wasn't making much sense as she was under heavy sedatives.

'Who came back?'

'He did. He did. He's here, in the UK.'

Petra was getting agitated — the monitor showed her heartbeats. 'You must rest. We'll talk about it later, my dear.' Christina wasn't sure what Petra was talking about, but the last thing she wanted was for her friend to get worse.

'I know we will, but there's something else.' Petra took a deep breath and stared Christina in the eyes, looking lucid for a second. 'You must tell her if I don't make it. Promise me,' Petra said in a broken voice before falling asleep to never wake up again.

Why? Why did you have to go like that? What were you talking about? And about her — why did you ask me that? I don't think I have the strength to deal with it, not now, Christina thought before falling asleep.

2

Christina

Christina had planned to take two months off work to deal with her loss. She'd feared that going back to work would throw her into depression since she'd have no alternative but to face the fact that her best friend and business partner wasn't there anymore.

Christina and Petra had had a passion for arts since they were children. They'd always had plans to study art and open an art gallery together. After finishing their A levels, they'd gone together to Brazil to meet their friend Teresa for a long holiday over Christmas and New Year's Eve, and that turned into a gap year.

Christina went straight to university when she returned, where she got a degree in fine arts, and Petra came home with a baby. Teresa, who was already enrolled in law school in Brazil, had a complete change of heart and moved to the UK with her friends, ending up with a master's in business studies.

When Marina, Petra's daughter, was seven, Petra

went to university and got a degree in art history. A few years later, together with Christina, she opened an art gallery on Upper Street, just a few blocks away from their houses, as they all lived near each other and their parents.

They'd been doing quite well. They had a good reputation in the art scene and had managed to make enough money to live comfortably.

A month after Petra's death, Christina decided that staying at home wasn't helping her grief. *An idle brain is the devil's workshop,* she thought.

'Morning, Patricia. How are things?' Christina greeted her manager, who happened to be Hugo's, Teresa's older son's fiancée. Patricia had worked as a graduate at Marina's gallery a couple of years back and they'd become friends. Marina was the one who'd introduced her to Hugo.

'Christina! I wasn't expecting you yet. How are you? It's so nice to have you back at work.' Patricia walked towards her with open arms and a smile on her face.

'Fine. It's been hard, but I'm hoping being back at work will help take my mind off the fact that Petra isn't coming back. Life goes on.' Christina spoke as if she were trying to convince herself.

'I guess that's the right attitude. You and your friends are all so strong.' Patricia gently squeezed Christina's hand as she spoke. 'I'd like to believe that I've managed to keep things in good shape here at the gallery. Let me know when you're ready and we can go over last month's sales. It's going well. We've sold several works, including two of yours.' Patricia sounded proud of how she'd managed the gallery without her bosses around.

'It's been a while since I sold any of my art. Which pieces?' Christina felt joy for the first time since Petra was gone. She was a great artist but hadn't invested much time producing anything new or promoting her work since her father had fallen ill a few years back.

'Well, we've sold "Wave" and "Sandstorm", two of your favourites, if I remember right? Both to the same buyer, that client of Petra's from South America.'

'South America? That's interesting. I don't remember that client. We usually sell South American art to British and Europeans, not the other way round.'

Christina was intrigued. Through Teresa's mother's connections, they represented a lot of South American artists, especially Brazilians. 'I wasn't aware that Petra had a south American client.' Christina made a gesture as if trying to piece together the new information.

'Maybe she forgot to mention it to you. She sold a piece to him when you took time off when your father passed away. That was over a year ago. He came in when he saw the Peruvian *retablos* on display and ended up coming back a few months later and Petra sold him a few more pieces.'

Retablos are exquisite Peruvian folk artworks that showcase miniatures inside boxes depicting history, dances and other cultural scenes. They were colourful and vivid, very different from Christina's work that had been sold, which were both monochromatic, blue and teal shades, very minimalist.

'Strange that Petra never mentioned him. We always talked to each other about our clients. Oh well, I'm happy to sell my work.' Christina turned to make her way to her office. 'Give me a couple of hours to read my emails. I'll have lunch with Karishma and after that we can go over last month's activities.'

'Sounds good to me. Bianca will be on the afternoon shift; she can see to the clients, and I'll be all yours.' Bianca was the art student they'd hired a couple of months ago to help them at the gallery.

Christina sat at her desk and took a deep breath. Her office and Petra's were divided by a glass wall with blinds. The blinds were half closed, but she could still see Petra's desk. She remembered them communicating with their eyes and gestures whenever they were on the phone with a demanding client or dealing with any unpleasant business. Now there was just silence, silence and emptiness. Christina felt as if she were missing a limb. She walked over and shut the blinds. *I'll ask Patricia to turn Petra's office into a meeting room. I can't do it myself,* she thought. Looking at Petra's empty desk was too much for her. *What were you up to, my dear friend? Who was this mysterious client?* Christina wondered if he was the man Petra had mentioned at the hospital.

Promise me. Petra's voice echoed in her mind.

When I'm ready, when I'm ready, my dear, Christina said to herself and she started checking her email, trying to stop her thoughts of Petra and the mysterious man.

Time flew by and it was noon before Christina knew it.

'Hello, ready for our lunch?' Karishma appeared at Christina's office door. 'Look who the cat dragged in.' Teresa jumped from behind her.

'Hi! I thought you were away for work!' Christina glanced happily at Teresa. 'And good to see you, too.' She gave Karishma a hug.

'I managed to dodge that ball; I sent someone else and have agreed that I won't travel for a while. I'm tired of jet-setting.' Teresa looked relieved, as she'd been constantly travelling for work.

'Good for you! Does that mean we'll have more time to see each other?' Christina said with her hands together in a praying gesture.

'Hope so.' Teresa gave Christina a hug and a kiss.

'It's been a while. I haven't seen you, my girls, since Petra's life celebration event.' Karishma said, avoiding the world funeral as per Petra's wishes.

'Yes, it's been a while and I didn't have breakfast, so let's go for brunch.' Christina grabbed her bag and led the way out.

'Are you back on your fast?' Teresa asked sceptically. She wasn't a big fan of diets.

'Sure, I am, have just started… again. Collagen coven, remember?' Christina said laughing. 'And I'm back at the gym as well. Trying not to stop this time. We always promised each other to try to keep fit and healthy, remember?'

Christina was self-conscious about her body. Menopause had hit her hard, and with her father's long time health issues, she'd been through hard times. George had struggled with Parkinson's disease until his death, and she'd helped her mother look after him. That plus Petra's death had taken a toll on her mind and body. She kept promising herself to exercise more and watch her diet, but she kept relapsing into bad habits.

'True, I've never stopped gym and I'm always on a diet,' Karishma said. 'We don't share your Brazilian genes, my dear.' She looked at Teresa.

Christina nodded.

'There's a new bistro on Highbury Grove. I noticed it when I went for a run the other day. Shall we try it?' Teresa suggested.

'Sure, sounds good. I'm starving.' Christina followed her, linking arms with Karishma.

'Wow, cosy. I like it,' Karishma said in a sassy voice as they entered the stylish new restaurant.

'Me too,' said Teresa.

'Me three.' Christina was impressed with the chic and minimalist interior design — pale walls with stylish design furniture, an elegant light wooden counter and lots of natural light. She was very particular when it came to anything related to art or architecture and was clear about what she liked or disliked.

'Can we start with a round of mimosas, please?' Teresa ordered.

'Wow, you mean business, don't you?' Christina asked. 'I have to go back to work. I have a long catch-up meeting with Patricia today.'

'You'll be fine. Just have one. It'll help you relax,' Karishma said.

'I *am* relaxed. And don't you have patients to see after this?' Christina gave Karishma a reprimanding look.

'Nope, finished for the day. My shift started at two am. I'm running on fumes, from here to bed.' Karishma was an anaesthetist and worked crazy hours, two days a week at A&E and the rest of the time, she attended private clients.

'How is Patricia doing? Is she any good?' Teresa asked.

'She's actually quite good. Too keen sometimes, but she's doing great. She puts in plenty of effort and I'm lucky to have her. I don't know how else I'd have managed since Petra left us without Patricia. Have her and Hugo set the date yet?'

'Not yet. And I think that's a good thing,' said Teresa. 'They should get to know each other better. They got engaged so fast.' Teresa sounded unimpressed.

'Teresa, you sound like my mother!' Karishma said jokingly.

'Hugo is an adult. They've been living together for a couple of months, and I think she really does like him.' Christina held Teresa's hand as she spoke.

'Well, you're right. You're right, I do sound like an old person, and it's their decision. They should know better than me. Don't worry, I'm not getting involved.'

Teresa was about to take a sip of her drink that had just arrived. 'Wait! Let's toast first!' Christina said.

'Of course, my bad.' Teresa raised her glass.

'To Petra and to the happy rest of our lives,' said Karishma.

'To Petra.' They all cheered.

Lunch was delicious. Karishma had the onion soup and Christina and Teresa both had a croque madame. They shared a bottle of Viognier.

'How does it feel to be back at work without Petra?' Teresa asked Christina.

'Not easy. To be honest, it's only been a couple of hours and Patricia and Bianca have been great. And seeing you guys helps a lot,' said Christina. 'Being home wasn't helping me. I've been thinking about life and the decisions I've made. Maybe I'm bored.'

'I've been feeling exhausted but I don't think I could stop working. I'd be so bored that I'd probably be grumpy and argue with Daniel all the time,' Teresa joked.

'I'd kill for time off. Not having to work long shifts, wake up in the middle of the night...' Karishma closed her eyes as she spoke, as if dreaming.

'Do you ever feel that you're living in a dream, like a parallel life? As if the real you were somewhere else, living the life your younger self had dreamt of instead of what reality turned out to be?' Christina asked seriously.

'Wow, you've been thinking a lot, haven't you?' said Teresa.

'I have. It's a strange feeling. I love my children more than life itself, but sometimes I wonder what it would be like if everything had been different. Remember when I wanted to travel the world?' Christina said.

'And I wanted to be a rock star.' Teresa laughed. 'Well, I've married a musician, at least.'

'You did, indeed,' Christina said excitedly. 'I don't know. I've been thinking, maybe thinking too much. I remember when we were teenagers — we had it all scripted. The idea of what our lives would be seemed so perfect before our lives happened. What changed? Did we get it all wrong?'

'Are you saying you're unhappy? What's wrong?' Teresa grabbed Christina's hand.

'Peter and I have distanced ourselves from each other. The kids are grown now and it's like they were the glue. They were what we talked about all the time. And now they're independent — well, Harry is only fourteen, but you know what I mean. Now it's like we have nothing in common. We don't talk anymore. We rarely have sex.' Christina's face was red.

'Well, who has time for sex these days?' said Teresa. 'Work, house chores, children, work. All that exhausts us and when the kids finally follow their own path, the libido has long left the building. And let's agree, menopause is a bitch.'

'I feel there's an abyss between me and Peter. He was never hands on with the children, which left me exhausted, and maybe I was never good at communicating. Maybe there are things I should have told him. It feels like the connection is broken, a chain link is missing, lost in secrets of the past.' Christina gave Teresa a cryptic look.

'I don't think you should go there,' responded Teresa, taking the hint.

'Go where?' Karishma asked. 'Did I miss something?'

'No. You didn't. Just things in general. I should have told him how I felt when I was left alone with the housework and looking after the kids while he worked. That's all.' Christina sounded convincing enough.

'I feel like that all the time.' Karishma looked down. 'I mean, like I'm living someone else's life. Like my own life was stolen, my plans, my dreams.' Karishma was now tipsy.

'I'm sorry Kari! I didn't mean to stir up the past.' Christina realised she'd hit a nerve.

'Don't be silly. I just feel that I've drifted away

from my own life sometimes. But the good news is that, most of the time, I do feel happy.' Karishma reassured Christina. 'I have you two. We've created an amazing family together, and that's enough. I'm just tired. Ignore me.' Karishma yawned.

Teresa looked at her stepsister and then at Christina. She was worried about them. 'How is Marina doing? I've been thinking about her. She and Petra were so close.'

'I know. I'm worried too. I always worry about her. Petra lived for her daughter and now she's gone, it must be so hard for Marina,' said Christina.

'I'll invite her for a drink at some point. We should all do it.' Karishma was nearest in age to Marina and they were close.

The three friends continued talking for a while and then walked together to the gallery, where they all hugged each other again and said their goodbyes.

'Sorry again. I was so silly today. It was good to see you,' Christina said.

'Don't worry, we're all a bit all over the place these days,' Teresa reassured her. 'I'm here if you need me, as always.'

'Oh, I almost forgot.' Karishma said. 'There was this guy at the life celebration event for Petra. He was looking for you.'

'A guy? Looking for me? Who was he?' Christina asked.

'I don't know. His name is Theo, and he was about thirty-five, tall, handsome. He said he was the son of one of your father's friends.'

'Hmm. Tall, dark, handsome? Is that a spark in your eyes? Did you get his number?' Teresa teased Karishma.

'I did, in fact. For Christina.' She gave Teresa a 'shut up' look. 'I'll share the contact with you when I get home — my phone is dead. And for the record, I'm not interested in romance anymore. I gave up on dating a long time ago.' Karishma had a bit of an aggressive tone in her voice.

'Well, you should get back on that horse. It's been too long, Kari. You're still young,' Christina said firmly.

'Bye, bye, girls. Believe me, I'm fine.' Karishma walked away, waving her hands in the air without looking back. She was far from fine.

'Do you think I upset her earlier?' Christina was now alone with Teresa. 'All that talk about life and dreams. Do you think it hit a nerve? I didn't mean to.'

'Karishma's fine. It was a long time ago. She needs to live her life a bit more, but she'll get there.'

'I worry about her sometimes. I guess I worry too much. I've just been thinking about everything. Our lives, our choices, you know.' Christina looked into Teresa's eyes as if saying, *You know exactly what I mean.*

'There's nothing to think about. Don't go down that rabbit hole. You know where it leads. Our choices are done. Some stuff is best left in the past where it belongs. We've lived our lives, and it's all good. Isn't it?' Teresa asked.

'I guess.' Christina was thinking about Petra's last words. 'It's just… too much.'

'I know. I know. I'm also suffering. We've all been through hardship at some point. But we've stayed together and now we need to be together more than ever.' Teresa gave Christina a hug. 'Now go. My future daughter-in-law is waiting.' She glanced at Patricia and waved with a smile.

◆ ◆ ◆

Later that night while she was at home, Christina's phone beeped.

Theo — invite to WhatsApp said the text on the screen, followed by a message from Karishma.

This is the guy that was looking for you. Sleep well. Love you, Kari.

Who are you, Theo? Christina thought. For a second, she wondered if he was Petra's client, the one mentioned by Patricia. Her thoughts were interrupted by her husband's voice.

'How was your day back at the gallery?' Peter joined her in bed and gave her a kiss on the cheek.

'Good, I guess. Patricia has done a great job this last month.' Christina was pleased with her. 'The girls came by for lunch. It was great to see them.'

'Coven lunch? Sounds good. You girls are bouncing back. I'm glad.'

They looked at each other and Peter started

kissing her neck softly. 'I've missed you. Glad you're back. You haven't been yourself lately.'

Christina was taken by surprise. She initially enjoyed the moment of intimacy; they hadn't had sex for almost two months now, but her mind was somewhere else, Petra, the gallery, the mysterious client and now this man looking for her.

Christina and Peter had a good marriage, but it hadn't been easy. They had three children. Samantha, the oldest, was now twenty-two and living by herself at university in Bath. Vanessa was turning eighteen soon and completing her A levels, and Harry was fourteen. Peter had been always present, but Christina was the one who'd carried most of the load of looking after the children and the house.

Peter was a successful businessman who'd dedicated most of his time to work. Even though the children were older now, and she didn't have to do as much for them, Christina was exhausted. She'd been exhausted for years.

She loved her husband, but since Harry's birth, her sex drive hadn't been the same. She'd had a complicated birth and was certain she'd had postpartum depression.

And after years of juggling, work, children, household chores, Christina lacked self-esteem and intimacy was difficult for her. 'Sorry, love. I don't feel ready.' She gently moved Peter away.

'You don't need to be ready. Just relax.' He moved

even closer and started kissing her again.

'Relax? Why do men think we just lie there and think of England, when it comes to sex? I mean, if my head isn't there, I can't enjoy it. And my head is not there,' Christina yelled with contempt.

'What do you mean? Where is your head?'

'Is that all you've heard?'

'I'm trying to tell you to let go, enjoy the moment. We rarely have moments like this.'

'I can't. I'm tired, I'm constantly thinking about the kids and work, and it hasn't been easy since my dad… and Petra.'

'So, what does it mean? We must have an abyss between ourselves because life has been tough?'

No, because I kept secrets from you forever and that's consuming me, she thought, but she simply said, 'I don't feel open, ready for intimacy, I don't feel great about how I look.'

'You look great. After all these years, I'm still very much attracted to you. You should be glad, right?'

'I should be glad you're attracted to me. What do you mean? Do you think you should be going after a twenty-five-year-old? Is that what you mean?' Christina had only focused on part of what Peter had said and was now upset.

'No, that isn't what I meant. Sorry. Look, Christina, I'm still into you. Despite you being so cold and distant. I'm still here, still loving you, desiring you, your body, all of it, and sometimes I feel like you're not attracted to me anymore.'

'This isn't all about you! I don't feel well and I don't feel happy right now. I'm not in a sex mood. Maybe I'm not attracted to myself right now, so I can't be attracted to anybody else. Give me space. I'll get over it. I just need space. I need to feel like myself again. Please understand.'

'You haven't been in a sex mood for a long time. I'm patient, but this is starting to affect me, my confidence, my mood and our marriage.'

'It's not you! Why is everything always about you?' Christina raised her voice in frustration.

'Everything's about me? It's all about you, all the time. I try to help you with the kids and the house, and you're never happy,' Peter yelled.

'Help me? Maybe if you didn't think you had to help me but instead if you realised you should share OUR obligations — maybe then I'd have time to be in a better sex mood.' She got off the bed and locked herself in the bathroom.

'Great! That's how it goes. All I did was kiss you! I'll sleep on the sofa!' Peter left the bedroom, yelling to make sure she could still hear him.

Christina was crying. She turned on the shower as she didn't want her children to hear her. They must have heard her and her father arguing and that should be enough. They didn't need to see their mother crying.

3

Karishma

The alarm rang promptly at one in the morning. Another day was about to start. Another early shift.

Karishma opened her eyes and within two minutes, she was already having a shower. She was a good, renowned professional, dedicated to her patients, but the life of a doctor isn't easy, especially in A&E. She lived close to the hospital where she worked a couple of nights per week. An hour was long enough to have a shower, a cup of coffee and check in at work.

Karishma loved her job, but sometimes she felt so tired that she questioned her choice of career. All she wished, in that moment, was to go back to bed. She even considered calling in sick, but her sense of responsibility and commitment to her patients was stronger than her exhaustion.

Christina's comments the day before had hit a nerve. Karishma had been hiding behind work for the last fifteen years. Now, at almost forty-six, she wanted to believe that motherhood wasn't for her, but it hadn't always been like that. As she got dressed, she couldn't stop thinking about Iain. It was a long time ago, but the memories were still so fresh in her mind, it still hurt.

She'd met Iain twenty-two years ago when she was a medical student; he was a great photographer and adrenaline junkie. It was love at first sight.

'Come on, please come with me to the party,' her university dorm roommate had insisted. 'That guy I fancy will be there, and I really want to see him. He has a brother who's very hot, and he's already a doctor. I'm sure he'll be there too, and you'll like him. Please!' The girl was persistent.

When she was at university, Karishma was always committed to her studies and rarely went out partying. She'd rather go out with her ten years older stepsister and her two best friends, or go home to her family whenever she had a chance.

But that night she'd given in. She'd been studying crazy hours for the last few weeks, eating breakfast, lunch and dinner in her bedroom and — to her own disgust — had even skipped showering on a couple of days. She could do with a break.

It didn't take long after they arrived at the party for her friend to get drunk and hook up with the hot doctor herself, the brother of her alleged love interest. The guy was indeed hot, but he wasn't Karishma's type. He was handsome but also arrogant and his Don Juan vibe gave away his intentions. He was interested in having fun with easy-to-impress medical students and was clearly trouble. Karishma wasn't interested in dating, especially getting involved with someone who was probably a player.

His brother, who was also very handsome, was the opposite. Quiet and apparently shy. As Karishma's friend and the hot doctor couldn't take their hands and mouths off each other, Iain, the brother, and Karishma — who were both visibly embarrassed — decided to get a drink and move away from the couple.

'Get a room,' Iain said jokingly as he and Karishma walked to the bar. They talked for a bit and quickly agreed that the party wasn't their scene.

'Want to grab something to eat? I'm starving.' Iain said, tapping his belly.

'Sure. I'm hungry too. But what time is it?' Karishma wasn't sure they could find anything edible in the middle of the night.

'Past midnight pizza! My favourite. Follow me.' Iain led the way through the Soho narrow streets in central London. He knew a place that served pizza all night long. *Not the best pizza on earth, but after a few drinks, any pizza is gold,* she remembered him saying.

The party wasn't far from the university campus in Bloomsbury and Soho was only a stone's throw away. To this day walking in central London at night is difficult for Karishma. Her and Iain would do it a lot, sometimes riding bikes looking for hidden places to explore or simply chasing the magical streetlights during the Christmas holidays.

Back to the present — Karishma had been so lost in her thoughts that she'd lost track of time. It had been a long time since she'd stopped to constantly think about Iain and the time they'd had together. But Christina's comments the day before had somehow brought the thoughts back. She quickly got ready and went to the hospital — she was almost late.

Karishma's shift was unusually calm that night. She even had time to have a proper break for a coffee and biscuits. Her shift finished at one in the afternoon. She was tired but too alert to go home and sleep. It was a beautiful day, and she'd not have another overnight shift for a few days, so she decided to spend some time alone and enjoy herself. Karishma decided to go to for a walk with her dogs, a Rottweiler called Otto and a cream Labrador called Star, in Richmond Park on the other side of the city — it was ages since she'd been there. When she was a child, Robert and her mum used to take her there to see the deer, and it was a place where she always felt happy. After a long walk and a lot of deer sighting, she went for a late lunch at a gastropub by the river.

Karishma enjoyed having lunch by herself. She'd got used to it since Iain had departed from her life. She'd go to nice pubs and restaurants and enjoy the food and a good glass of wine, sometimes even a cocktail, all by herself while taking the opportunity to think about her life, her goals and so on. It was her way to meditate and try to mentally put her ducks in a row.

She ordered a martini to start. *Why not?* It was her favourite drink, and she deserved it. She ordered a pumpkin soup for starters and the sea bass for her main course. Halfway through her meal, she noticed a man staring at her from the bar. She didn't recognise him at first but after a closer look she did.

The man had clearly recognised her and made his way to her table. 'May I?' He pointed at the chair.

'Theo, isn't it? Please, sit down.' That was unusual for her. Karishma had always been conscious about strangers. She wouldn't even dare try online dating, not after all the true crime podcasts she'd listened to where the culprit was, in most cases, the hot date who the victim had met online. *At least I didn't meet him online*, she thought.

'Yes, Theo. And you are? Sorry I didn't get your name the other day. How rude of me.'

Handsome and polite.

'Karishma. My friends sometimes call me Kari,' she answered. 'Has she called you?'

'Has who called me?' He paused for a second. 'Wait, of course, Margaret Lanyon's daughter. No, she hasn't, not yet. I assume you passed my number onto her?' He seemed lost for a minute and that was a red flag in Karishma's mind. *He could be a serial killer, after all. He could be making it all up.*

'Where do you know them from, again? You mentioned your father knew her father?' Karishma said in a colder tone of voice.

'My mum. I mean my mum knew her father.

Look, I know it sounds strange. Me coming out of nowhere asking for your friend, I mean, I assume Christina is your friend? It is Christina, right?'

'Why are you looking for her when you don't even know her name? What's this about?' Karishma was now agitated.

'It's nothing bad. I mean… it's complicated.'

Theo paused for a second. 'My mum, she was good friends with George Lanyon, Christina's father. I met him several times. My mum and I were very fond of him, and we only recently learnt about his death.'

'And what do you need to talk to Christina about?'.

'My mum used to date him… a long time ago. Before my father. And she's shaken by his death. I thought I could find out more about what happened to him and ask if he ever mentioned my mum, that kind of thing. Do you understand?'

'Not really. You're chasing the daughter of your mum's ex-boyfriend to ask if he'd ever mentioned her?' Karishma couldn't make sense of it. 'He passed away about a year ago and it was a hard time for Christina and for Margaret. He had Parkinson's and his last year was tough.'

'I'm sorry. I didn't mean to cause pain. I thought it would be nice to connect, that's all.' Theo sounded as if he was being honest.

'I understand, kind of. But please be careful if Christina calls you. As I said, they've been through a lot.' Karishma was no longer thinking he was a psycho, but she wasn't sure he was telling the complete truth, and she didn't want her friend to suffer even more.

'I will. I don't want to cause any pain, I promise. I just wanted to know more about him. He used to come round sometimes, and we shared good moments, I mean, my family and George.'

'What about your father? Was he around? What did he think of your mum's male friend coming around to hang out?' Karishma wasn't scared anymore but was still puzzled.

'My father died when I was a baby. And as I said, George was a really good friend to my mum.' Theo's voice quivered with emotion.

'I get it. I hope Christina calls you and you can get whatever it is you want without causing any distress to her or Margaret.'

Karishma looked at her fish that was cold by now.

'Oh, sorry. I interrupted your lunch. I'm sorry… again.'

'You say sorry too much,' Karishma noted.

'I do, don't I? Sorry.' Theo laughed. 'Oops, did it again.'

They both laughed.

'I wasn't that hungry, to be honest. I was planning to save space for dessert, anyway.' Karishma pushed her cold dish away.

'If you don't mind, I'd love to share dessert. I mean, order my own but have it here, with you, not eat your dessert, to be clear.' Theo smiled and looked at Otto and Star sitting by her feet under the table. 'I hope they don't mind. I hadn't noticed your dogs.'

He was even more handsome when he smiled, and Karishma couldn't help but feel charmed by him. She responded fast, before she had time to think it over, and surprised with herself, she said, 'Great! I mean, Otto is the kindest dog you'll ever meet and Star wouldn't hurt a fly. He looks scary but is sweet as anything.' She patted Otto's head. 'I wouldn't mind the company. Lemon pie for me, you?' she said as the waiter approached the table.

'Warm chocolate brownie with salted caramel ice cream, please.'

'I'm jealous now.'

'I'm happy to share. If I can try the lemon pie? It was my second option.' He laughed.

'A brownie was mine.' She stared at him. Something about this man was attractive to Karishma. It was like a magnetic force. She'd felt it the first time she'd seen him at Petra's life celebration. And now he was there, staring into her eyes. That made her feel happy and uncomfortable at the same time.

'Bids of a feather.' Theo continued.

'I beg your pardon?'

'Sorry, I meant we have the same taste for dessert. Birds of a feather flock together, as they say. And oops, I said sorry again.'

'Yes, you did. And yes, I get it. I had an early start

today and feel a bit tired. It's my turn to say sorry. Do you live around here?' she asked, to break the ice.

'Yes. We live round the corner. I always come to this place; I love their coffee. And their dessert.' He smiled.

'We? Do you have kids?' Karishma asked.

'Yes, I have one. He's seven. David is seven.' His face brightened as he spoke his son's name.

'Seven, an interesting age.' Karishma tried not to show her disappointment on her face. *Of course he has someone.*

'He's a handful but a lovely boy. What about you? Any children?' Theo glanced at her hands — no rings.

'Nope, just me. I mean, me, Star and Otto. I don't have kids.' She felt her cheeks grow hot. 'How come you're having a pint in the middle of the afternoon? No work?' She immediately realised she was being intrusive.

'I know. Odd, isn't it? But I do work. I have a small graphic design company. We develop graphics for TV, for live broadcast. We've just finished a big job, worked overnight with my team for a deadline earlier today. I've sent everyone home to rest and came here to reward myself with a pint... and dessert.'

He grabbed a spoon full of brownie with dripping ice cream. 'What about you?'

'I'm a doctor. Anaesthetist. Had an overnight

shift and here I am, rewarding myself with a stroll in the park, a cocktail, a nice lunch and dessert with a stranger.'

'Wow. A lot of rewards.' He smiled. 'Do you live around here?'

'No. I live in northeast London, near Petra's parents' house, the house where the funeral — life celebration— was.'

'Why don't you say funeral?'

'It's a thing between my friends and me. We agreed, long ago, that funeral is a heavy word. We decided to call it something else whenever one of us died.'

'I see. And why did you come all the way here? Have you looked me up? Are you stalking me?' Theo smiled.

'Of course! What would you expect-me to do? I had to find out who the man looking for my best friend is,' she said in a serious tone.

'Really?'

'Of course not! I came for the park. It's one of my favourite places. I needed to calm my mind for a bit.'

'I see. Shoot, you scared me there for a second.' He looked at his watch. 'I didn't realise it was that late. I must go; I completely lost track of time!'

'You don't want to leave the missus waiting.' Karishma regretted saying that as soon as the words left her mouth.

Theo glanced at her and offered a big smile. 'No missus, just my mum. I live with my mum and my son. Not that I'm a mum's boy, but she isn't well, and I decided to move back with her after David's mum and I separated so I can keep her company and she can help me look after David.'

'Sorry, I didn't mean to assume.'

'No worries.' He stared into her eyes. 'Let me get the bill, please.'

'No way, you only had dessert.'

'I insist. It was a pleasure to meet you properly. You can pay me back with a coffee sometime?'

Her cheeks were totally red now. 'Coffee would be good, thank you.' She was relieved there was no missus in the picture.

'You have my number. Call me.'

He left the table, paid the bill at the counter and looked at her one more time, making a goodbye gesture with his hands.

What was that? Karishma was still surprised with herself as she took the tube back home. Since Iain, she hadn't dated anyone. Not seriously, though she'd had a handful of short romances with men who were as emotionally unavailable as herself. Not that the dessert sharing had been a date, but this guy, Theo, he'd caused feelings that she hadn't felt in a long time. It had been a lifetime since butterflies had flown in her stomach and she'd forgotten how good it felt.

Later that night she decided to send a text to Theo. After all, what harm could it cause?

Thank you for lunch, I had a good time.

She got a reply immediately.

> It was my pleasure, had a good time too. Looking forward to being invited for coffee.

She didn't know why, but she felt guilty, guilty about having fun and feeling happy because of a man. *What am I thinking? He must be ten years younger than me and I know nothing about him.* Karishma's mind was trying to find a way of sabotaging her, punishing her. *Why do I have to be so hard on myself?*

She remembered the last time she'd spoken to Iain. 'I'll call you as soon as we get back from the top. Love you.' And then… pain, only pain and sorrow.

She tried to block her thoughts and shifted her mind to the surprisingly good day she had. *I have the right to be happy and it wasn't a date. I'm just meeting new people, that's it,* she tried to convince herself. It was like she had voices in her head, as if Jiminy Cricket and his evil twin were having an argument in her mind. *I won't tell the girls yet. Not until he speaks to Christina, at least. I think there's more to that story. I'll wait and see how this plays out.*

That night Karishma slept better than she had in a very long time.

4

Teresa

Teresa had been married to Daniel for thirty years. She was twenty-six and a young professional when they got married. They had three sons; besides Hugo, Patricia's fiancée, she had Alan who was twenty-five and Alex, seventeen.

Daniel and Teresa were very different, but somehow managed to live a good life together, rarely having an argument.

Teresa was a fierce businesswoman, the CEO of a cosmetics company, while Daniel was a music teacher. She was doing well and at the beginning of her career when she fell pregnant with Hugo. She then took a break of four years, staying at home with the kids until Alan, her second son, was two. She went back to work, and by the time Alex was born, she was already in a good position at her company. With Alex, she managed to return to work after only ten months.

Daniel's work was much less glamorous and demanding. He only worked a few hours per week and was more like a stay-at-home dad. He didn't make a lot of money, but he was lucky to come from a wealthy background, so they managed well even when Teresa was on maternity leave.

She'd always thought it was great to have Daniel look after the house and the kids while she pursued her career. But sometimes it bothered her that Daniel seemed to lack ambition. Sometimes, she wanted him to be more proactive and succeed in life. He enjoyed teaching primary school children, but she always had the feeling that he felt unfulfilled and that he'd somehow left something behind — his dreams of stardom, for instance — to be a fully committed father.

Teresa worked hard. Although Daniel did most of the house and kids' work, Teresa contributed a lot. But in her head she'd always blamed herself for not dedicating time enough to the boys. She'd always felt torn between building her career and raising her children.

Often, she thought about what would have happened if she'd never left her hometown, Rio de Janeiro, and her home country, Brazil. If she'd stayed with her mum instead of moving to the UK with her friends after that gap year. She enjoyed the way things seemed to function much better in the UK as a country than in Brazil, but she could never get used to the weather.

Teresa had only lived in Rio until she was twenty, but she'd never forget her life growing up by the beach, in what, she now fantasised, was like an eternal summer. When Teresa was a teenager, her school was only a block away from the beach and it was usual for her and her friends to wear bikinis under their uniforms and go to the beach after school.

Teresa was crazy about the sea. That was her element, the place where she felt whole and happy, and yet she'd decided to live most of her life away from the sunny beaches where she's grown up. Even though she didn't regret it, part of her wondered what would have been like if she'd never left, if the collagen coven hadn't happened.

Her mother, Ines, still lived in Brazil and Teresa, Daniel and the boys went every year to visit. They'd been there for the last time six months ago and Teresa was feeling homesick already.

A childhood friend from Rio whom she hadn't seen in a decade was in town and had invited Teresa for lunch. Renata was an English teacher. She was very good looking with blonde hair and piercing green eyes, tall and incredibly fit. They met at a lovely restaurant on Charlotte Street.

'Renata, I'm here!' She waved as she noticed her friend coming in.

'Hello!! How are you? Oh my God, you look amazing!' Renata gave Teresa a big hug.

Teresa did look amazing. She was tall with a toned body and flawless skin. Her mother, Ines, was a beautiful black Brazilian woman and her father a fine Englishman with a James Bond way about him. As a result, Teresa was a mixed-race goddess.

'I don't! You do. What's in your water? I want some of that.'

'It's so good to see you. How are Daniel and the kids?'

'They're fine. The boys are all grown up. Hugo's engaged, Alan's moving to the US for work and Alex has a boyfriend. What about you and Miguel? Still together?'

'Oh, my dear, we have a lot to catch up on. How long it has been? Me and Miguel divorced six years ago after he got his twenty-something old secretary pregnant. Typical, isn't it? I never expected him to be such a cliché.'

'I'm so sorry to hear that. How are you feeling?'

'I'm feeling amazing. I got some work done on my body with the divorce money.' Renata pointed at her eyes, breasts and tummy. 'And hold your breath — I'm getting married again in two months.'

'Oh wow! You look gorgeous! Who is he?'

'She. She's called Maria Luisa, Malu.'

'I didn't know you were, I mean, girls?'

'Me neither. But it happened. Things have changed and I'm happy. Really happy.'

'And I'm happy for you. Let's have a toast, to happiness.'

'How are your friends? Collagen coven, isn't it?'

'Yes, you remembered that? They're fine. I mean, Karishma and Christina are fine. Petra passed away.'

'I'm so sorry. I didn't know she was sick. She was so young.'

'She wasn't sick. It was a heart attack. Very sudden and sad.'

'How are you all coping?'

'I'm fine. We're all fine. Not easy, but we're managing. The only thing we can do is to move on, and that's what Petra would have wanted us to do.'

They were chatting away and enjoying their lunch when Christina saw Daniel outside on the street. She knew there was a guitar shop nearby where he went for strings and imagined that was where he was headed. She was about to try to grab his attention when she saw him wave to a tall woman wearing a big hat and sunglasses, as if trying to disguise herself. She was walking in his direction. They briefly hugged and continued walking towards Oxford Street.

Teresa froze.

'Hello, are you there? You look like you've seen a ghost.' Renata grabbed her hand.

'Me? No. I mean, I'm sorry. I just remembered that I have a meeting in half an hour, completely forgot.' Teresa gently tapped her own head.

'No worries. I must go soon as well. Malu is meeting me at the Tate Modern. It's her first time in London.'

'You should come and have dinner with us at my place on Thursday. It's Daniel's birthday and we're having cake and prosecco. Bring Malu.'

'I will do. Well, great to see you.'

'You too, darling. Sorry to rush off in this way. See you on Thursday.'

Back in her office, Teresa couldn't focus on her work. The image of the blonde woman hugging Daniel was too vivid and disturbing. She called Christina.

'Hello. How are you?'

'I'm fine, just busy with the gallery. So much work to catch up on. I recognise this tone in your voice. What's wrong?'

'Can we meet for coffee? In an hour or so? I can come to the gallery.'

'Sure, come. I'll be here all day.'

Teresa went quickly back to her office. She sent a couple of urgent emails, made up an excuse to leave early, and went to the art gallery.

'Hi Patricia, is Christina here?' Teresa greeted her future sister-in-law with a hug as entered the gallery.

'She's in her office. Do you want me to call her?'

'No need, darling. I'll go there if she's free?'

'Yes, she's alone. Just go in.'

As soon as Teresa entered Christina's office, she started crying.

'What's happened? Sit down.'

'I'm fine. Close the blinds, please. I don't want Patricia to see me. I don't want Hugo to know.'

'Know what? You're scaring me.' Christina said, closing the blinds.

'I think Daniel is having an affair.'

'What?'

'I saw him with a woman today.'

'What the fuck? Saw him where? Doing what?'

'I was having lunch with Renata. Remember Renata, my friend from Rio?'

'Yes, of course I remember her. Didn't know she was in town.'

'Yes, she is. Anyway, we were sitting by the window at that cosy restaurant you like, near my work. And then I saw Daniel outside, across the street. Before I called him, I saw that he was looking and smiling at someone.' Teresa paused and grabbed a tissue.

'What happened? Did they kiss?'

'No. I mean, not that I saw. They hugged, briefly.'

'That's all?'

'They hugged, exchanged a few words and walked together towards Oxford Street.'

'Did he see you?' asked Christina.

'I don't think so.'

'Maybe she was a colleague?'

'A colleague? He teaches guitar and piano to pre-teens, for God's sake. The woman looked like a top model.'

'Maybe she works at the school. Maybe she's a teacher.'

'And what would they be doing together? He never mentioned any young, gorgeous friend from work,' said Teresa.

'Don't jump to conclusions. Why don't you talk to him?'

'No. Not yet. It's his birthday on Thursday, remember? You're coming, right?'

'Sure. But I'm sure there'll be an explanation.'

'I don't think so. We've been distant lately.'

'How? You've always been my dream couple.'

'Come on, you know things aren't perfect.'

'Nothing is perfect. No couple is perfect, we know that.'

'I know, but you're my favourite "not perfect" couple.'

'I don't know if we'll be a couple anymore,' Teresa sighed.

'Of course you will. You're being dramatic. I'm sure there'll be an explanation.'

'Please don't say anything. Not even to Karishma. I'll talk to him after his birthday. I don't want to change plans now. Everyone's coming, and the boys are excited about it.'

'I know they are. Alex came to see Vanessa last night and the party was all he talked about.' Christina sat next to Teresa and kept her hands on her shoulder until she'd calmed down.

'I feel better now. Talking to you made me feel better, as always.' Teresa hugged her friend. 'Maybe you're right, and this will be nothing.'

'I hope so. I don't know what's going on. Peter and I had a big fight the other night.' Christina took a deep breath. 'Maybe we're all having a mid-life crisis.'

'Why did you fight?'

'Over nothing, really. It was after Petra's life celebration party. He wanted to have sex, and I didn't feel like it. Haven't felt like it since Petra's death. I mean, I feel so sad. Sex is the last thing on my mind. We started saying things to each other and ended up having an argument. We haven't spoken much since.'

'Relationships are so hard.'

'After all this time together, life gets boring and somewhat sad if we don't keep working on ourselves. We get set in our ways, bottle up our feelings and then, the emotional cracks get bigger.'

'I know. I feel the same sometimes. The other day I was thinking of our gap year in Brazil.'

'Me too. I think about it all the time, lately.'

They exchanged a look.

'Do you regret it? Our choices, I mean. The coven…?' Teresa asked.

'No. I don't. Not all of it. I do wonder though how things would have been if —'

A knock on the door interrupted their conversation. 'Sorry to bother you,' Patricia said as Christina opened the door. 'I have that new artist here for you. Andrea from Peru.'

'Yes, sure. I forgot. She's amazing, a promising artist. Could you show her around? Give me a few minutes to finish talking to Teresa.'

Teresa was looking down, trying to avoid Patricia, seeing that she'd been crying. If Patricia noticed, she was discreet enough to pretend she hadn't.

'You were saying?' Teresa said.

'Nothing. Just that sometimes I try to imagine how things would have been if a couple of different scenarios had taken place, you know.'

'I do too. Do you think Petra was happy? Do you think she ever questioned things?' Teresa looked pensive for a second.

'I think she was happy, yes. Very happy. She gave up so much for Marina, but I think she was happy in the end. And I think she was seeing someone lately. Did she mention anything?'

'Not specifically, but she was cheerful lately, you're right. It would make sense that she was seeing someone. And before she died, she said we needed to talk, that she had something important to tell me. We didn't have time.'

'We didn't have time...' Christina wiped away a tear. 'Honestly, I don't regret any of it. We probably wouldn't have had the coven if things had been different.'

'You're right. I'd have been a lawyer in Brazil. I wouldn't have met Daniel and wouldn't have my boys.'

'And I have no idea what would have become of me. My life would have been different without all of you,' Christina said.

'But you know what? I wouldn't change having you, Petra, Kari, our kids — any of it. I wouldn't change it for anything.' Teresa hugged Christina.

'Me neither. Love you!'

'Me too. My sister from another mister! Now go see your artist from Peru. This sounds exciting.'

'It is. She's a good friend of mine and Petra's. We've met a few times in Peru. She does beautiful paintings, and we've been meaning to sell her art for a long time. Come, I'll introduce you.' They walked towards the gallery reception where Andrea was waiting.

After the introductions, Teresa said goodbye and went back home. Daniel was already there when she arrived, and so was Hugo. He had his own place, but he'd come round for dinner at least twice a week.

'Hi, Mum. Is everything alright?'

'Yes, sure, why do you ask?' *Patricia must have said something*, Teresa thought.

'Nothing. I mean, Patricia said you spent the afternoon with Christina. I was wondering if all was good at work.'

'All good. We miss Petra too much and decided to talk for a bit.'

'That makes sense.' He gave his mum a hug.

'How was your day?' Teresa asked Daniel.

'Mine? Good, all good. Had three lesson sessions at the school and then back home,' he lied.

'Well, that's good, I guess. New students?'

'Yes, I mean, not new. One was new, two were from another teacher who was sick. Younger students, I was covering for them.'

He could have at least pretended that he went to the guitar shop in case I saw him, since he was so close to my work.

'I'm exhausted,' said Teresa. 'You guys clean up, please. Leave a plate for Alex, he'll be late, and Alan is having dinner out. I'll have a shower and sleep.'

Teresa left the two men in the kitchen and retired to her room. She couldn't stop thinking about the woman with Daniel.

I'll confront him after his birthday.

5

Cake and Prosecco

It was Thursday and Teresa was busy organising the party. She had no time to prepare anything herself, so she ordered a big cake shaped like a guitar, cupcakes with keyboard cut outs on top, an amazing grazing board and, of course, *pao de queijo* – Brazilian cheese bread, something Teresa couldn't live without. She only had to go and collect the prosecco from her local wine shop.

Teresa and her family lived in a nice townhouse in Highbury, overlooking the park, not far from Christina and Karishma.

'Could you please organise the cakes in here?' Teresa gave instructions to the ladies she'd hired to help serve the guests. Most of their birthday parties were low key, but since it had been years since Daniel celebrated his birthday properly, and he was turning sixty, she'd decided to splash on a nice party. 'Alex? I'll go and get the wine. I'll be back soon. Would you please help these lovely ladies if needed?'

'Sure, Mum. Vanessa and Louisa are coming and they can help me as well.'

'Oh, are they coming early?'

'Yes, we'll hang out until it's time for the party.'

'Fair enough.' Teresa was happy that the children of the collagen coven were so close. Christina, Marina and Teresa had been pregnant at the same time. Christina gave birth to Vanessa first, Marina to Louisa a fortnight after, and Alex finally came two weeks after that. Petra became a grandmother, and Karishma had a new nephew, so they had plenty of new life to celebrate.

As Marina was so young, Petra had practically raised Louisa, with the help of her friends, of course. They all helped so Marina could continue to study. The three kids grew up together and became inseparable and the fact that their children — and grandchild, in Petra's case — were so close brought great joy to the group of friends.

'Hello, ladies. Do you want to come in? My mum asked us to help set up the party,' Alex said as he opened the door to Vanessa and Louisa.

'I didn't come here to help; you said you had something urgent to say to us,' Louisa reminded him.

'Don't you see? We've been scammed.' Vanessa lightly punched Alex in the chest, joking.

'I do have something to say and that's why I called you here. But Mum asked me to help so I figure you could all chip in — please?' Alex pulled up an irresistible begging face.

'You lazy ass! What can we do?' asked Louisa.

'You can spread the flowers around. I know you love flowers.'

'Yay!' Louisa was happy as she saw the pile of flowers waiting to be arranged into vases around the living room.

'And me? Should I manage her?' Vanessa asked hopefully.

'Nope. You should help arrange the plates and the prosecco flutes.'

'Boring!' she protested.

Once the flowers, plates and flutes were set, the three of them went across the street to the park to talk.

'I want to share something with you two,' Alex started.

'Oh no! You broke up with Oliver,' guessed Vanessa.

'Or he broke up with you?' asked Louisa.

'No. Ollie and I are fine; he's coming tonight. It's something else, something serious that may concern you, Lou.'

'Me? What happened? Is it something about my mum? Do you know something?' Louisa panicked for a minute. She'd just lost her grandmother, who was like a mother to her, and the last thing she needed was for something to happen to her mum. Marina was the first person who came to her mind.

'Your mum's fine. And it's not a life-or-death thing. It's your granddad.'

'What about Marcus? Is he ill?' Vanessa asked.

'No. Not ill. It's something else. Something I saw.'

'Please tell me! You're driving me crazy, you piece of shit!' exclaimed Louisa.

'Hey! No need to be rude.'

'I'm joking, but please say it. What happened to Grandad?'

'I was out with Ollie the other day and I saw him. You know?'

'No, I don't know! You saw him where?'

'We were grabbing some food at a cafe in Soho. He was there cosied up with a man. I think Marcus is gay. There, I said it.'

'Gay? How come? I mean, I don't care if he's gay, but what about my grandma? They were married for a long time. This doesn't make sense,' Louisa said.

'Maybe it does. I mean, maybe he realised he was gay and that's why they divorced,' said Vanessa.

'I don't know. He was with this guy, and he saw me,' said Alex.

'Did he? Did you talk to him?' Louisa asked.

'No, I felt embarrassed. I pretended I hadn't seen him and then Oliver and I left.'

'I'd never think in a million years that my grandad was gay. And if he is, why did he never say anything? I mean, we're all open-minded, and he knows that.' Louisa was intrigued.

'I don't know, Lou. But I always sensed something there,' Vanessa said carefully.

'Really? I never suspected anything.' Louisa was

trying to digest the new piece of information.

'I'm gay, and I swear the possibility of Marcus being gay has never crossed my mind,' said Alex. 'Marcus is coming tonight. What if he wants to talk to me about it? What do I do?'

'You talk to him and tell him he must come out. He must tell my mum,' said Louisa.

'I can't say that. It's his choice to come out or not. Don't be like that.'

'I disagree. Maybe he's been hiding and this is hurting him. And my mum is his daughter. She has the right to know.'

'Sorry, honey, but I don't think we can make it about your mum. It's his own self, his choice, his right to come out or not,' said Vanessa.

'I can't keep this from my mum. If you don't say something to him, I will,' Louisa firmly told Alex.

'If you do, you' put me in a tricky position. Please don't.'

'He knows we're close. And from what you've said, it looks like he saw you seeing him. Of course, he'll join the dots. Tell him I' tell my mum unless he tells her first,' Louisa insisted.

'You're such a bully!'

'Because I want to support my grandad and not keep secrets from my mum? That's not being a bully. It's called protecting who you love,' Louisa said angrily.

'Stop. Both of you!' Vanessa said. 'I agree he'll figure out you've told Louisa and me. But don't threaten him. Just say you think it's best if he tells Marina before Lou does.'

'I can do that. But only if he approaches me.'

'If he doesn't approach you today, I'll approach him.' Louisa was adamant.

◆ ◆ ◆

Everything was now ready for Daniel's sixtieth birthday party. The guests started to arrive. Karishma was the first, with a card and a bottle of a fine, expensive, eighteen-year-old whiskey. She looked stunning in an emerald green midi dress. Karishma was half Indian, from her mum's side. She was of a small build, skinny and not very tall, and had big dark brown eyes, long natural lashes and lush black hair. She was sweet and delicate; her voice was soft, and she always chose her words with care.

Christina came straight from the gallery with Patricia, and Bianca tagged along. Peter arrived shortly after, with Margaret, Christina's mum, Samantha, his and Christina's eldest daughter, and Harry, their youngest.

Robert and his wife, Purnima, Karishma's mother, arrived almost at the same time as Peter. They brought Declan and Ellie, Petra's parents.

Marina was the last to arrive with her partner Anthony and their children, Gabriel and Archie. Louisa's father, Joe, and Marina had parted ways for good when Louisa was three, after years of an on-off relationship. Louisa had kept in contact with her dad, but was much closer to Anthony. He'd been her stepdad since she was eight.

A few of Daniel's colleagues from the school where he worked came by. So did Renata, Teresa's friend from Rio, and her partner Malu.

Daniel had impeccable taste in music. He'd made an amazing playlist for the night. The food was delicious, there was plenty to drink, and the cake, an amazing sponge with chocolate ganache, was to die for.

Their town house was cosy and elegant. It had five levels. The lower ground was Daniel's studio. He had all sorts of musical instruments, including a piano and several guitars. They'd made the walls soundproof so he could play music as loud as he wanted without bothering the neighbours. Daniel occasionally gave private lessons at home, and composed for several artists, some of them relatively famous.

The ground floor was elevated from street level. It had a guest's bathroom, an impressive open-plan lounge and dining room integrated with a modern kitchen. At the back, big doors opened to a small balcony that had stairs to the good-sized and well-landscaped back garden — good-sized for London, at least.

Everything was going well; guests were dancing, chatting, having fun. At one point, Teresa, Karishma and Christina had a moment to themselves. They sat on the comfy garden chairs while everyone else stayed indoors. It was the beginning of spring but there was a chilly wind.

'I wish she was here,' Christina was the first to say.

'Me too.' Teresa said, followed by a 'Me three,' from Karishma.

'Me four.' Marina had arrived to join the others.

'Darling, come here.' Christina gave Marina a big hug.

'Christina, have you been drinking?' Marina said, kissing Christina on the head.

'Maybe I have. It's just that you remind me so much of your mum.'

'She does. She reminds us of Petra. We love you, my dear. You're a bit ours too,' Teresa said, looking at Christina and then at Karishma.

Of all of them, Christina was the least affectionate. Despite loving Marina, she was never one to hug and demonstrate her love.

'It's the first family get together since she left. I thought it would be harder, to be honest, but it isn't. Look at them all,' Marina said as she looked inside the house through the glass doors. 'We're a family, a loving family. We've had our ups and downs, but look at this, look at what you've built. The four of you.'

At that point they were all crying. Christina wiped away a tear and raised her glass. 'I have an idea! We should go to Rio at the end of this year. New Year's Eve in Rio de Janeiro. Like we did thirty-six years ago when the coven started.'

'What a fuckingtastic idea!' Karishma almost jumped up with happiness. 'I was too young back then. Now I can drink champagne.'

'Perfect! And we can lay flowers in the sea. Like the witches in Brazil.' Marina was excited.

'They're not witches. They're from a different religion,' said Teresa. '*Candomblé*, which means *dance in honour of the gods*. It combines different religions with traditional African beliefs, and it's common in parts of Brazil.'

'Why did you call your group a coven? Was it inspired by them?' Marina asked.

'Yes. In the past they were accused of witchcraft and they still are these days by people who don't understand or respect different views, and because they believe in spirits — *orishas*. The flowers, food and drinks they lay on the beach at New Year's Eve are offerings for those orishas,' Teresa explained.

'But we meant no disrespect. We were fascinated by them and, to be honest, I'd love to be a witch with magical powers like your mother wanted when she was a child.' Christina spoke with nostalgia.

'Strong women who weren't afraid of speaking their truth or defying the status quo,' Karishma completed.

'I'd proudly be a witch,' Marina said. 'Am I allowed to take my mum's place in the coven? I wasn't there thirty-six years ago, but I'd love to be this time.'

'Of course you were there!' said Christina. 'I mean, you were just a foetus, but you were there that night with us.'

'True!' Teresa made a face as if it was a big discovery. 'You were in your mum's belly. With us. And of course you're part of the coven. You always have been.'

'That's true.' Christina had a big smile on her face. 'You've always been a part of the coven. That was the night your mum decided you were the best thing that had ever happened to her. And we were celebrating you.'

'I'm so happy! I've always wanted to go to Rio. It will be like bonding with mum. And what was that with the flowers in the sea? Each flower has a meaning, right?' Marina couldn't contain her excitement.

'Yes, you're right! Each flower symbolises something according to their tradition,' Teresa said with excitement.

'Red for passion. Yellow if you want success and prosperity. Pink for love and harmony. And white for peace and purity, white was the colour of the flower that Petra and I offered at sea that day.' Christina remembered it well. 'White for us to live in peace with our choices forever. Ines told us. '

'Wasn't white also the colour of our clothes?' Karishma was trying to remember; she'd only been ten years old at the time.

'Yes, most people wear white on New Year's Eve in Brazil. Sometimes gold or yellow but never black.' Teresa was, of course, the expert. 'And do you remember the underwear? You must wear brand-new underwear. Its colour has the same meanings as the flowers plus green for hope and good health, blue for serenity. I miss it so much.'

'We should go buy underwear together!' Marina was still the most excited. 'I can't wait to tell Louisa. She'll love it!'

'I'll ask my mum to look for accommodation for us. She'll be over the moon to have us all there,' said Teresa.

'Ladies, please come inside. I have an announcement to make,' Daniel said loudly from the top of the stairs.

Teresa froze and looked at Christina.

'I'm sure it's something good. Maybe a new job?' Christina said, trying to calm Teresa down. Of course, Daniel wouldn't announce that he had a mistress in front of the whole family; that would be insane. She made a gesture of *breathe* to Teresa.

When they arrived inside, Daniel was standing next to a tall blonde woman with the figure of a supermodel. 'Everyone, this is Valerie Evans, but I guess some of you will have recognised her already,' Daniel said.

'OH MY GOD, I'm dead!' Vanessa screamed.

'I'm dead too!! Is this for real?' Louisa screamed too, followed by Alex.

'Fuck me! Valerie Evans, in my house! This is amazing,' he yelled.

Valerie Evans was a pop star, famous amongst the Gen Z crowd. She'd smashed the Grammys last year and was all over the radio. She had the voice of an angel.

'Hello. Welcome. I'm Teresa, Daniel's wife. Sorry, I didn't recognise you. I wasn't aware you were working together. You're working together, right?' Teresa was still suspicious and a bit jealous.

'Mum, you're showing your age now.' Alex was embarrassed.

'You must be Alex. Please don't be rude to your mum. It's totally normal to not know me, or at least my face. I'm not that famous.' Valerie smiled. 'I'm pleased to meet you, Teresa. Daniel talks about you a lot. And no, we don't work together, not yet, but… Daniel?'

Daniel took the cue and started talking. 'An old friend of mine, a drummer, introduced me to Valerie. We've talked a few times and even had a couple of jam sessions. Valerie's invited me to tour with her as one of her musicians. And I've invited her to come here tonight to celebrate my birthday, to meet my wife and our amazing made-up family— of course, I couldn't miss that look on the faces of those four.' He pointed to Alex, Vanessa, Louisa and Ollie. They were still in shock, gasping in disbelief.

Laughter, followed by clapping, echoed around the house. Teresa looked at Daniel in shock as he approached her with open arms. 'I thought you were having an affair.' The words came out of her mouth as her husband hugged her.

'Me? Never! I love you, Teres., I'd never change you for any woman — or man.' He kissed her. 'Are you happy for me?'

'I guess I am. I mean, I am, of course, but why didn't you tell me first?'

'I wanted it to be a big surprise, and I know that if I'd told you before, you wouldn't keep it from Christina and Karishma.'

'You're full of surprises. I love you too. But tour? What does it mean?'

'We can discuss it later; it'll be fine. I promise, and you can be my groupie.'

'That sounds sexy. But what about my job?'

'Take a sabbatical. I know you're tired and not that happy at work.'

'Yes, you're right, I'm not as happy at work as I used to be but if I take a sabbatical, as soon as I'm out of the office door, there'll be a twenty-something trying to get my place.'

'That's not possible. You know that. True, they might hire someone and there's a risk they could permanently replace you over time, but, who cares? You'll find another job. Or not. I can be the breadwinner with this new job. Let's not think about it right now. Let's enjoy the party, please.'

Teresa nodded and held his hand as they walked towards Valerie. 'Are those kids annoying you? I can call security,' Daniel joked. Valerie was surrounded by not only the four teenagers but also Patricia, Alan, Hugo, Samantha and Harry.

'See? It's all good, isn't it?' Christina wrapped her arms around Teresa.

'Yes, I guess. I'm still shocked and a bit upset

that he didn't tell me first. And this tour thing, he wants me to join them.'

'Like a groupie?'

'Yes, can you imagine? A fifty-six-year-old groupie.'

'I can, yes. You'd make a gorgeous, mature, and confident groupie. That's so exciting, and if you don't go, I will. I could do with a big change in my life,' Christina joked.

'What about my work, my career?'

'It's time to have fun! You've been bored for a long time. And you don't need it. You can be a freelance consultant once the tour is done, or do online masterclasses for young entrepreneurs with all your experience. That's what I'd do. Think about it.'

'I guess I can. But what about Rio? We can't cancel that. What if the tour dates coincide with New Year's Eve?'

'If, and it's a big if as you don't know the dates yet, if that happens, we'll find a way, I promise. Think how exciting this could be for you.' Christina knew how bored Teresa was and how things had gone cold in her marriage to Daniel. She wished she had an exciting opportunity like that herself. Her own life felt stagnant and dull lately.

They touched their foreheads in a tender way. They felt truly happy for the first time since Petra had left.

As Daniel took Valerie around the room to

introduce her to his colleagues and family, and to get her away from the young mob that had surrounded her, Marcus, as predicted, approached Alex. 'Hello, Alex. How have you been?'

'Hi, Marcus. I'm fine. You?' Alex was as red as a tomato. He had an idea what Marcus was about to say and he was so embarrassed.

'Would you mind having a quick word?'

'Sure, I guess.'

They walked to the garden. 'Look Alex, I know you saw me in Soho.'

'Marcus, I did but I don't want to get involved. I understand. Me, more than anyone. I understand.'

'I'm afraid you don't. You're lucky. Your generation, you can be who you are, you don't have to hide. At least not here in this country. I had to hide my whole life, and I've built a life that isn't mine, and now I'm not sure I can lead this fake life anymore.'

'Your whole life? What about Auntie Petra? Did she know? You were together for so long. Did you lie to her?'

'No, I never lied to her. It's complicated. I was confused to start with. We were friends, even before being husband and wife, we were friends. She knew I was confused and she accepted me. And when we finally decided to part ways, I could have come out, but I didn't. I wanted to protect Marina.'

'Protect Marina? From what?'

'From stigma, from judgment, from society. Not so long ago, being gay carried a heavy load, much heavier than you can imagine. As I said, you're lucky.'

'It's still not always easy today.' Alex looked down. 'I have a supportive family and nice friends, but I wouldn't say it's been an easy ride.'

Marcus realised he was being harsh on the young boy, for no reason other than feeling that he needed to defend himself. His fear of the family finding out about him. He spoke again; his voice softer this time. 'I know, kid, I know. But multiply that bumpy ride by a thousand and you'll have an idea of how it felt for me.'

'I understand, I do. Can I ask — who is that guy, the guy you were with?'

'My partner. My secret partner, I guess. We've been together, unofficially, for fifteen years now and I love him.'

'Wow. Fifteen years? And is he fine with being kept a secret?'

'Not really. He wants me to come out, and I'm considering it. I always tried to protect Petra. Now she's gone, at least I won't hurt her.'

'Do you think it would have hurt her before? How? She was your friend; you said she supported you.'

'She was my best friend. And yes, she did support me. But I know it would have been difficult for her if everyone knew. People would scrutinise our lives, ask questions. Maybe some questions we wouldn't be comfortable answering. Maybe. Maybe not, I don't know. Do you think Marina will be fine?'

'Louisa will.' Alex looked into the living room and saw Louisa and Vanessa staring at them through the glass doors.

As Marcus looked at them, they quickly dispersed. 'You told them, didn't you?' Marcus said.

'Yes, I did. I'm sorry.'

'And what did they say?'

'They said they're cool with that. Vanessa said she always suspected.'

'Really? I thought I had never given it away.'

'You didn't. It never crossed my mind, not until I saw you and now I know, it kind of makes sense, somehow.' Alex spoke cautiously. He didn't feel comfortable having this conversation with one of his best friend's grandad.

'What did Louisa say?'

'She wants you to tell her mum. Or she will. She asked me to tell you that.'

'Did she? But you said she wasn't mad — and to be clear, I'm not mad at you?' Marcus said, noting the distress on Alex's face.

'I'm glad you're not angry at me, but I wish I hadn't been the one to see you. And I'm sorry for all you must have been through.' Alex sounded more relaxed.

'Sorry? For what?' Marcus asked.

'I don't know. For you not being able to be yourself, for hiding all this time. It must have been so hard.'

'Don't be sorry. I'm happy now. It wasn't always easy, but I've been happy most of the time. Petra was the best life partner I could have asked for and Marina made me a father. I always wanted that. One of the main things in my head when I was young was that I wouldn't be able to have children if I came out.'

'How come? You could adopt, surrogate, whatever.'

'Again, not an easy thought to have thirty years ago. The thing is, I'm glad you saw me. I feel relieved. Maybe I needed this push to take the courage to show my family who I really am.'

'Cool. Does it mean you're ready to tell Marina?'

'I am and I will. And I'll talk to Louisa too. Just not tonight. This is Daniel's night. Let's go back to the party.'

Vanessa and Louisa weren't the only ones watching Alex and Marcus talk. Christina was also puzzled. She approached him as he came back inside. 'Marcus. Do you have a minute?'

'For you, always, my dear,' he said with a smile.

'Sorry to intrude, but what were you talking to Alex about?'

'Nothing important. I was just asking him if he could help me organise a party for Louisa for her birthday. A surprise party for my granddaughter.'

'Her birthday's in July. Still a few months to go. And I thought the three of them always celebrated their birthdays together. Eighteen is a big one,' said Christina.

'I know. I'd completely forgotten, and that's exactly what Alex said.' Marcus continued to improvise on his lie. 'They're throwing a party together. But I offered to help them, anyway.'

'I see. That makes sense. Well, I can help too. Let me know how.'

'I will. Let's meet the superstar now.' He grabbed Christina's hand and walked towards Daniel, Teresa and Valerie.

Christina was puzzled. It was obvious that Marcus was lying. He wouldn't have forgotten the fact that since they were young, all the birthday parties for Vanessa, Louisa and Alex were celebrated together.

She was concerned that Petra had been talking to Marcus about telling the family, about their past. And seeing Marcus acting suspiciously and talking to Alex made her wonder if he'd said anything to him. But perhaps she was being paranoid. *Maybe he was being honest. Let's see,* she thought as she followed him back to the party.

6

Marina

Like her mother, Marina had studied art. But despite her mum having an art gallery, Marina had always wanted to be independent and build her own career without the help or influence of her mother or Christina.

She had a passion for sculpture, and she'd had some work exhibited in prestigious galleries, and had even sold a few pieces a few years back. But since she'd had Gabriel, Marina had stopped sculpting and had been working at an art gallery for the last five years. She was happy with her work.

Daniel's party had gone on until after midnight, and Marina was exhausted and late for work. As she arrived at her gallery, Marcus was waiting for her, cup in hand. 'Iced chai late with oat milk, your favourite, madam.'

'Dad? What are you doing here? I mean, it's great to see you but also unexpected. A nice surprise.' Marina gave her dad a tender hug.

'I had to run a few errands and thought I'd come

and say hi.' Marcus gave his daughter a long, pensive look. 'I'll be done in a couple of hours. Are you free for lunch?'

'Yes. Sure. I'd love to have lunch with you, Dad.'

'It's a date. How does half-past twelve work?'

'Can we make it quarter to one? I have a meeting until half past, so in case it runs over?'

'Perfect. I'll take you to that Italian restaurant you love. It's not far.'

'Amazing. Can't wait. See you soon, Dad.' Marina gave him a kiss on the cheek.

The morning was busy as Marina was preparing an art exhibition and had lots to do with back-to-back meetings. She was happy and hungry when her meeting finished at twelve-thirty, excited to be seeing her dad. They hadn't spent much time together since Petra's death.

'Hi, Naomi. I'm having a long lunch with my dad. Could you cancel my next meeting? And the courier will come to pick up the last pieces for the exhibition. I should be back by then, but if not, please hand them over.' Naomi was Marina's assistant, a young, talented art student.

'I will, don't worry. I have it all under control. Enjoy your lunch.' Naomi was excited about the exhibition and had been great at helping Marina.

'Thank you. Bye.'

Outside, Marcus was waiting. He was visibly anxious.

'What's going on, Dad? You look nervous.'

'I'm just tired and hungover. I had a bit too much to drink last night. It was a good party, wasn't it?'

'It sure was, and what a surprise. Valerie Evans? That was amazing.'

'Did you know of her?' Marcus asked as they started to walk to the restaurant. The gallery was in Marylebone and so was the restaurant, a pleasant less than ten-minute walk.

'I did, actually. Louisa listens to her music all the time. She seems talented; I like her music. Did you know of her?'

'Nope. Not until last night. I guess I'm too old. I listened to some of her songs as I was getting ready this morning. They sound nice, catchy. I was surprised that Daniel's joining a pop singer. I always thought jazz and bossa nova was more his style.'

'Me too. But she has some jazzy stuff as well. I'll share some playlists with you. She seems to be a versatile artist, very creative. She writes her own music.'

'I'd love to hear good stuff from her. Please share; it would make me feel cool.' They both laughed.

When they arrived at the restaurant, they got a nice table by the window.

'How lucky are we? This is my favourite table, but it's usually impossible to get it,' Marina said with joy.

'It wasn't luck. I called to book and asked for this spot specifically. I know it's your favourite.'

The table was right in the corner by the window and isolated from the others. It gave some kind of privacy, and privacy was what Marcus needed. The last thing he wanted was for the whole restaurant to hear him coming out to his daughter. It would be embarrassing, and he wasn't sure how Marina would react.

'Shall we have wine?' Marcus suggested.

'Didn't you say you had too much last night?'

'Yes, but it's been so long since we got together, just the two of us. And I need to tell you some things, delicate stuff, so I want to relax.'

'Now you're worrying me.' Marina grabbed her father's hand. The first thing that crossed her mind was that he might be ill or something.

'I'm fine, don't worry. But there are things. Things about me and your mum. Don't worry. Let's order our food first.'

'Now it's me who needs to relax. You've got me worried.' Marina chose the wine and ordered a bottle of sparking water.

'Look, darling. You know I love you, don't you?'

'Yes, I do, and you're scaring me now. Please say it, whatever it is. Are you ill?'

Their drinks arrived and Marcus took a long sip of his wine and then looked Marina in the eyes. 'There's no easy way to tell you this… I'm gay.'

It was Marina's turn to have a big sip of her drink.

'Don't panic, please.' Marcus was sweating.

'I'm not. It's just — it's just a big thing. Not a bad thing, I think. I mean, what about Mum?'

'She knew. And she supported me. She accepted

me, I promise.'

Marina gulped down a full glass of water.

'What do you mean by she accepted you? Did you guys live a fake life? An open marriage? What was the deal? Sorry, I'm confused.'

'I understand. I'll tell you everything. We lived separate lives, yes, but not always.'

'Not always? Sorry, I'm not angry but confused, very confused.'

'Your mum and I have always been friends, best friends. Since school. We dated for a while.'

'For a while? What do you mean? You were married for years.'

'We dated when we were young, in Rio. That was when you came. We were still young, and I was confused. Confused and scared about my own feelings and emotions. I was attracted to your mum and I loved her. I always had, but I also felt attracted to men.'

'That must have been confusing. How did it happen? Sorry, again, I'm not angry, but you don't get your girlfriend pregnant when you're confused, do you?' Marina paused. She was trying to sound at ease about Marcus's revelation, even though she was shocked.

'When we finished school, your mum and Christina decided to take a gap year in Brazil. They were going to spend some time with Ines, Teresa's mum, and then travel around South America for a bit. You know that story.' Marcus paused for a second to ensure Marina was following. 'Your mum had a boyfriend who was a piece of work, and she wanted to get away from him. She suggested I go with them for the gap year. We'd always been good friends. I decided it was a great idea. A couple of my mates had always wanted to go to Brazil and joined me. We rented a small apartment and got odd jobs, like washing dishes and some office work.'

The waiter approached to take their order. He noticed the tone of the conversation and politely offered to give them more time to decide. Marcus nodded, and they watched the waiter depart.

'So you didn't go together?' asked Marina once the waiter had left.

'We went at the same time, but I wasn't going to stay at Ines's house with the girls. I did my own thing, but we were always together.'

'And how did you and Mum hook up?'

'She'd confessed that she liked me, not just as a friend. I liked her too, and I guess I was trying to convince myself that I was straight. I was trying to fit in. It was 1988 and it wasn't easy to be gay at that time. AIDS was a big issue, there was fear, there was a lot of stigma and my parents were conservative. They'd have never accepted me.'

'So you got together? You decided you weren't gay and off you went?'

'It wasn't that simple. Your mum and I, we ended up getting together one night, not long after we'd arrived in Rio. We were young and free and we were experimenting. You've been a teenager; you know the drill.'

'Do I? I've been a teenager but I've never experimented with girls. Not that I think it's wrong, but I've always liked guys. What I'm trying to say is that I wasn't confused. Not that I have any kind of prejudice, but this is a territory that I'm not familiar with. I can't understand what you and Mum were going through,' said Marina.

'I was unclear about what I wanted, about what I liked. And I guess your mum was as well. She liked me as a friend. She'd broken up with a guy who she'd been sort of dating for a while. She wasn't sure about her feelings for me, if I was a friend or more than that, and then…'

'Then?' Marina was already halfway through her second glass of wine.

'You happened. We found out just before New Year's Eve. We talked about it, we considered the options, and we decided we wanted you. We wanted to try to be parents.'

'You considered the options? You mean aborting me?'

'No, not really. Your mum and I always wanted you from the moment we knew you were there. We had to decide what we were going to do and how. We were two teenagers enjoying a gap year in a foreign country. How would we tell our families, our friends? How would we raise you, financially and all?' Marcus was telling a story close to the truth, but not exactly the truth. But it was as far as he could go without implicating other people.

'And then what happened? I was born in Brazil. I've always wondered why you didn't come back straight away. Why was I born there?'

'Well, Teresa and Christina jumped in and vowed to help raise you, as if we were all a big family, or coven like they later said. We'd also decided you'd never be a reason to stop us from doing anything and we'd enjoy our gap year as much as we could. Ines supported and helped us.'

'What about the parents? Yours and mum's parents. What did you say to them?'

'Well, Declan is the best father ever. Your mother told him, from the beginning. And he was supportive from the moment he knew. Declan was always on your mum's side. Your Grandma Ellie was having her own gap years. You know that story.'

'Yes, Mum told me — it really bothered her.'

'That's why she didn't tell her mum about you for a couple of years, not until Ellie was back together with Declan; Ellie was away at the time, and Petra thought she didn't care.'

'Did she?'

'Yes, in her own way. Once she came back, she fully embraced the role of dedicated mother and grandmother. Declan had always been in love with her, and I guess he knew that being with a free-spirited woman ten years younger than him was going to be challenging. He took his time but ended up forgiving her and taking her back.'

'Did Mum forgive her?'

'Deep inside she did. Petra was much closer to Declan, of course, but she did forgive Ellie, and she loved her.'

'What about your parents?'

'I think my parents always feared I was gay, and so did my older brother and sister. When I came back from my gap year with a daughter and a bride to be, they were so relieved that they didn't care that I was still basically a child.'

'You're right. You and Mum were too young. The same for me when I had Louisa. Why didn't you get mad at me? I was basically a child too. Only eighteen.'

'I did get mad, not at you, but at the situation. I was worried for a while, especially as I always knew deep down that Joe wasn't going to be very present. But at the same time, your mum and I hadn't set you the best example, so I had to suck my frustration up and be there for you. Just like Declan had.'

They noticed that the waiter was impatiently circling around them and decided to order their food. As soon as the waiter was gone, Marina returned to her questions. 'And how did you live in Brazil? During the pregnancy, I mean.'

'Ines was a godsend. She was there all the time for us. The girls lived with her, and she took care of you for the first couple of months. She was with your mum when you were born. She was amazing.'

'I've always liked Ines. I guess you guys were

lucky there was no internet and no one would figure out the pregnancy. Not until you told them.'

'True, no Facetime or WhatsApp for parents to see what their kids were up to. Ines had a Polaroid camera, but it was so expensive to buy the film that there are only a few photos of that time.'

'That's a shame. I'd have loved to see photos of you all together in Rio. I've never been back there but have always wanted to visit my birth town. I bet you had fun.'

'Yes, I wish we had photos too. But we have memories, good memories. And you should go to Rio. You'll love it.' Marcus took hold of Marina's hand. 'Are you upset at me? Do you forgive me?'

'I'm not angry, Dad. And there's nothing to forgive. I just worry if Mum suffered if she loved you as a husband and you weren't there for her.'

'Your mum knew. And she was fine with it. We decided together to dedicate our lives to raise you. And at one point, we decided you were big enough to understand that we'd continue our lives separately. But your mum and I have always remained close.'

'Do you have someone? Did Mum have someone? I always felt that she was lonely.'

'I know your mum was seeing someone for a few months before she died. But she never told me much about him. For some reason, she'd decided to keep it private, and I respected that.'

'And what about you?' Marina asked gently.

'I do have someone. Since a few months after

your mum and I separated, I've been with someone. His name is Paolo, he's half Italian, and we love each other. I want you to meet him.'

'I need time to digest all this. I'm not mad, but I need space. It's a lot to process. Once I get my head around it, I'd love to meet him.'

'One more thing. Louisa knows. Alex saw me with Paolo the other day. He told her and Vanessa.'

'Of course he did. Those three are thick as thieves. How did she react? Do you know?'

'I haven't spoken to her yet. I wanted to tell you first. But Alex said she was fine with me being gay.' Marcus spoke with joy in his voice.

'I bet she is. Louisa is a great kid; her heart is in the right place and she loves you so much.'

'I love my grandchildren. And I love you.'

'Does anyone else know? Teresa? Christina?'

'Nope, no one knows. Your mum and I had an agreement that she'd never tell anyone until I was comfortable with it, and until now, I wasn't. It was my secret to keep before it became our secret, and I'd like to think your mother understood that.'

'Are you telling them all? The rest of our big extended family?'

'Soon, I promise. For now, enough talking. Let's eat.' Marcus smiled; he seemed relieved.

After they'd finished their lunch, Marcus walked Marina back to the gallery. 'Thank you for understanding. Love you, kid.' Marcus kissed Marina on the head.

'Love you too, Dad. Thank you, for everything.'

As Marina sat back at her desk, her head was spinning. She wasn't angry at Marcus. She was a disappointed — not because he was gay but because he'd kept this from her for so long. She wished he'd told her before, but she couldn't lash out at him. They were still hurt by Petra's death, and he'd always been there for her. She owed it to Marcus to be supportive.

Marina decided she wasn't going to tell anyone — except for one person. 'Naomi, please cancel all my meetings. I have to go somewhere.'

'But I have people waiting for you here.'

'Say something urgent came up – a family thing.'

'No worries. Hope you're alright.'

I will be, it's all fine, don't worry. I just need to talk to someone.'

Marina went to see Christina at work. 'Hi Patricia. Is Christina here?' she asked without even saying 'hello'.

'Marina! What happened? You seem flustered.'

'Sorry Patricia, hello. I'm fine. I just need to speak to her.'

'Of course. She's in her office. You can go in.'

'Thank you. By the way, I haven't forgotten about our get together. I'll call you next week — are you free then?' Marina had realised she may have been rude and wanted to fix things.

'Yes, free next Friday if you are.'

'Perfect!' Marina said, making her way into Christina's office. 'Hello Christina. Can we talk?'

'Marina! What a nice surprise! Sit down, let me get you a glass of water. Do you want a coffee? Cup of tea?'

'No, water's fine.'

'What's happened?' Christina was worried. Marina was usually so calm.

'Did you know?' Marina asked abruptly.

'Did I know what?' Christina panicked for a second.

'About my dad?'

'What about Marcus?' Christina remembered seeing Marcus and Alex talking the night before and she knew something was off.

'Dad is gay.'

'What? Marcus is gay?'

'You didn't know? Didn't Mum tell you?'

'No. I didn't know. Did Petra know? She wouldn't have kept that from me, from us, the coven, I mean.'

'Well, she did know and by the look of it, she did keep it secret. Dad asked her to. He said it was his secret to keep, not hers.'

'Typical Petra, always so loyal. She was the best of us all at keeping secrets.' Christina spoke with a loving nostalgia. 'What about Alex? I'm sure he knows. I saw him talking to Marcus at Daniel's party last night.'

'Yes, Dad had to tell him. He saw Dad with his partner at a bar.'

'Ahh, that makes sense. But wait, *partner*? Does Marcus have a partner?'

'Yes, he does, apparently for the last fifteen years.'

'Of course. Since he and Petra separated, I never got the lonely vibe from him. I suspected he had someone, but not a man. How are you feeling about this?'

'I'm not sure. I'm not angry — I mean I don't care if he's gay. I want him to be happy, but it hurts me that he kept this from me for so long. And if Alex hadn't seen him, he'd have probably kept it secret forever. It feels like I've been cheated on by him and my mum. I told him I'm OK, but I'm not sure I can forget the fact he didn't trust me. This is a big secret to keep from your daughter.'

Christina's head was about to explode. *You must tell her.* Petra's last words kept echoing in her head like a broken record. *What would Marina think of the secrets they'd all had kept?*

'It's a big secret to keep, but he must have had his reasons. He probably wanted to protect you and your mum. I know it's hard, but harder for Marcus than for anybody else. And it's an honourable thing for him to keep this for so long. I can see why he did it. Marcus was always protective of you and Petra. It must have been so hard for him, and to have a partner and hide him for years.'

'You all knew him all your lives, and he kept it from you as well. So did my mum.'

'I'm sure they had their reasons.'

'Of course you're defending them.' Marina sounded upset.

'It's not about defending. They're not criminals. There's nothing to defend from. I'm just taking myself out of the equation and trying to put myself in their shoes. Sometimes we keep secrets to protect the ones we love, that's all.'

'Do you have a secret as well?'

'Me?' Christina was red as a rare cooked steak. 'I don't have any secrets.' She had plenty. 'But I'm looking at this from their point of view. Once you digest all this, I'm sure you will too.'

'I'm not sure I will. I don't care if Dad is gay, if Mum had a boyfriend or ten. It's just that I've been lied to. I feel betrayed.'

'Don't. This isn't only about you. It's about your mum and dad, too. Their lives, their challenges and believe me, they have had a few.'

'It hurts, you know.' Marina looked at Petra's desk through the glass that divided hers and Christina's office. 'I wish she was here. I wish I could shout at her and ask why she didn't tell me. Or maybe I just wish she was here so I could be angry at her and have her explain it to me, why they've kept that from me.'

'I wish she was here, too. Come here.' Christina hugged Marina, a tight, loving embrace.

A loud bang came from the reception. Marina and Christina left the office to see that a child had broken a large vase. The mother looked incredibly embarrassed. Patricia was telling them not to worry while she cleaned up the mess. When they returned to the office, Marina looked around. 'How can you work looking at her desk?' she asked.

'I can't. I'm turning that into a meeting room. If you agree, I mean.'

'Me? Why me? It's your gallery.'

'No, it isn't. It was mine and Petra's and her share is now yours.'

'I guess it is, but I've not thought that through yet.'

'I have. I think you should come and work with me. Continue your mother's work. She'd be proud, and it would bring me great joy.'

'I've never wanted to depend on her. I've always wanted to do my own thing. You know that.'

'I know and I admire that attitude. So did Petra. But she's not here anymore and there's an empty space that's yours. I have Patricia as a manager and Bianca has been amazing, but with your experience and contacts we could do even better. Your mum would have loved that.'

'I don't know. And I wouldn't be able to work from her office.'

'You wouldn't have to. We can refurbish the space. We need an upgrade, anyway. Petra and I had been thinking of doing it for a long time. We can change the layout, share an office maybe.'

'I don't know, sorry. There's too much going on in my head right now.'

'Promise me you'll at least think about it?'

'I will. And thank you for listening to me. Doesn't it bother you that my mum didn't tell you about dad? Not at all?'

'Maybe a bit, but I agree with your dad that it was his secret to share. Come here. You look better, calmer now.' Christina hugged Marina.

'I am, thanks to you. And please don't tell the others. Let Dad do it. Not even Teresa or Karishma.'

'Of course. Marcus must be the one to do it.'

'I've always thought of you, Teresa, and even Karishma as my aunties, since you and mum were like sisters from other misters.' Marina spoke from her heart. 'But now, I feel that you're my friends more than anything, not my mum's "soul sisters" for some reason.'

'We are. We have always been.'

'Dad told me about Brazil.'

'What about Brazil?' Christina's heart was racing again. She tried not to show any emotion.

'That you all decided to do this, I mean, to raise me together, and that you decided to enjoy more of your gap year and that Ines was amazing and looked after you all and took care of me. He also told me how supportive Granddad was. Mum never told me much about Brazil. Only that she and Dad fell in love in Brazil, which now I know was a lie, and I was born there but not much else. She never liked to talk about that.'

'It's a big decision to have a child as a teenager. You, better than anyone, know that. Your mum maybe didn't want to revisit everything. I remember we were all happy, but those were hard times.'

'Maybe you're right. As always.'

'Oh no. I'm not always right. Believe me I've been wrong.'

'Well, I don't remember that happening.' Marina smiled. 'Anyway, thank you again for listening. I must go now. Poor Naomi, I've dropped a heavy load on her today with the exhibition coming and all.'

'How's that coming along? I'm sure it'll be great. I'm even a bit jealous. Are you showing any of your own work?'

'Not really. It'll be great, yes, but none of my work this time. Anyway, I'd better get going.'

'Will you think about my offer? For you to come work with me?'

'I will. Maybe not immediately but I will. After the exhibition perhaps. See you soon. Bye.'

'Take your time. Bye. See you soon.'

When Marina had left, Christina took a deep breath. She considered calling Teresa and Karishma to talk about Marcus and wondered if they knew. But she quickly convinced herself that Petra wouldn't have done that and if Petra had told anyone, it would have been her. Besides, Marina was already feeling betrayed by Petra and Marcus. She didn't want to go behind her back.

◆ ◆ ◆

Later that night, Marina told Anthony everything.

'Marcus? I'd have never guessed. He must be relieved to be telling the truth, don't you think?'

'You know, Anthony. I hadn't thought from that perspective until I spoke to Christina. I was only thinking about me. But you and Christina are right. I must try to understand how Mum and Dad felt about this all, this must have been hard for them to keep for so long.'

I must be ready to meet his partner earlier than I imagined, she thought.

7

Christina

After work, Christina walked home — she needed to think, clear her mind. On the one hand, she was glad that Marcus's conversation with Alex was related to his own personal stuff and not about anything related to their 'gap year' but on the other, she worried about how Marina felt betrayed. She also tried to imagine how Petra must have felt for years. She'd always thought that Petra was lonely, despite her best friend reassuring her that she was happy being alone. But now, knowing that even her relationship with Marcus had been non-existent from a romantic point of view, she realised how Petra had been alone all her life.

It was hard to know that Petra had kept that a secret for so long. Christina knew that Petra was infatuated with Marcus when they went to Rio for the gap year, and in her mind, it was like they were in love, for a while at least. Petra and Marcus had difficult moments — no relationship is perfect. They had arguments, disagreements, but they always found their way back to each other. They'd spent twenty years together, after all, before the divorce. The thought that it had all been a lie was unsettling. How painful it must have felt for her and for him.

She knew deep inside that they'd done it all for Marina. And she felt guilty as Petra's best friend. She should have noticed, questioned, whatever. But no. Christina, Teresa and Karishma all kept living their lives, as people do, without questioning much, taking things for granted, avoiding questions, avoiding stirring the waters. They'd convinced themselves that Petra was a private person when it came to her romantic life and had decided, long ago, to respect that.

They had noticed, of course, how both Marcus and Petra had a strange vibe about them sometimes. Even before their divorce, they gave an air of friendship, not romantic or sexual energy. Now Christina knew why.

And that was exactly how she felt about Peter right now. They'd been together for years, but she'd never felt so distant from him as she'd been feeling since Petra's death. They'd raised three children together and were good parents, but everything was always done as a big family with Petra and her family, Teresa and her family. Looking back, she realised that Peter and herself hadn't spent much time where it was only them and the children, let alone just the two of them. She wasn't even sure anymore if they had much in common. It had always been a big group of people getting together and taking holidays together, but it was never her own family alone, never just her and Peter. Whenever they weren't with the family, he'd be working and she'd be looking after the kids or working.

As she walked home and thought about her life and her marriage, Christina concluded that Petra's marriage hadn't been any more fake than her own. Peter and herself always lived either their own individual lives or family life. Never their life as a couple.

'Hello. Long day at work? You look tired,' Peter said when Christina arrived home and walked through the door.

'Yes, a long day. I'm exhausted. What about your day?'

'Same old. Boring, long busy workday.'

'Are the kids home?' She put her coat over a chair and walked to the kitchen to get a bottle of wine and two glasses.

'Wow, wine. I'm in. I'll make a cheese board for us. Harry is at a friend's house and Vanessa is out with Alex and Louisa.'

'Good. Just us.' Christina started pouring the wine.

'Just the two of us.' Peter added a few grapes to the board.

'This looks great. It's been ages since we've done that.' Christina pointed at the board.

'Have we ever done this? Just us? Cheese and wine?' Peter asked.

'Have we? I don't remember. We probably did, but clearly not enough.' Christina looked sad.

'You're right. There are a lot of things we haven't done enough. We did raise amazing kids, and we had amazing moments with our big extended family, don't get me wrong. But I don't think we've dedicated enough time to each other. At least, I haven't dedicated enough time to you.' Peter grabbed her hand.

Christina was impressed that apparently she and her husband had been having the same thoughts. 'I feel the same. How bad is it that we're on the same page but struggle to communicate with each other? What went wrong?' Christina squeezed his hand. Despite their troubles as a couple, she still loved the man standing in front of her. 'Hang on, let me put some music on.' They were having a nice moment, and she thought she'd make it more special. 'I don't know, we were always so busy. And I believe we did take each other for granted in the end, didn't we?' Christina started playing a song from her phone's playlist on the speaker.

'We did, but we also stuck together. Isn't that better than most couples?' Peter asked as he pretend played piano with his fingers, following the bossa nova song selected by Christina.

'It may be. I don't know. I've only been married to you.' She smiled softly.

They kissed. It was a short kiss, not a passionate kiss, but one full of tenderness.

'I don't even remember the last time we kissed,' Christina said.

'I do. Our wedding anniversary a couple of years ago. We were all, the whole family, in Portugal. Remember the resort by the beach? Dinner at the restaurant, feet in the sand, moonlight over the sea. That was a special night for me.' Peter sounded nostalgic.

'For me too. I remember it now.' Christina nodded in agreement.

'Do you?' he asked.

'I do. It was the night Alex came out to Teresa and Daniel.'

'That's all you remember?' Peter sounded disappointed.

'No, of course not. I remember we had a happy night, a great night. Everyone was surprised by Alex's news. They all went to the pool to talk, and you and I stayed at the beach restaurant, drinking wine. We had a lovely night.'

'I'm glad you remember. I'm sorry about the other day. I didn't mean to upset you, but I miss you; I miss us. And I worry if there is still "us".' Peter seemed unusually emotional.

'Me too. Sorry about the other day. I don't want to make you feel rejected or whatever I made you feel, but I think there's an abyss between you and me, and we need to build back a bridge if we want to connect again. But I don't know how. Not right now.'

Christina felt like a heavy weight had been taken from her back as the words came out of her mouth. Even though there was still a lot left unspoken and secrets that could cause pain, being able to tell how she felt had helped a lot. Christina looked at her husband as he poured more wine into her empty glass. She could see his affectionate gaze on her. It was obvious Peter still loved Christina. *You must tell her.* Petra's voice continued to echo in her head. Would Peter still love her if he knew everything?

'Building bridges, eh? I'm up for that.' Peter tenderly moved a strand of hair from her face behind her years. 'Are you?'

'I'm up for trying; I can promise you that,' Christina lied. She knew deep inside that she wouldn't be open to truly connect with Peter or anyone. Not for as long as she was carrying the weight of her biggest secret. Her fear of losing everyone, everything, if the truth came out was too intense. It was easier to keep her relationship incomplete, unfulfilled, as if it had never been real. That way the loss wouldn't be real as well. *I can't lose what I've never had.*

That night, they had sex, and it felt special. Christina credited it to the bottle and a half of Beaujolais. For the first time in a long time, she let herself go with the moment. She felt present there with Peter.

The following morning, Christina woke up early and prepared a full breakfast for Peter and the children, as she used to do every weekend when kids were in primary school.

'Wow, that looks delicious. How many of us are you expecting?' Peter asked when he saw the feast Christina had prepared. There were eggs, avocado on toast, burrata, cheese, bacon, fruits, cereal and her signature kale-mango-coconut smoothie.

'Morning all!' Alex's head popped out from the sofa.

'Alex? Did you sleep here?' Christina was surprised. 'Does your mother know?'

At that moment, her phone rang. It was Teresa. 'Hello dear, good morning. Sorry to call so early on a Saturday, but do you have any idea where Alex is? It freaks me out when he doesn't say where he is. While he's still under my roof, he must let me know…' Teresa's words were coming fast.

'Morning, calm down. I understand. I'm the same with Vanessa, and yes, I'm looking at him right now. He spent the night on my sofa.' Christina looked at Alex with a reprimanding look.

'Oh. OK, thank you. How are things with Peter? I didn't even ask.' Teresa sounded much calmer now.

'All good, tell you later. Listen, I've made a massive breakfast like I used to, remember? Why don't you and Daniel come over? I can fry a few more eggs.'

'That sounds incredible, on our way. Should I bring anything?'

'Some sourdough please, and maybe more eggs?' Christina said as she saw Vanessa enter the living room with Louisa. Apparently, she'd also spent the night there.

'Does your mum know you're here? ' She gave Louisa a hug.

'Yes, I texted her last night. I'm not irresponsible as some are.' Louisa pointed jokingly at Alex, and he threw a cushion at her head in response.

The doorbell rang. 'Who could that be?' Christina said before asking Vanessa to open the door. Teresa lived only a few blocks away, but there's no way it would be her.

'Hello! Surprise!'

It was Samantha, Christina's oldest daughter, and she'd brought her grandma. Apparently, she'd decided to come home from university for the weekend and surprise her parents, but had forgotten to bring her own keys.

'Sam! Darling! What a fantastic surprise. And Mum, so glad Sam brought you, I was going to call you next.' Christina kissed her mum on the forehead.

'Impromptu family breakfast, and here we're all together again.' Peter looked at Christina and smiled. She knew exactly what he meant.

'At least we had a great night!' Christina whispered in his ear before smooching his lips.

'Now, that's new!' Samantha said. 'I don't think I've seen you guys kissing since I was a kid.'

'Someone must have had a great night.' Louisa said and quickly regretted her words. 'I'm so sorry; it's not my place to say.'

'Don't worry darling — you're family, you can say anything.' Christina took a long look at Louisa. In the same way they'd all helped Petra raise Marina, Christina and her friends — the collagen coven — had done the same for Louisa. She'd always been like her own grandchild, especially since Vanessa and Louisa were the same age. Christina remembered all the occasions where she'd have Louisa over for the weekend so Marina could enjoy a bit of her own youth. And, to be honest, so Christina could have some time for herself. It was easier to entertain a toddler with another child the same age. Christina could read a book while the girls played. And sometimes there was Alex as well.

'Who had a great night?' Harry had arrived in the living room still in his pyjamas.

'No one. Are you hungry?' Christina hugged her boy. Harry was fourteen but still affectionate towards his mum.

'Now I'm hungry. You haven't made a breakfast feast in ages. This is amazing.' Harry grabbed a plate and started serving himself.

The doorbell rang again. This time it was Teresa with Daniel, a couple of sourdough loaves and loads of eggs.

As they ate breakfast, chatting away and laughing, Christina looked around at Margaret, Samantha, Daniel, Peter and Teresa around the table and Alex, Louisa, Vanessa and Harry with plates on their laps on the sofa. Her heart warmed. That was how she remembered most of her life with her big, boisterous and happy family always around.

That moment made her miss her father, George. He'd been a big part of the family. Even though he travelled for work, whenever he was around, he told jokes and played with the kids giving them piggybacks. Christina missed him a lot.

She couldn't imagine life without them all and for a second she panicked, thinking once again about Petra's last words. *What if they all leave me? What if they never forgive me?* she thought and told herself that it wouldn't happen as long as the past stayed in the past. *Sorry Petra, but I don't think I can tell them.*

Peter and Daniel offered to clean up after the feast. It was almost noon, and they'd all had a happy morning.

'Should we go for a walk in the park?' Daniel suggested.

'I'm in.' Teresa agreed straight away, followed by the youngsters.

'You all go ahead. I have to sort out some stuff, but I'll catch you up in a bit,' Christina said.

'Are you sure everything is alright?' Teresa asked her in a low voice.

'I'm great; all is well. I just want to call that man. The one that came during Petra's event asking for me. Remember? Karishma gave me his number. I'll give him a call, maybe invite him for a coffee.'

'Who is he? Be careful.' Teresa was worried.

'I will be. I'll meet him in public. Besides, Karishma said she'd got a good vibe from him.'

They all left for the park, leaving Christina alone. 'Hello? Hi, my name is Christina, Christina Lanyon. My friend Karishma gave me your number. She said you'd come looking for me at a family event the other day.'

'Sure, hi. Christina. I'm Theo. My mother knew your father and I recently learnt of his death; I'm sorry for your loss.'

'Thank you. How did your mum know my father?' Christina was confused.

'It's a long story. I'd rather talk to you in person.'

'Are you free later? We can meet for a coffee.'

'I'm free at four. Would that work for you?' Theo asked.

'Sure. Where are you? I mean, what part of London? You *are* in London, right?' Christina wanted to find more about the stranger.

'Yes. I am. Southwest London. You're in Highbury, right? Near where the event, I mean funeral for your friend took place, correct?'

'Live celebration, yes. We're across the city from each other. We can meet halfway if you want.' Christina preferred to meet him away from her neighbourhood. She wasn't sure exactly who he was and didn't want anyone to see her with a stranger on a Saturday afternoon.

'Are you sure? I could come to you. It's not a problem,' Theo offered kindly.

'Don't worry. I'm happy to travel a bit. What about near Charing Cross station? Would that work?' Christina suggested.

'Perfect! Do you have a place in mind?'

'Yes, there's a great Italian café. I'll text you the location. See you at four.'

'See you at four, bye.'

Christina hung up the phone. *Who are you, Theo?*

She went to meet the family at the park. They spent a couple of hours there. It was a lovely sunny spring afternoon, and the park was full of children playing, dogs running around and people having picnics and playing ball games. Daniel went home with Peter at one point to grab picnic blankets, snacks and wine. It was a perfect day.

At half past three Christina apologised and said she had to sort something out at the gallery. She looked at Teresa who picked up that Christina was meeting Theo.

'Oh, are you meeting that new artist, the friend of yours?' Teresa tried to help with the cover up.

'Yes, a quick meeting. I may take her for a coffee but I'll be back soon.' Christina grabbed her bags and said her goodbyes.

'You're leaving? It's a shame you must go. It's Saturday, darling. Stay, please.' Peter asked his wife.

'I'd love to, but my friend is leaving tomorrow. She's a great artist, and I want to sell her work. I'd promised that I'd meet her today — I'd totally forgotten. But I'll be back soon, I promise,' Christina lied.

'I understand. Shall we have dinner out later?' Peter asked, smiling.

'Sure. I'd love that,' Christina replied without giving it much thought and left, blowing him a kiss.

She arrived at the Italian café ten minutes late and texted Theo.

> Sorry, I'm late. Have you arrived?

> I just arrived. Don't worry. Table at the back. Red t-shirt.

Theo stood up, waving.

> I see you, she texted back as she made her way towards him.

'Hi, I'm Christina. Sorry again I'm late.'

'No worries, I'm glad you agreed to meet me. Thank you.'

They sat down. Christina looked at the young man in front of her. She didn't have a clue who he was or what he wanted with her, but something about him felt strangely familiar.

The waitress approached them with a menu for Christina. Theo already had a menu lying on the table in front of him.

'Have you ordered anything?' Christina hung her bag on the back of the chair.

'Nope, not yet. I was waiting for you. Do you suggest anything? The food looks delicious. I wasn't going to eat but I may now.' Theo glanced at the display with pastries, desserts, paninis and arancini balls.

'The pistachio latte is a must. And I'd go for the pistachio rum baba or the cannoli if you fancy something sweet.' Christina said as her mouth watered up. This was one of her favourite cafes.

'I'll have the latte and a hazelnut cannoli.' Theo ordered for himself. 'You?'

'I'll also have a latte, pistachio latte with oat milk, please. It's nice to meet you, Theo, but I'm not sure what this is about, and I'm curious.'

'Well, I'm not sure where to start, to be honest.' Theo was visibly tense.

'From the beginning, maybe?' Christina suggested. 'How do you and your mum know my father?'

'It's a long story. Your father's younger brother and my mother went to school together. They lived in the same street for a while and saw each other a lot when they were growing up.'

'What's your mother's name? Maybe my father mentioned her.' Christina was fishing.

'Emma. My mother's name is Emma. Has he ever mentioned her?'

'No. Not that I remember, sorry. And did they keep in touch?'

'Not really. For a long time, they lost contact. And in 1987 they kind of bumped into each other on the street and became friends again.'

'Ah — 1987. I remember that year well. And did they become good friends again? Close friends?' Christina was suspicious and concerned about where the conversation was going. The man in front of her looked like he was in his mid-thirties so he must have been born around 1987, maybe 1988.

Oh my God, is it possible? But my dad — oh God. Christina's heart was pounding.

'Two pistachio lattes, one with oat milk, one pistachio rum baba and one hazelnut cannoli, is that all?' The waitress asked as she placed their drinks and desserts on the table.

Theo was staring into Christina's eyes; it was clear by the look on her face that she knew exactly what he was about to say.

'I think you've figured…' Theo said in a choked voice.

'I'm not sure. Please tell me. How do you know my father?'

'George was… he was… my father too. I'm your half-brother, Christina,' he said, bracing himself for her reaction.

'Could I have a glass of water, please?' Christina asked the waitress, as she held herself stiffly.

The waitress promptly brought her a jug and a couple of glasses. Christina drank all the water in the glass at once and refilled her glass. She stayed silent for several minutes, staring at Theo. She thought about challenging him, and hoped he was lying for a second, but it was all so clear. He looked a lot like her father. Same blue eyes, light brown hair and a turned-up nose, features she also shared.

'Please say something. I'm a bit freaked out here,' said Theo.

'I don't know what to say. Not yet. Give me a few more minutes.'

They sat in silence, each eating their dessert and drinking their latte without speaking a word, digesting the delicious treats and the words that had been exchanged.

'OK. I'm sugared up now. Let's talk.' Christina's face had recovered some colour.

'Well. As I said, my mum and your father reconnected after they met again. It happened in Spain. That was when they saw each other again. I think your father was travelling for work and my mother was living there for a while. She was divorced from her first husband. They had no children. She was thirty-six at the time and had decided to try a change of scene. It turns out that your father had a colleague at the same company where she'd managed to get a job. One day your father was on a work trip and came to see his friend and that was how they met, in Seville,' Theo said.

Christina was silent as she listened. As Theo talked, she recalled that phase of her life. If she remembered right, those were the most difficult years in her parents' marriage.

'They got together and my mother got pregnant.'

'That's it? Tell me more, did my father saw you growing up? Did he continue to see your mum? I'm sorry, but I have so many questions.' Christina's head was running at a thousand miles per hour at that point.

'They never told me much. I was born and grew up in Spain until I was ten. Dad came and visited every month. He always told us he had to travel for work and that's why he couldn't spend much time with us.'

'Sounds about right. He wasn't around much after he got the job at the Spanish company.' Christina ordered another latte. 'Do you need another drink?'

'Yes, another latte for me too, please. When I was about ten, my mother decided to move back to the UK. I remember that around that time I didn't see Dad much. For a year at least. My mother later told me that they were separated. After a while, he started to come back to visit me. My mum and him weren't together, but I saw him a lot. Football games, school plays, he even took me on work trips a few times.'

Christina was still listening carefully. She felt a bit jealous. School plays and work trips. It didn't sound like the same father. Although George was kind whenever he was around, always laughing, joking and having long conversation with her, always interested in her life, he wasn't a sports day or school choir events father, not for her. 'And did he continue to see you as you became an adult? Where were you when he got ill? Why didn't you contact me before?' Christina was trying to join the dots.

'After I had my son, David is seven now, Dad was still around for a couple of years, but he then started to come around or contact me less and less. I wasn't happy, and we ended up having a big fight about four years ago. I was in a bad place. My partner, David's mum, had left for good and my son stayed with me. I moved back in with my mum so she wouldn't be lonely and she could help me raise David. Dad stopped calling and I was so angry, I stopped talking to him.'

'Didn't you suspect something was wrong? That he had another family? Wait, you knew?' Christina was confused.

'I found out. I saw him once with his wife, your mum, and you at a restaurant — he didn't see me, but I confronted him after. That's why we had a fight. We only talked after that so he could check on David, but we stopped seeing each other and we stopped talking.'

'What about your mother? Did she know?' Christina asked.

'Yes. She found out after we moved back to the UK. He told her, and that was when they broke up. He told her he loved her and me, but he had to stay with his first family. She was depressed for a while, but she never even considered taking him back. I know my mother suffered a lot, but she's dedicated her life to me and now she dedicates herself to David. I forgave her for never telling me. I made peace with it. I understand that she wanted to spare me from hating my father and from all the grief.'

'I guess that didn't work, did it?' Christina had noticed how sad Theo looked.

'Nope. He broke my heart, but what hurts the most is that I didn't speak to him for years and now he's dead. I could have forgiven him.' Theo had tears in his eyes.

'None of this is your fault.' Christina could see clearly. 'Don't be too harsh on yourself. It's a lot to process. It must have been hard to find out all you knew while growing up was a lie.' Christina was pensive as she remembered, again, Petra's last words to her.

'It was hard, but he must have had his reasons. And I didn't know he was sick. I should have been there for him. I only found out he was dead a few months ago. And that was when I decided to come looking for you.' Tears were rolling down Theo's face as he spoke.

'I'm glad you did.' Christina didn't think before speaking, but despite being somewhat shocked, she was happy to have a brother. 'You know, I had a brother. Did Dad tell you that?'

'No, he didn't. Never. Do I have a brother as well?'

'You did. Not anymore. He died when I was fifteen, before you were born.'

'I'm sorry to hear that. I never knew. I don't even think my mother knows.'

'It was a long time ago. A freak accident. I don't like to talk about it.' Christina always felt sad when talking about her brother. 'He was nine at the time. My mother never really recovered and my father, well, I think he didn't either, but he managed better than mum and now, after learning about you, your story, I think it was probably because of you.'

'Why do you say that?'

'When Ralph died, Dad kind of started travelling more and more for work. We rarely saw him for a good five years. My mother was devastated and that wasn't fair on her. She always defended him and tried to convince us that his way of dealing with his loss was to travel for work, and he travelled a lot. By what you told me, that was when he reconnected with your mother, and you were born. He continued to travel but after a while he was more and more at home until he changed and became the best husband and father, when I was already an adult and probably by the time you moved back to the UK with your mum.'

'That makes sense; he broke my mum's heart and came back to mend your mother.' Theo sounded bitter.

'I think he felt guilty. He wasn't there to support my mother in her own grief after losing a son. It just took a long time for him to realise it. I think he loved her but for what I recall, he wasn't "in love" with my mother.' Christina's voice was faint.

'I'm sorry, I really am. I think our mothers suffered from his actions, but I'd like to think he wasn't a monster.'

'He wasn't. All in all he was a great loving father. You know what's funny? I thought about him this morning. Not that I don't often think of him but this morning I specifically missed him.' Christina remembered the breakfast with the family.

'And now, you've met me. I'm not asking you to

suddenly be my big sister, but it took me a long time to gather the courage to come here, to finally look for you and I'd like to be part of your life if I can. I understand if you don't want anything to do with me, but I'd love to have a big sister. And for what it's worth, I miss him too, a lot.'

Christina felt an urge to hug the man in front of her. He was a stranger, of course, and for all she knew he could be making everything up, although that seemed unlikely. But despite the shock and feeling of betrayal, she felt warm towards Theo. She imagined everything that Theo and his mum must have gone through. It was like she knew from the moment she laid eyes on him that there was something, a connection between them.

'I'd like to get to know you better too. But I need to process all this. It's been a hard year so far. Petra, the friend whose funeral — I mean life celebration… Sorry, she hated funerals. Petra was like a sister to me. I'd known her all my life and we shared so much. She was my best friend and so much more. I'm still grieving and there's so much going on in my life. I hope you understand.'

'I do, I honestly do. Let me know when you're ready.'

'I will. I promise.' Christina realised she'd been making a lot of promises lately.

They left the restaurant and shared a quick hug before going their separate ways. They both felt some kind of joy even though there was so much pain involved in all that situation. But somehow there was something more that ran deeper than the pain and grief. Underlying all their stories, there was love. Love for their father and who knows maybe they would come to love each other as brother and sister as well, only time would tell.

◆ ◆ ◆

When Christina got home that evening, Peter was waiting for her on the sofa. 'You took so long. I was worried. I tried to call you,' he said as soon as she came in.

'Let's go out for dinner, please.' Christina stood by the door with her bag.

'Wait, what happened? You don't look alright. What is it?'

'I have a brother. My father had a son, with another woman,' she said with her eyes fixed on the wall.

'A brother? How?' Peter was the one in shock now.

'I'll tell you. Let's go, please.' Christina went out the door.

She told Peter everything that happened, how Theo had come looking for her and what they'd talked about. Peter wasn't impressed with her lying to him and going alone to meet a stranger, but at least Teresa and Karishma knew, though that made him jealous. The girls had always shared everything with each other and often he felt excluded, left out. But he quickly realised that it wasn't the moment to complain. Christina needed him now and he was there for her. They talked for hours that night as she recalled her upbringing and many moments shared with her dad, questioning how she'd never suspected anything. *Did Mum know?* was the question lingering in her mind that night.

8

Karishma

Since their dessert sharing date, Karishma and Theo had seen each other a couple of times. She did invite him for a coffee and then lunch after that. Every time they met, they got closer. They'd talked about their work, what food they liked, places they'd been, places they wanted to visit.

'As I told you… we're birds of a feather,' Theo said as they were saying goodbye after lunch. 'Have you noticed how much we have in common?'

'We do indeed,' Karishma said looking into his eyes. And, as if the world had stopped, they moved their faces closer. They were about to kiss when Jimmy the Cricket's evil twin said in her head. *What are you doing? He's half your age.* That wasn't true. Theo was thirty-six, and Karishma was forty-six. A big difference, but so what?

Karishma moved her face away as the battle in her head continued. She was unconsciously trying to sabotage her own happiness as she used to do. It was as if she felt guilty for having a life after Iain.

As if the part of her that had died with him was trying to drag the rest of her to a joyless life as a punishment, as if she didn't have the right to be happy without him.

'I'd better go; I have a long shift starting soon,' Karishma said before turning around and walking quickly towards the tube station.

'Call me,' was all Theo could say as she walked away from him.

Karishma didn't call him for a few days. She wasn't sure why. She did want to see him again, of course. And that almost-kiss moment was stuck in her head like a car advert jingle. Karishma could still feel butterflies inside her stomach – there were a lot of butterflies every time she thought about Theo.

Karishma was happy and definitely falling for Theo, but at the same time, she was scared. She was terrified of falling in love again. If things didn't go well for some reason, she didn't think she could survive a broken heart again. On top of that was the age gap and, of course, the guilt, the strange feeling that she was betraying Iain.

She hadn't seen her therapist in years. When Iain died, sixteen years ago, Karishma went to a dark place. His death took her off the tracks. She was still a young doctor, and she almost gave up on her career. At the time, she took six months off work due to her depression. Petra, Teresa and Christina had been with her all the way. They'd taken turns staying with her, cooking for her, pushing her to get out of bed on her darkest days, and just being present in silence when all she needed was not to be left alone.

Karishma was glad to have her friends by her side, and for a while that was all she needed. But as time passed, she'd decided that seeing a professional would accelerate her healing process. That was what she felt after losing Iain, that she was wounded and needed healing. She did heal, with time, and slowly got back to her work, her life. She continued to see her therapist for a few years, but about five years ago, she stopped. After meeting Theo and with the swarm of emotions she'd been feeling lately, she felt it was time to see her therapist again.

Mia, her therapist, was specialised in bioenergetic therapy, a method that explores the interconnection between mind, body and spirit. Walking back into Mia's clinic was like a trip to a painful time in the past. All the pain and despair rushed back to Karishma's mind as if a switch had been turned on, bringing back the memories of those unbearable days. For a moment, she thought of giving up, turning back round and making an excuse not to see Mia. Then she remembered how she felt with Theo, how he'd made her laugh on the couple of occasions they'd seen each other and how she wanted to see him all the time. Deep down, she knew that without getting her mind in the right place, she wouldn't be able to give herself the chance to at least get to know Theo. That gave her the strength to knock on the door. She deserved it; she deserved to be fine. It was as simple as that.

'Hello! It's so good to see you, Karishma. It's been what? Five years?' Mia had a big smile on her face.

'Give or take, yes. A long time. How have you been?' Karishma asked.

'I've been well. Had a couple of minor health issues, my back playing up, but all good now. But more importantly, how are you?' Mia led the way towards the consulting room.

'Not bad, thanks.' As Karishma stepped into the consulting room, she noticed that everything was different — Mia had redecorated. 'Wow, you've changed things here. It looks amazing.' The place now boasted sage-green wall with black and white framed photos and new modern furniture, including a lovely comfy chaise longue. It was a relief to Karishma to feel she was in a completely different place than the room where she'd spent hours crying and grieving Iain.

'I've changed everything. My old space was so outdated. Same building but a new space, new energy. Glad you like it. Please sit down. Make yourself comfortable.' Mia pointed at the chaise longue.

As soon as Karishma sat down, she started talking. 'I've met someone.'

'I see. And that's good, I assume?'

Without being able to contain the big smile that took over her face, Karishma told Mia all about Theo, how they'd met and how she felt about him.

She shared her fears about getting involved with someone again and that she was concerned about their age difference.

'Well, I find it unfair that society sees an older woman with a younger man as a violation of nature. People get way less shocked to see an eighty-year-old man with a twenty-year-old woman than seeing a woman with a man a few years younger. Why is that? Why do we have to be seen as if we have an expiry date? Ten years, so what? I don't see any problem with that, honestly,' Mia said.

Karishma also talked about Petra's death.

'I'm so sorry to hear that. I know how close you all were.'

They talked for a while. Karishma tried to share her feelings as much as she could, then they did a few grounding and breathing exercises. As the session was about to finish, Karishma decided to address something that was bothering her even more than her and Theo's age gap.

'We can talk about this during the next session, but there's something else on my mind,' Karishma said as if begging for Mia to push her into talking — she needed a push.

'Go ahead. We still have a few minutes. I knew there'd be a lot to cover. That's why I suggested a double session.'

'A couple of months ago, I was out with Teresa and Christina. And Christina said something about how different their lives were from the plans they'd had when they were young. They'd become mothers instead of travelling the world or becoming rock stars. They'd settled for a quieter and more conventional life.' Karishma's voice was breaking.

'And? I guess it stirred some feelings?'

'It did, yes. It made me think that my life had also been different from what I'd planned, but not for a good reason like having children or because of an unexpected career direction.' She took a deep breath. 'But because my fiancé, the love of my life with who I shared those plans, had to fucking die.' Karishma was crying now.

Mia passed her a box of tissues.

'I feel so lonely for most of the time. And I keep those feelings inside me, and I can't do it anymore. All the feelings I've kept locked in are eating my soul. And I've been thinking about the embryos,' Karishma said in between sobs.

When Karishma and Iain were together, they'd decided to have embryos frozen, partly in case something happened like early menopause or one of them getting ill, but mainly to avoid struggling to conceive if they left it too late to have children. She was at the beginning of her career after years studying, and Iain was an adventure seeker with plans to travel, take as many pictures as he could and climb many mountains. Until he climbed the last one, the Matterhorn. Iain was one of the over five-hundred climbers to perish trying to conquer one of the world's deadliest peaks.

'I called the clinic where they're frozen. I'm thinking of hiring a surrogate. I'm old, but I want to have Iain's baby. I know it sounds crazy, but I think I owe it to him and to myself. I think it will set me free.'

'I don't think you owe anything to Iain. However, if this is something YOU truly want, you should go ahead with it.'

'What about Theo?' Karishma asked.

'What about Theo? It should be your choice. If he loves you, he may even help you along the way. He may want to be involved. But one step at a time. Sometimes things happen for a reason that we can't explain, but somehow they make sense. You need to be present in every moment and avoid trying to control things that haven't even happened yet. That can only bring anxiety and anguish.'

'I'll think about it. And I'll see Theo again.' Karishma wiped her tears and nose. 'Talking to you about it makes me feel better and not like a lonely old lady with a crazy dream.'

'You're not old or crazy, Karishma. And if you don't dream, you're likely to pass by life without living, like a visitor. It's about time you start to dream again.' Mia looked at the clock on her desk. 'See you next week?' Mia gave Karishma a hug before she left.

The session with Mia did make her feel lighter, more relaxed and somehow present in her own life. She questioned why she'd stopped doing therapy in the first place.

◆ ◆ ◆

That night, Karishma invited Theo to dinner. They met at a bistro off Kensington High Street.

Theo told her about his son and his relationship with David's mum. He explained that they were together for five years, and that he'd always had the impression that he was way more in love with her than she was in love with him.

He told Karishma that he'd always wanted to have a big family, as growing up it had just been him and his mother. He'd always wished he had siblings. Theo said that David's mum was a free soul, and she'd never wanted to have kids. Her dream was to travel and explore the world, and once she got pregnant, Theo had to work hard to convince her to keep the child. Once David was born, his mum was totally in love with him, but as time passed, she started to feel depressed and — *suffocated*. She struggled trying to juggle between the mum she thought she should be or who David needed her to be and the person she wanted to be for herself.

'When David turned three, she couldn't do it anymore. She wasn't happy and I wasn't happy. I'm sure David could sense the bad energy around us. We decided to part ways. David stayed with me and now we're all better. She still sees him a few times a year between her travels. She does a lot of humanitarian work, but I'm the one who raises him, and my mum helps.'

'Does David miss her?'

'Yes, he does. But I try to fill the gaps, and when she comes to visit, they always have a good time. I always try to paint a positive picture of her. She does love David, in her own way. Showing any disapproval or anger towards her myself would only make him suffer more.'

'That sounds noble of you. Do you have any resentment towards her?'

'I did, for a while. Not anymore.' Theo paused as if trying to find the best words to say next. 'I came to terms with the fact we can only love people for what they are, and now I understand that we can only take what they're capable of giving for as long as they can. She never pretended to be something she wasn't and if for a second I thought she'd change and become a different person or that I could change her, that's on me.'

'Wow. You're an old soul, Theo. I'm impressed. And when did you figure all that out?' *Handsome, polite and an incredible human being, I'm in trouble...*

'I didn't figure it out alone. It took years of therapy.' Theo told her.

'Really?'

'Yes, why? Are you against therapy?'

'No, not at all. I have a therapist myself. Saw her today.'

Theo grabbed both her hands inside his and kissed them. At that moment, Karishma felt the hair in her arms rise and she noticed that Theo's arm also had goosebumps. She felt as if all the butterflies left in the world were inhabiting her stomach. She was definitely falling for Theo.

'Your turn now. Tell me more about yourself,' Theo said gently, and he listened as Karishma described her past.

'That's how the collagen coven started. I was ten and felt so important because my older sister and her friends treated me like one of them.'

'Collagen coven, that sounds interesting.'

She told him about that New Year's Eve in 1987, and added that she believed that Teresa and her friends probably thought it was annoying to have a child with them at the beach but she was sure that years after, as she became a young woman, they were happy to have her as a friend.

'I'm sure they love you. Who wouldn't?' Theo said with an embarrassed smile.

'They do. I'm sure they do.' Karishma didn't mind his cheesiness; she liked it.

She told him about Iain and how they'd been crazy about each other. How they'd had plans to get married and build a family but only when they were older and had ticked a few boxes on their bucket lists. Adventures for him and a medical career for her. And she talked about his accident and how lost she'd felt ever since.

Theo grabbed her face in both his hands and kissed her. This time, Karishma had no chance to think or try to stop him. She let herself go and kissed him back. Karishma felt as she hadn't felt in such a long time. It was like someone had opened a big window so the sun could illuminate her soul.

That night, they went back to her apartment and made love all night. They gave themselves away completely, exploring each other's bodies and exchanging sentiments and emotions that had been buried deep inside them.

The next morning, they had breakfast and stayed cosied up on the sofa for hours. It was as if they'd known each other forever.

It was Saturday morning, the same Saturday morning when Christina cooked a feast for the family after a long time when they were interrupted by Theo's phone.

'It's Christina,' Theo whispered, covering the phone.

'Don't say you're with me, please.' Karishma asked him, also whispering.

After he'd hung up, Theo asked, 'Why don't you want me to say we're kind of seeing each other?'

'Because you haven't told me yet what you're doing with her, and I don't want to mess up things. Talk to her first and then tell me.'

'I'll meet her later today and after I speak to her, I'll tell you everything. There's a chance she'll hate me, though.' His face wasn't so happy anymore.

'What have you done?' Karishma's heart jumped.

'Nothing, I promise you it's nothing serious. I mean, I haven't done anything, but I'll tell you. I'll meet see you after I've spoken to her.'

'Deal. I honestly don't know why, but I trust you.'

They kissed again and again until it was late and Theo had to leave to take David for lunch and meet Christina.

◆ ◆ ◆

That night after meeting Christina and telling her everything, Theo returned to Karishma. He told her about his father, the conversation he'd had with Christina and how happy he felt. He'd finally met a sister who for a long time he hadn't known existed, and as a bonus, Christina had led him to Karishma.

Karishma was happy too, but also concerned. Christina had been acting differently since Petra's death. Karishma wasn't sure if it was grief or if there was something else bothering her friend, but the truth was that Christina had seemed bitter lately.

She feared that Christina might not be happy to find out that her best friend was getting close to her newfound baby brother.

9

Teresa

Teresa had a big meeting at work, overseeing the acquisition of a celebrity's makeup brand. The celebrity was a diva and wanted more money than the brand was worth. Not to mention that a revamp would be needed, as some of the products didn't comply with Teresa's company's high quality and consumer safety standards. After a three-hour meeting with her acquisitions team, lawyers and the celebrity diva, they finally came to an agreement.

Teresa felt drained from the meeting and thought about the conversation she'd had with Daniel when he'd announced he was going on tour with Valerie Evans. She was indeed bored with her work. She used to love being involved in developing new products and all the hands-on activities but since she'd become a CEO, she was much more involved in boring discussions usually involving lawyers, the group board and a lot of problems to deal with.

Of course, being a CEO gave her that feeling of power that every businessperson enjoys. But ego aside, Teresa started to question what she really wanted. She wasn't a child anymore and Petra's death had shown her how in a minute it all can be gone. She began to question her life choices and then realised that most of the time she'd made decisions guided by her ego or to prioritise others, like her children or her friends.

She'd been thinking a lot about Daniel's new career direction and decided that it could be a good opportunity to do something more than spending the rest of the best years of her life in an office with boring and competitive corporate people. Besides, although she trusted Daniel, she did feel slightly jealous of him and Valerie. He was old enough to be her father, true, but they seemed so close to each other during his birthday party that Teresa was concerned. How would she not be? Valerie was a gorgeous and talented young woman, and she and Daniel shared a passion — music. Teresa didn't think anything was going on between them, but the thought of letting him travel the world alone with the girl bothered her.

◆ ◆ ◆

'Hello,' she said when she recognised her husband's voice as he answered the phone.

'Teresa? What's happened?' Daniel responded, sounding alarmed. She usually never called him in the middle of the afternoon.

'I'm fine. I just think it's time for us to have that conversation about Valerie's tour.'

'Really? Should I be happy about this?'

'Maybe.' Teresa paused with a smile on her face. 'Dinner tonight?'

'That sounds great.'

Teresa knew Daniel would be excited and hopeful after her suggestion of dinner. Whenever Teresa made an occasion out of a conversation, it meant she was excited about it. 'I was thinking about that restaurant I've been wanting to go to. You could meet me at the office…'

Daniel interrupted her. 'I'll cook tonight. I'll tell Alex to go sleep at Marina's or Christina's. How does that sound?'

'Perfect, just perfect. See you at seven.' Teresa hung up. She felt happy.

She got up from her seat and stood in front of the floor to ceiling window of her spacious and impeccably decorated office. She stared at the vast city skyline with the gloomy sky background. *It's time for a change of scene,* she told herself and smiled again. Teresa thought that the biggest power she could feel, bigger than the one of being a CEO for a big company, was the power to be the boss of her own life, her own time.

Teresa got home at seven on the dot. As soon as she opened the door, she noticed that Daniel had put in a real effort for the night. Candles and a marvellous fresh flower bouquet were adorning her eight-seater round table.

The delicious smell of food made Teresa even hungrier than she already was.

'You're here.' Daniel walked towards her and kissed her on the lips. 'Sit down. I've prepared a three-course menu. You'll love it.'

'Wow. It looks amazing.' Teresa saw the big paella pan sitting on the stove.

'First, courgette flowers with caramelised goat's cheese.' Daniel served her starter and a glass of wine.

'This is delicious,' Teresa said after tasting the exquisite dish. 'It's been a while since you prepared this kind of amazing food.'

'Indeed, but tonight is a special occasion, isn't it?' He looked at his wife.

'Is it? You don't know what I have to say yet.'

'But I have a good feeling about it. I can see it in your eyes — they've changed.'

Teresa felt an excitement that she hadn't felt in a long time. The same kind of exhilaration she used to feel when they'd first met, every time they'd planned a holiday together or when she came to his first gig. The anticipation of being thrilled, of waiting for something special.

'You may be right. But be patient, I'm still hungry, and the paella will go cold. Let's eat first.'

They ate the paella, drank wine and for dessert had home-made chocolate mousse. After dinner, they sat down on the sofa next to each other. 'It's been so long since we've made time for each other like this,' Teresa said.

'It has. Does it mean you have good news? Should we start making more time for us?'

'I haven't made my mind up yet. I want to discuss things with you first. First, tell me more about the tour. How long is it going to last? What cities, countries? Where will you stay? Are there any breaks?' Teresa had a million questions.

'One thing at a time.' Daniel sat upright and rubbed his hands before he started talking again. 'The tour starts in New York on the twelfth of October. There' be ten major cities where we'll perform, one each week, then two weeks' break over Christmas and New Year's Eve. And I've thought of something special for us to do together over that period... Hawaii.'

Teresa adjusted her position. She loved the idea of going to Hawaii, but not for New Year's Eve. She remembered the plans made with the girls to go to Rio. She thought she'd mentioned them to Daniel, but he must have forgotten as he'd been so excited and busy preparing for the tour. *Better not mention say anything now. I'll decide what to do later.* She brought her attention back to what Daniel was saying.

'After Hawaii, we'll do eight cities in South America. By then, it will be mid-March. From there South Africa, Europe, India, Japan, Australia and finish with six shows in the UK in December. We'll travel the world together.' Every muscle in Daniel's body tingled with excitement; he couldn't contain his enthusiasm. 'And we'll be in amazing hotels, all paid for, and I'll be well paid for that.'

'It's tempting.' Teresa was excited but at the same time hesitant.

Daniel noticed and said, 'But?'

'How do you know there's a "but"?' Teresa asked, making air quotes with the fingers.

'I can see it in your face.'

'You know me well, I'll give you that.' Teresa moved closer to David. 'I have a condition. Well, not a condition, but there's something I've been thinking about for a long time, and I think now is the time to share it with you.' Teresa's body was now stiff; she was tense.

'Do you want something in return for giving me that time? It feels like I'm taking something from you and not giving you a once-in-a-lifetime fantastic opportunity.' Daniel wasn't impressed.

'You are. Of course you are. But I'm giving up my work and I'll be away from my children, my friends, my father. It's a lot to ask.' Teresa stood and started walking in circles around the living room.

'Hey. Calm down. There'll be breaks and we'll see them all. Just not every week, all the time, as we do now. A year will fly by, you'll see.'

Teresa sat down, this time on the floor, facing Daniel. 'It's not only that.'

'What is it, then? Your work? Once we're back, you can start your own business. You have the contacts and the knowhow, and we'll have money to invest.' Daniel took her hand.

'It's not work. I can't stand work anymore,' Teresa confessed.

'What is it then?'

'After the tour, maybe I don't want to be back, not for a while. I want to spend at least a year in Rio, close to my mother.'

'Rio? You never mentioned you wanted to go back.'

'I know. I didn't, not until recently. I've been thinking about it a lot. I kind of miss my mother, the lifestyle, the weather.'

'I thought you'd never looked back. You have been here for what? Thirty-six years? '

'Exactly, I came here thirty-six years ago. And I did it for the girls, for our "coven". We made a pact. I don't regret it, but looking back, my decision was made on a whim. I never thought it through or thought about what I wanted to do. I just did it.'

Teresa was typically pragmatic and controlled. But that night, with tears in her eyes and hands wrapped around her legs, she felt vulnerable, unlike her usual strong self.

Daniel was listening quietly and attentively.

'Of course I was used to the culture here, since I've spent the summer with Dad for as long as I can remember, but moving here as a young adult and leaving everything, including my mum, behind wasn't easy. I've always had a feeling of *what if I'd stayed?*'

'You wouldn't have met me; we wouldn't have our amazing kids.' Daniel went to get more wine.

'True. And boy, aren't our kids amazing? Talking about them, what about Alex? He's still young. We can't leave him.'

'Of course we can. Alex will be eighteen soon. He's not a child anymore. Your father and Purnima live so close they can give him some support. And besides, he can come and meet us during the tour.'

'I guess he could, but what about his studies? He's going to university.' Teresa wasn't yet convinced that leaving her baby boy behind would be a good idea.

'That can wait a year. And he can take the time to be sure. Alex is very responsible and having some space without us would be great for him. Besides, he loves music — he'd love to be with us in some of the shows.'

'You have a point. I guess he'd love it. But about Rio. I need to fulfil that dream of living there again, for a while, at least. I have all these ideas of what it would be like to live there again, go to the beach every day, enjoy the sun, see my old friends, their families, my mum's side of the family. I always fantasised that living in Rio is like living a dream, a tropical dream.'

'You know it isn't. It must be great to live there, but it's not easy, let alone perfect. You know that. Your mother is always complaining that Rio is unsafe, that life is hard over there and so on.'

'I've heard that. I don't *know* that. And I feel like I need to know that to be sure I'm not missing out on anything. I need to live it to know it so I can differentiate between my romantic ideas and reality.'

'Only unfulfilled dreams can be romantic, as they say...'

'It's not only that. I want to be with my mother, I really do. She's older now and I don't know how much time we have left together.'

'This is all very tempting.' Daniel was smiling.

'The boys can come and visit. What do you say?' Teresa was hopeful, but at the same time, unsettled. 'I know this is a big step to take, completely different from our calm predictable routine. But I want it so much.'

Teresa couldn't recognise herself. The idea of going on the tour and living in Rio for a while suddenly made her feel more alive than she'd felt in a long time. It was as if she was twenty-five again with her whole life yet to happen.

'I say, yes. Let's go travel the world with a superstar and let's live in a tropical country for a year or two. Who wouldn't? Wait? Why are we still debating it? It sounds so perfect! How lucky are we?' Daniel hugged Teresa.

Teresa hugged him back and they stayed in a long embrace for a couple of minutes.

'There is one more thing.' Teresa said, pushing Daniel slightly away.

'Go for it. I'm so happy that nothing will be an issue right now.'

'There are things... things from the past between Petra, Christina and I that may come up,' Teresa said hesitantly.

'Is it something that could affect us?' Daniel had changed from a relaxed body language to a tight posture. He couldn't stop fidgeting with his hands.

'Maybe, not directly. I mean, yes and no. Not something involving me, or you or our kids, but something I'm part of. I need you to try to understand, when the time comes, why I never shared any of it with you.' Teresa was biting her lips.

'Why don't you share it with me now?'

'Because I can't, for the same reason I haven't shared it before. It's not mine to share.'

'What's not yours? A secret?'

'Yes, it's a secret, a big secret.'

'Is it about Marcus? If it is, maybe I know already. Alex told me.'

'What did Alex tell you?' Teresa's heart was racing now.

'That he saw Marcus at a gay club. Did you know? Marcus is gay.'

Teresa's jaw dropped. 'Marcus is gay? I didn't know. I know he'd never been with anyone, not that we know of, at least, since he divorced Petra, but gay?'

'Yes. He's gay. That's all I know. Alex didn't want to say anything, but I saw him talking to Marcus on the night of my birthday and I knew something was up. I asked and he told me. But please don't say anything, not even to the girls. Alex said Marcus will tell Marina first and then the rest of us.'

'No. I won't, of course. I'm just shocked. I had crossed my mind that it was a possibility, a long time ago, but I never believed it was true. It must have been hard for him and Petra all this time. Do you think she knew?' Teresa's mind was now racing as fast as her heart.

'I don't know. Let's wait until he decides to tell us. Now, about the secret — I'd be lying if I said I'm not worried. If not Marcus's news, what could it be?'

'Please forget about it for now. I'm not telling you. It doesn't directly affect us. If anything, in a way, it brought us together. You'll understand when and if it comes out.'

The dinner, the upcoming tour and the idea of Teresa joining him and even the idea of secrets raising to the surface had inspired Daniel. Together with Teresa, he spent the night in his studio composing a song, something he hadn't done in a long time. When they'd first met, almost thirty years ago, Daniel used to compose songs while Teresa listened to him and contributed a few words and ideas. He used to say that she was his muse. As the years passed and the children came, they rarely shared moments like that. It was a special night.

Teresa woke up late for work the next day and decided to call in sick. She hadn't done that in many years. Even with a bad dose of flu, Teresa would work even if it was from home. But now she'd decided to quit her job, join Daniel and live abroad for a while, it was as if a massive load had left her shoulders. She'd had only a few hours sleep and was tired, but the prospect of such a change in her life filled her with enthusiasm that she'd forgotten existed within herself.

She decided to call Karishma, Christina and Marina to break the news.

They agreed to meet for lunch.

I have something amazing to share. Teresa texted on their group chat.

I don't want to steal your thunder, but I have something to share, too. Christina texted back almost immediately.

It will be a long lunch then. Marina texted back and added a couple of wine glass emojis followed by one of girls dancing.

They met at an exclusive restaurant in central London. It was one of their favourites, with a five-star menu, unique art inspired décor and a quirky atmosphere.

I know it's expensive, but we deserve it. I'm paying. Teresa had texted before they all complained about the expensive choice of venue.

Christina was the first to arrive after Teresa. 'I love this place. I haven't been here in years,' she said.

'Me too. Isn't it great? I love the interior design,' Teresa said as she looked around the room.

'Hello. How are you both? Teresa, thank you for inviting me. I always wanted to come here,' Marina said excitedly.

'I can't believe you've never been,' Christina said as they said their helloes.

'I haven't. I know you've all been here a few times, and that always made me jealous, but I was never invited before. Thank you, Teresa.' Marina gave Teresa a special hug.

'Karishma should be joining us shortly; she had a long surgery this morning but will be here soon,' Teresa told the other two as they ordered drinks. They ordered a drink for Karishma as well so she could get *straight into the mood* as per Marina's suggestion.

Karishma arrived twenty minutes later and, like the others, made it clear how happy she was to be there. 'How did you get a table? It's impossible to book here last minute.'

'I have my contacts.' Teresa winked. 'Alan is friends with the manager. They went to school together, and I've known her since they were tiny. I bumped into her the other day, and she told me she'd been hired here and offered to book me a table whenever I needed. How lucky was that?'

'Do you want to spill the beans or order first?' Christina asked.

'If you're going to order first, do it quickly.' Marina said.

'Order first, I'm starving. I won't be able to process anything on an empty stomach.' Karishma made the decision for them all.

They ordered their starters and mains and as soon as the waiter walked away from their table, all heads and attention turned to Teresa. She'd realised that though the others would be happy for her, they'd probably also be sad as Teresa would be gone for a while and their lunches, dinners, family gatherings and wine Thursdays wouldn't be the same. 'Maybe

Christina wants to go first. You said you have news too, right?' Teresa wanted more time to prepare for her sister's and friends' reaction.

'Nope. You go first. Don't throw me under the bus. You called the meeting, your agenda,' Christina said in quick response.

'I don't want you all to be sad, but I've made a big decision,' said Teresa.

As Teresa started to talk, Christina brought both her hands to her cheeks. 'Is this about our conversation at Daniel's birthday party?' she asked.

Teresa looked at her and smiled before continuing. 'You know that Daniel has been invited to tour with Valerie Evans, right?'

'OH MY GOD!' Marina didn't wait for Teresa to finish. 'You're going with him?'

'I am.' Teresa took a deep breath.

'Wow, this is big news!' Karishma almost choked on her drink.

'I know. Big news. We had a long conversation last night and we decided it's time for us. I haven't been happy at work for a long time and could do with a change of scene.'

'Change of scene? This is a complete change of world. Where are you going? When are you going? Wait, does this mean we're not going to Rio for New Year's Eve?' Marina's face went from mega excited to mega sad in a second.

'One thing at a time. We'll go to all the continents, which is amazing. The tour starts in October and there's a break for the December festivities, so I can still join you in Rio.' Teresa had decided not to tell them about Daniel's Hawaii plans. At least, not yet, and to be honest, she'd decided to figure out how to do both.

'I'm so jealous! Can I carry your bags?' Christina joked.

'You can, dear. Or at least you can come and meet me in some of the cities where she'll perform. You all could. That would be amazing. I could try to get you tickets, VIP tickets.'

'Oh, that would be a dream.' Marina closed her eyes as she spoke.

'But that's not all.' Teresa's voice was now serious.

'What? Are you pregnant?' Christina joked.

'Can you imagine? At fifty-six? I'd kill myself — just joking, but of course I'm not pregnant.' Teresa laughed at the joke and noticed that Karishma had an awkward look on her face.

'Please tell us. You're killing me here. I'm dying of curiosity,' Marina said.

'After the tour ends, around December next year, we'll move to Brazil for a bit. A year or two maybe. I want to be with my mum, and I want to live in Rio for a while.'

'Wow! That I wasn't expecting,' Karishma said in shock. 'I thought you never wanted to live there. You've always said it's an amazing place but too hot and dangerous. What's changed?'

'A few things. I miss the weather, blue sky, warmth

and the sea. I miss my mother. And since I moved to the UK, I've often thought about how my life would have been if I'd stayed — what I've missed.' Teresa was trying to figure things out as she spoke. *I don't want to die suddenly like Petra without embracing all the opportunities and living all the dreams I can.*

'I thought you'd never looked back,' Christina said in a disappointed tone.

'I haven't. I'm glad we did, I mean, that I decided to come here with you and Petra at the end of our gap year.'

Teresa looked at Marina.

'What? I wasn't there. Why are you looking at me?' Marina asked.

'I'm not. I did look at you, but I'm talking with all of you. And yes, we've already established that you were there. In your mum's belly, but you were there. To be honest, you were one reason I came here. We'd decided we'd all raise you together. You know that,' Teresa said.

'Should I feel guilty?'

'Of course not. You were there, but you didn't have a voice. Besides, I've never said I regretted coming to this country. I came because at the time it was what I wanted. And I got to be with my father, to see Karishma grow up and to meet Daniel. All good.' Teresa said, grabbing Karishma's hand.

'I helped your life to be better than it was supposed to be, didn't I?' Marina was back to smiling.

'Of course you did. I love you. We all do. But

enough of me. Christina?' Teresa looked at her friend as if saying, *your turn.*

Christina took a long sip of her drink before she started talking. 'Where to begin? Karishma, do you remember that guy who came looking for me at Petra's life celebration party?'

Karishma's heart was exploding in her chest, but she tried to keep a straight face, not letting out any emotions. Teresa was the only one to notice that something was going on, as she knew her stepsister way too well not to.

'Theo. His name was Theo, I think. I remember.' Karishma was trying hard not to give away any hint of what was going on between her and Theo.

'Yes, that's him, Theo. Well ladies, Theo is my brother.'

'What? A brother? George has a son? I mean, I assume it's from George, not Margaret. How come?' Marina was perplexed.

'Dad had an affair. Remember when he used to travel for work? Apparently, he met this woman in Spain and lived a double life. It was after my brother died.'

'How do you feel about that?' asked Karishma.

'At first, I was shocked and angry at Dad, but now I'm happy. Very happy, to be honest. He seems to be such a nice person. He has a son and his mother, didn't know that my father was married for a long time.'

'Have you told Margaret yet?' Teresa asked.

'No, not yet, but I will, soon. I want to get to

know him first. I want to find out more. I want to meet my nephew, and then I'll share him.'

Karishma was feeling progressively more uncomfortable and now she'd convinced herself that Christina would be jealous if she found out about her and her brother's affair.

'Do you think your mum will be fine with that?' asked Marina. 'I imagine it's not easy to find out your husband had a second family. Not nice to be cheated on.'

'Of course it will be a shock for her. But I have a feeling that Mum will see beyond the betrayal. I hope she'll be able to see that it's not Theo's fault and that she'll eventually appreciate him. She never really recovered from Ralph's death, and maybe Theo and her can connect. I know it sounds twisted, but life has a strange way of showing us new paths sometimes.'

'I hope so,' said Teresa. 'But be careful how you tell her. It will be a shock for Margaret. I think she may eventually like Theo, but maybe not as fast as you expect.'

'Maybe you're right. But for now, I'm happy to have met him.'

'How old is he? Is he married?' asked Marina.

'He's about your age, Marina. And he's not married. He was apparently crazy about this woman, the mother of his son, David, but she was, according to him, a free soul. She's currently doing humanitarian work in Africa.'

'How can a mother leave her son like that? How old is David?' Marina asked.

'Seven. Theo says she's a great mother despite not being much around. Who are we to judge?' Christina said.

'I'm not judging,' said Marina, slightly aggressively. 'But I don't understand how a mother could leave a small child behind to go help other children. I had a baby very young, and I've never left her behind. And believe me, at times I thought about it.'

An awkward silence dominated the table for a while. Karishma was eating her food and looking down. Christina and Teresa exchanged brief looks and kept quiet for a minute. Marina was munching her food and had a serious expression on her face.

'Let's not let our opinions spoil our appetite.' Teresa broke the ice. 'You and Theo's ex are different people; Christina has her own views and Karishma is still hungry.'

They all looked at Karishma as she devoured her food — she hadn't said a word for a while. They all laughed.

'What?' Karishma spoke with her mouth full. 'I told you I was starving. I've been in an operating theatre since five this morning.'

'So that's why you've been so quiet all night?' Christina asked.

'Yes. I'm hungry and tired,' Karishma said and she blew Christina a kiss.

They finished their food, shared a couple of

desserts, laughed and celebrated Teresa's and Christina's news. Once they'd said their goodbyes, Karishma offered to share a cab back with Teresa while Christina and Marina went back to work.

'I have something to tell you, sister.' Karishma called Teresa 'sister' sometimes, usually when she needed her to be her older sister and not her friend.

'I thought so. You were acting strange all through lunch. What's up with you?'

'I don't know how to say it. So many things.'

'Shall we go for a coffee?' Teresa suggested.

'I don't think I can fit any more drinks or food in me, but you can have a coffee while I talk.' Karishma brought her hand to her stomach.

They got out of the cab a few blocks before their houses and went to a small coffee house nearby.

'I've been thinking about Iain.' Karishma had tears in her eyes as she spoke.

'Oh, dear. Of course you have, come here.' Teresa wrapped her sister in her arms. 'It's normal to think about him, darling. What happened was devastating. It's normal to have highs and lows.'

'It's not like that. I've been thinking about him not only because I miss him, which I do, but because I want to have a baby, his baby.'

'Sorry, I'm confused. How could you possibly have Iain's baby, darling?'

'We froze our embryos before Iain died. We always wanted to have children, but we weren't ready. As I was almost thirty and we didn't know how long it would take for us to have our ducks in a row, we decided that freezing embryos would be a good way to avoid my eggs getting old.'

'You never told me that.'

'I never told anyone. Iain died not long after that and I tried to forget it for a while.'

'But you've kept the embryos.'

'I did. And I've learned this week that they're healthy and in a good condition to be implanted.'

'Would you get pregnant? I'm not judging but you're not so young anymore. To be pregnant is wonderful, but it takes its toll.'

'I know. I wouldn't get pregnant. I'd hire a surrogate. Do you think it's wrong?'

'Wrong? Me? Not at all. All forms of love are worth it. There's too much judgement in this world. One thing we don't need is to judge love. If you decide to have Iain's baby, I'll be there all the way for you.'

'From Brazil? You're leaving.' Karishma's tears were now rolling down her face.

'I know. But I'll come and visit. And your mum and our dad, they'll help, I'm sure. Christina, Marina, everyone will help. It takes a coven, remember? Our coven.' Teresa passed her a handkerchief.

'It's not only that. It's the timing.' Karishma was sobbing.

'Timing? It's the perfect time.' Teresa was confused.

'I've met someone, Teresa. I think I'm falling for him. He's younger and I think the last thing he'd want is the baby of my dead fiancé.'

'You've met someone? When? Where? Why didn't you tell me before? Who is he?'

'It's Theo. Christina's brother.'

Teresa looked up, took a deep breath and closed her eyes.

'I knew you'd disapprove.' Karishma shook her head.

'I don't disapprove. Not at all. I'm just surprised. There's been so much going on since Petra left us. Everything is happening. Daniel joining a band, Marcus, Theo.'

'What happened to Marcus?' Karishma had stopped crying now.

'Nothing. You'll find out but not from me. He's fine. Let's focus on Theo. How did it happen?'

'Well, I'm the one who opened the door when he came looking for Christina. There was a spark when we met but I didn't think much of it until one day when I started thinking more and more about Iain and the embryos. I went to Richmond Park to clear my head, and I bumped into him. That's where he lives. We talked and one thing led to another. Do you think Christina will hate me?'

'Hate you? Of course not. She may get a bit jealous and protective of both of you, but she'll be fine. You should tell her.'

'Not yet. And please don't tell her yourself. I'll give her space and let her tell Margaret first. To be honest, I'm not sure where this is going and if I decide to have the baby, I'll have to stop seeing him.'

'Why? Have you spoken to him about it? Stop being so self-defeating. You always do that. Please don't be your worst enemy.'

'I'm not; I'm being rational. Of course, I haven't told him. We've only just met.'

'And how do you think he feels about you?'

'I think he likes me back. I don't think he's prepared for me to go and decide to have the baby of another man, a dead man. Too much to process for a new relationship or whatever is it that we have.'

Teresa looked Karishma in the eyes. 'Again. I'm not sure I agree. I don't think there's a set of rules for relationships and love. Of course, there are things that can be delicate to talk about, but when there's a strong bond between two people, I believe things can be sorted. Even the hardest things.'

'I never took you for the sentimental type.' Karishma laid her head on Teresa's chest.

'You'd be surprised.'

The stepsisters stayed together for a while before going to their parents' house where they stayed until late.

Teresa wasn't the religious type but that night, before going to bed she thought, *If I were more gullible or religious, I'd think you're somehow looking down at us, Petra. I'd believe you're making things happen here to fill our lives with joy to fill the gap you've left in our hearts. If only I could believe that.*

10

Marina

The weeks were passing by, and Marina was incredibly busy with the art exhibition she was curating. Finally, the day of the preview arrived. She'd put together a very exclusive list of guests and had overseen all the planning and installation, but she was so glad for her assistant, Naomi. The young girl had been brilliant in making sure that everything was perfect and that all the parts involved in the organisation of the event were seamlessly coordinated.

Marina had selected the artwork and was the creative flair, but Naomi had sent the invitations, coordinated the marketing and promotional efforts. She'd also had set up the space and hired a catering company. Everything had fallen into place, and all efforts had culminated in a terrific event.

Teresa, Alex and Karishma were there, and so was Anthony alongside Louisa, who was thrilled to support her mother. Marcus came with Petra's parents, Declan and Ellie. Christina also attended the event and brought her daughter Vanessa and her mother Margaret.

Alberta Laurent, the prestigious gallerist and Marina's boss, effusively congratulated her and Naomi.

Marina was happy with her job, and despite finding Alberta obnoxious at times, she enjoyed working with her and all the glamour that came with it. Alberta was well regarded in the art scene and had phenomenal contacts — some of them had become well acquainted with Marina. Working at the gallery was a great enhancement to Marina's CV, but since her conversation with Christina, when she'd shared the news about Marcus, Marina had been seriously considering leaving Alberta's gallery and joining Christina, taking the position left by Petra.

After the preview, Anthony proposed that they went for a drink. Marcus said he'd love to, but he had to take Declan and Ellie home. Declan was in his mid-eighties and was still in a good shape, but since Petra's death his health had visibly declined. He'd become more reclusive and had had a couple of bad episodes of flu, one of which had led to pneumonia. He'd recovered but somehow wasn't the same. Alex, Vanessa and Louisa had a party to attend for the birthday of one of their close friends. Karishma had an early surgery to assist the following morning.

Teresa, Margaret and Christina were up for a drink, but Marina decided that since half the group had left, she'd rather go home with Anthony. She was exhausted and they'd left Gabriel and Archie with a babysitter who'd agreed to only a certain number of hours.

Teresa, Margaret and Christina went for a drink, anyway, and Marina went home with her partner.

When Marina and Anthony got home, the children were already in bed. They paid the babysitter, and Marina went for a bath. Once they were in bed, Marina rested her head on Anthony's chest. 'I'm glad the preview is over. I've been so immersed in putting the event together that I haven't had time to think about much else lately.'

Anthony was running his fingers through her wet hair. 'I know. We've barely seen each other lately. The kids miss you. Louisa was a great help all the nights you've worked late.'

'You're right. At least tomorrow is Saturday and I'll spend some time with them. Let's take them to the park?'

'I think that's a phenomenal idea.' He kissed the top of her head. She turned back and kissed him on the lips. With two young children in the house, sex wasn't a common occurrence, but they hoped that night would be different when they started to get in the mood. That was when they heard the door open and a little voice come from behind it.

'Mummy! You're home.' Archie was peeking through the small gap of the now slightly open door.

Marina managed to quickly put back on her

pyjama top that Anthony had removed seconds earlier. 'Come here honey, why aren't you in bed?'

Archie jumped into his parent's bed enthusiastically. 'I had a bad dream. I miss you, Mummy.'

Marina looked at Anthony as if saying, *No sex for us tonight.*

Anthony rolled his eyes and grabbed Archie, pretending to bite his feet. 'What's this little monster doing in my bed? I'll eat you!'

They nestled Archie between them and told him a bedtime story until he fell asleep. Anthony fell asleep right after.

Marina looked at them and started thinking back on her own life and how lucky she was to have Anthony in it. They'd met ten years before when a mutual friend had introduced them. Louisa was almost eight at the time. Marina and Joe, Louisa's father, were teenagers when they started dating. They were each other's first sex experience, and it didn't take long for Marina to get pregnant.

At first it was a shock for her, and she remembered telling her mother that her life had ended. She wasn't ready to be a mother. 'I'm still a child; how can I have a child of my own?' Marina said when she first told her mother and father about her pregnancy with Christina by her side.

Christina and Teresa were both themselves pregnant when Marina got pregnant. Their children were born at two-week intervals, first Vanessa, then Louisa, a bit early, and then Alex. Marina was embarrassed by being a pregnant teenager at the same time as her mother's thirty-something friends.

Petra and Marcus weren't angry or sad. On the contrary, they were thrilled by the prospect of being grandparents. 'I was a child when you were born and it didn't ruin my life.' Petra had said, hugging Marina tightly. 'Of course, it would have been better if you were more mature and could have planned your family, but these things happen.'

'I'm not sure I want to keep this baby.'

Christina and Petra exchanged a long look. They'd had the same sort of conversation eighteen years earlier. Petra and Christina told Marina that the decision was hers and hers alone to make. There was no right, no wrong, only a young woman with a tough decision to make over her body, her future.

Marina considered an abortion but ended up deciding to keep the baby. Deep inside, she always thought she'd got pregnant not by accident but by being subconsciously careless, almost as if she wanted to follow in her mother's footsteps. She felt that she'd stolen something from her mother, her youth, since she was old enough to understand that an eighteen-year-old girl is way too young to be a mother. Petra, with the help of her best friends, had been a great mother and hugely mature for her age. Despite having to postpone her studies and a lot of plans, she'd been present throughout and never showed any sign of regret about having Marina.

But even with that knowledge and certainty that she was the best thing to happen to Petra, part of Marina felt that she owed something to her mother and maybe getting pregnant at an early age, like Petra did, was a way of paying back, her youth for her mother's youth.

Marina had always known that Joe wasn't the fatherly type. He was childish and — beyond any doubt — not a nurturing person. He was at her side when Louisa was born and they rented a small studio with the help of their parents, trying to be a family. That didn't work out. After only a few months of sleepless nights and mountains of dirty nappies, Joe was less and less present, spending nights out with friends as Marina struggled alone at home.

She finally told her mother and her friends, the collagen coven, that her relationship had collapsed and she desperately needed their help.

Marina moved back into her mother's home. Joe moved in with friends and that was the end of their relationship. Joe still saw Louisa occasionally as she grew up, but he wasn't what anyone would consider an exemplary father.

Teresa and especially Christina helped Marina a lot with Louisa since they all had babies of their own at the same time. That was why Vanessa, Louisa and Alex were so close. They'd grown up together and were raised by a group of mothers and a grandmother.

Meeting Anthony was unexpected and amazing.

Marina had dated a few guys after Joe and was convinced that she'd never marry again or have other children. But Anthony was the opposite of Joe — mature, kind, protective, and, without a doubt, crazy about Marina.

Only three years after they met, they welcomed their first child, Gabriel, and then Archie. They were happy together.

♦ ♦ ♦

The next morning, Marina and Louisa prepared sandwiches and brownies and packed a big bottle of freshly squeezed orange juice. Together with Anthony and the two younger children, they went to London Fields for a picnic. The park wasn't close to their house but also not a long way to travel. They took the bus.

As Louisa played in the grass with Gabriel and Archie, Marina and Anthony sat down on their big picnic blanket, watching. 'I'm thinking of calling my father to come and join us with his partner. What do you think?' Marina asked Anthony.

'I think it would be a great idea, but only if you're ready for it. Are you?' He looked at her deep in her eyes.

'I think I am.'

'You think or you are?'

'I am. I'm calling him.' She dialled her father's number.

'Hey. How are you?' Marcus asked as soon as he heard his Marina's voice. When children reach a certain age, their parents are no longer on their priority list of people to call. In fact, parents are often the last ones on such a list. Maybe for that reason, parents often believe an emergency is the reason for the call. It was no different with Marina and Marcus.

'All fine. Just calling to find out what you're up to.'

'I thought something had happened.'

'Come on, Dad. I don't only call you when I'm in trouble.'

'You're right, you don't. But parents always worry about their kids.'

'I'm not a kid.' Marina laughed.

'To me you are and will always be. How are you doing?'

'I'm fine, Dad. We're at London Fields. Anthony, myself and the kids.' Marina paused to think for thirty seconds and make sure she was ready for what she was about to say. 'I was wondering if you wanted to join us. We have food and drink; it's a picnic.'

Another pause.

'That sounds fantastic. I'd love to.'

'There's one more thing.' Marina took a deep breath. 'I want you to bring your partner. I want to meet him.'

It was Marcus's turn to pause. 'That would make me so happy, but I need to check with him first. I'll call you back.'

Marina was excited, excited and anxious. Since

her mother's death so much had been going on. It was as if her life was turning upside down, but not in a bad way. Of course, it was a big surprise, her father coming out at that point in life, but it gave her comfort to know he was happy and that he could be himself around her. She'd worried that he'd suffered by keeping his true self for so long and having someone in secret for fifteen years. That must have been hard. But Marina's biggest worry was what that situation had meant to her mother. Did she love her dad? Had she tried to be in a romantic relationship with him? Was her heart broken? Was she lonely? Marina had so many questions and it was now too late and she'd never be able to have that conversation with her mother, to find out how she'd felt and to tell her that she loved her no matter what and that she was there for her. That was the only part of the story that was causing sorrow for Marina.

'Your father is calling you back.' Anthony pointed at her phone, bringing her back from the deep thoughts she'd been immersed in for the last few minutes.

Anthony had a calm and balanced personality. He knew exactly when to give Marina space and at the same time give her the assurance that he was there, waiting for her to be ready to talk.

'Hi, Dad. Did you talk to him?' she asked, her heart pounding.

'Yes, I did. He'd love to meet you, too. We're on our way.'

Marcus and Paolo arrived at the park and followed the dropped pin that Marina had sent from her phone to find them. It was a lovely sunny day and the park was full.

'Grandpa!' Gabriel, Marina's seven-year-old, ran towards Marcus as soon as he and Paolo approached them.

'Come here, little bunny.' Marcus grabbed Gabriel and raised him in the air.

'Who's that?' Gabriel asked, pointing at Paolo.

'It's Paolo. He's my partner.'

'Very nice to meet you, Mr Bunny,' Paolo joked.

'I'm not a bunny; my name's Gabriel. Grandpa calls me bunny because he likes being silly,' Gabriel responded with the honesty that only a child is capable of.

'Are you saying I'm silly? Come here.' Marcus started tickling him.

'Stop! Stop, I'm going to pee!'

'Believe me, he will.' Marina walked towards Marcus and Paolo. 'Hi, I'm Marina. You probably know that. It's nice to finally meet you.'

'Likewise. Your father has told me amazing things about you.'

'This is Anthony, my partner. This is Archie and this is Louisa.' Marina introduced her family.

'What's a partner?' Gabriel asked with curiosity.

'A partner is someone you share things with. Your life, your business. Anything.'

'I sometimes share my toys with Archie, but only

if he behaves. Is he my partner?'

'Nope, he's your brother, and brothers share things as well. Now come here and let's give Grandpa and Paolo something to eat.'

Marcus and Paolo opened their garden chairs and positioned them next to Marina's and Anthony's. 'Here, we brought some stuff, too. I got that truffle cheddar you like as well as nice crackers, olives and a bottle of wine.' Marcus opened his backpack and started taking things out.

'We also brought doughnuts for the kids,' Paolo said, picking up a package and showing it to Gabriel, who immediately jumped on him to grab his treat.

Louisa was lying belly down on a blanket with her chin resting on her hands. 'I've been so keen to meet you, Paolo, since I heard Grandpa had a partner. Tell us more about you,' she said.

'Louisa, this isn't an interrogation. Don't be intrusive,' Marina said.

'Don't worry, I don't feel intruded on. I'm happy to share and to learn about you all too.'

'See?' Louisa looked at her mum.

'I'm a hairdresser; I have a hair salon not far from here. I have two dogs and a goldfish. I'm half Italian — Mum's side — and I do speak Italian.'

'You have two dogs? And you haven't brought them? How come?' Louisa was clearly disappointed.

'They're with my daughter today. She takes them sometimes. It makes her children happy, but she doesn't want to have a dog of her own. I understand why. It's a lot of work, and she works hard and looks after twins. She has two five-year-olds.'

'Sad. I hope to meet them sometime,' Louisa said.

'You will,' Marcus reassured her.

'You have a daughter? Does my dad know her?' Marina asked.

'I do know her,' Marcus said and then looked at Marina.

I wish I'd also knew about you two. It's not nice being kept out of the loop. Marina looked back at her father, trying to hide her disappointment.

'My ex-partner and I adopted her when she was five. She's twenty-eight now,' Paolo explained. 'We broke up when she was about ten. But we shared custody and stayed on good terms. He's since re-married.'

They continued eating and chatting for over an hour. Paolo told them about his daughter and promised a haircut to Louisa. She told Paolo that she'd bring along Vanessa and Alex as they'd been dying to meet him since they'd learnt that Marcus had a partner.

After devouring the cheese, olives, crackers, cured meat, dips and pastries they'd brought for the picnic, Louisa and Paolo went to kick a ball around with Gabriel and Anthony took Archie for a stroll in the park, leaving Marina and Marcus alone.

'Why didn't you tell me earlier?'

'I knew you'd be upset.'

'I'm not upset. I'm sad.' Marina's face crumpled.

'I'm sorry. Your mum and I, we weren't strong enough to tell you the truth. And I never really thought about what this secret could do to you. I always thought it was my issue; my problem and I was to carry all the burden of it. I guess I was unwittingly selfish,' Marcus said.

'I feel jealous of Paolo's daughter. I feel sad that I missed all those years. I could have been part of your life, of your story with Paolo.'

'You were. You were always with me. You're part of me, my life, my story.'

'I wasn't there, Dad. Nothing you do or say will change that. I always had this feeling that somehow you and Mum weren't happy together. All that time I could feel your loneliness, yours and Mum's and — I've never told this to anyone — I thought something was wrong and it was because of me.'

'Don't. Please never ever think that. Your mum and I had hard times, yes. It was tough for us, but you were never part of the bad things. Everything involving you was the best part of it all.'

Gabriel kicked the ball, and it landed in Marcus's lap. He quickly threw it back to Anthony who was standing near them. Anthony mouthed the words 'Are you OK?' without making a sound. Marina nodded and blew him a kiss.

'Dad, I don't understand why you and Mum did everything you did. Why you've kept the secret, the sadness and the anguish you must have felt all these years.' Marina wiped away a tear and continued.

'But it was how our lives unfolded. I feel sad we'll never get a second chance, that moments that could have happened, happy moments, never will. But it wasn't your fault. Society can be a bitch. How can a collective of miserable, unhappy and unfulfilled people create rules and stigma to make everyone feel equally not enough so they feel less lost, less miserable? If only we could live our own lives and let people be. If only you'd never had to hide. You and Mum wouldn't have lied, and life would be different. But as I said, I accept what it is. Let's move on — I'm glad there are no more secrets.'

Marina stood up and extended her hand to Marcus in a gesture to call him to go and play with the kids. 'Let's make good memories, shall we?' She wasn't crying anymore and a timid smile appeared on her face as she spoke.

Marcus stood up and ran up to play tackle Gabriel for the ball. They played all day in the park.

Marcus was happy, but at the same time felt tormented. Not all the secrets were out, and he knew that the longer they were kept, the more damage they'd cause — for everyone. *We need to tell her,* he thought.

11

Christina

'Morning! How are you, Patricia?' Christina had arrived at the gallery in good spirits.

Christina had always felt like a sister to Petra, Teresa and Karishma and an auntie to their children, but finding out that she had an actual brother had brought her great joy, and the fact that Theo had a son made it even more special. Christina couldn't wait to start spoiling her nephew. Theo would never replace her lost brother, Ralph, but having a sibling had brought new purpose and energy into Christina's life.

'I'm fine and it looks like you're happy too. That makes me happy. It's been a while since I've seen you in such a good mood.' Patricia smiled. 'You have a visitor.' She pointed at the sofa in the small reception area of the gallery.

'Marina!' I'm so glad to see you. What's going on? Shouldn't you be at work?

'I quit,' Marina replied with a big smile.

Christina was lost for words for a second. 'Does

that mean you've considered my offer?'

'Yes. I have and I accept. I'll join you at the gallery and take my mother's place.'

Christina gave Marina a long, affectionate hug. That took Marina by surprise. Not that Christina was a cold person, but this felt different. Marina concluded that Christina must have been missing Petra. And having Marina there, side by side with her would fill some of the empty space left in Christina's life by the death of her best friend. Marina didn't want to feel like a replacement, but since she also missed her mother a lot, being closer to Christina would be good for her too. Christina had been a constant presence in her life for as long as she could remember. Even if she tried to, her mother and her friends never let her forget that she'd been raised by them all. It takes a coven, they'd always repeat.

'Patricia, Bianca, I have some fantastic news.' Christina had put a closed sign at the door and gathered the two employees together with Marina in her office. 'As of today, Marina works here with us. She'll take her mother's place.'

'Well, I still have a month's notice at my old job, and I may need a little time before I start,' Marina said politely, trying to curb Christina's enthusiasm.

That didn't work as Christina continued with, 'Sure, honey. But in the meantime, we'll change everything around here. Please, Bianca, call Julio. See when he can come over for us to draft the new layout.' Julio was a close friend of Christina's and a great architect and interior designer. He'd help Christina re-imagine the gallery space.

'I'm thinking of making the reception bigger, bringing all the exhibition space to the ground level and moving our offices upstairs. A complete make over,' Christina said.

The gallery was located in a small building that comprised two floors with a patio at the back. Downstairs was a small reception area with two desks and a pair of chairs opposite them and a small sofa in a corner near the entrance. Behind the reception was the exhibition space, and at the end were two offices with glass partitions to the exhibition area and between them. A small staircase led to the upper floor, where they had a small exhibition area, a tiny kitchen and a lot of storage space. The patio was empty and not properly connected to the main exhibition hall except for an old door that they used to hide with art displays since the outdoor space wasn't much used.

Christina and Petra were both organised with money, and though they'd struggled at the beginning, they'd managed to save every penny they could to invest in the gallery. The sacrifices they'd made had paid off, and the business became so successful they could afford to buy out the building they'd once rented. Christina always attributed their success to the fact they were unique. They'd worked with a lot of artists from South America that brought some originality and a lot of colour to the artwork they showcased. They also had a strong link to local communities and young artists. Both of them had an eye for talent and whenever they found an artist with good potential, they supported them and started a partnership. That way, the artist had a channel through which to market their work and the gallery had a special original flavour. A win-win situation.

'Julio can come over tomorrow at noon. Does that work?' asked Bianca.

'I'm free. That's perfect. Can you make it too, Marina?' Christina realised she was moving way too fast when she saw Marina's expression. 'Sorry dear. I'm so excited. I'm moving too fast.'

'A bit fast but it's exciting.' Marina smiled. 'Yes, I can make it. It's a date.' Marina was animated by the thought of her new work and the prospect of having her own space and more decision-making power. 'I'm still on gardening leave, but I can make it tomorrow. I'm hoping to be here full time in about a month and a half. What do you think?'

'I think it's fantastic! Start whenever you're ready! You're the new boss of your life now, darling. You make the rules. Let's see what Julio says about the timeframe for the refurbishment, and we can plan accordingly. I'm so happy that you've accepted the offer. It'll be great to work with you. I've always admired you as a professional. The preview the other day was fantastic. By the way, how did Alberta take it?'

'Well, she wasn't happy and of course she's afraid I may take some of her clients with me,' Marina explained.

'That wouldn't be bad for us, I guess.' Christina saw an opportunity there.

'I know, but I'm a professional and I'll be careful how I deal with it. I was thinking of an event once we finish the refurbishment. I can contact some of the artists I know and invite my clients — the ones I've made MY clients. I'll respect Alberta's own clients, those she had way before me, of course.'

'That's fair. She may have been expecting it. With Petra passing away, it's only natural that you'd inherit her business since you're in the same line of work.'

'You're right. She was expecting it but she still hoped I'd stay with her, especially because I was so invested in the preview. I guess that was my farewell gig.'

'And what a gig. I loved it.'

'Look, it's been great, but I must go now. See you and Julio tomorrow.' Marina gave Christina a kiss on the cheek.

'Bye, sweetheart.' Christina briefly hugged Marina in return.

As Marina was about to leave, she remembered something and turned back to face Christina. 'Oh. I almost forgot. Christina, do you know someone called Ricardo?'

Christina's heart stopped for a second. She

was livid as she heard the name and tried hard to compose herself without letting Marina notice. 'Ricardo? Maybe. I think we have a client called Ricardo… yes, we do. Why?'

'This guy called Ricardo called me. He said he wanted to visit the gallery to buy some art. He said he knew my mother. I'll meet him later today.'

'Will you? Why? I mean, of course, if he's a prospective client.' Christina had to think fast. 'But wouldn't it be better to meet him after you've completely moved here? That way he'd become our client, if he's not the same Ricardo. It would make things easier with Alberta, don't you think?'

'You have a point. I'll call him and postpone our meeting. Thanks for the suggestion. I hadn't thought about that. Bye.'

Once Marina had left, Christina remained in her office, stunned. She should have made the connection before. *Could it be the same Ricardo? Could he be Petra's client who Patricia had mentioned? Could he be also the man she was seeing? After all this time, how could it be?* She had to find out before Marina did.

Patricia was showing paintings to a woman who was looking for a large artwork for her dining room.

'Hello, sorry to interrupt. I need Patricia for an urgent matter, but Bianca here is the expert on this artist's work and can show you more options from our catalogue.' Christina whisked Patricia away from the client.

'What's happened? I've never seen you interrupt a client like that.'

'Do you remember the other day when you mentioned a client of Petra's? A South American who came for the retablos and bought some of my work?'

'Yes. What about him?'

'What was his name? I need his contact details urgently, please.' Christina was visibly agitated. 'And please keep it between us. Don't tell Hugo or Teresa.'

'Of course I won't. But is everything OK?'

'It will be. But I need to sort some things out. Thank you.' Christina said as she took the piece of paper from Patricia with the man's name and contact details.

Ricardo Goncalves. I knew it. Christina felt her world tumble down. She'd planned to meet her mother after work, take her for dinner and tell her about Theo. But this was more important. She had to find Ricardo and talk to him. She called the number.

'Hello, Ricardo speaking.' A familiar voice answered in English with a heavy accent.

'Hi, Ricardo. This is Christina. Teresa's and Petra's friend...' She paused, waiting to hear his reaction. He'd obviously remember her.

'I was expecting you to call me,' he said in an emotionless voice.

'We need to talk. Are you free? Now?'

'I knew you had something to do with it.' Ricardo's tone made it clear he wasn't impressed.

'What did I have something to do with?'

'Marina. I was supposed to meet her. She cancelled. Did you put her off?'

'Of course I did. What are you doing? You can't approach her like that. What do you want to tell her?'

'The truth. That's what Petra wanted.'

'How do you know what Petra wanted?'

'We were together, Christina; we'd been seeing each other.' Ricardo's voice was softer as he mentioned Petra.

'We can't talk about that over the phone. Let's meet up, please.'

They agreed to meet in a pub near London Bridge. Christina told Patricia to cancel all her appointments for the day and left in a hurry to meet Ricardo.

◆ ◆ ◆

Christina took the underground. During her journey she was filled with anticipation and apprehension. Over thirty years had passed since she'd last seen Ricardo. But as soon as Christina entered the pub, she recognised him sitting alone at a table by the window. He looked older, of course, but despite his now salt and pepper hair, his slightly wrinkled skin and the more defined angles contouring his face, his physiognomy still held the essence of the boy she once knew. She'd recognise him a mile away.

A multitude of feelings invaded Christina. Seeing Ricardo brought back memories of her, Petra and

Teresa in Brazil. A surge of nostalgia and memories of their youthful time, carefree moments and adventures mixed with recollections of bitterness and disappointment.

'You haven't aged at all.' Ricardo said politely as Christina approached his table. He stood up and pulled out a chair for her.

'You're too kind, but I've aged, and so have you. What brings you to London?' Christina was cold and direct.

'What do you want to drink?' Ricardo asked.

'A glass of wine, please. Red.'

'I'll get one for me, too. Give me a minute.'

Christina watched as he went to the bar to get the drinks. Her mind was all over the place. During the last thirty-six years she'd imagined the many ways an encounter between them would go. She'd thought about the thousand things she'd say to him, most of them not nice. But now that he was in front of her, she had no words.

'Look, I know you're not happy to see me,' began Ricardo. 'Not after everything that happened, but you don't know all the story.'

'I don't want to know all the story. There's no story to know. I don't want you to bring things back that should be buried in the past. I don't want Marina to get hurt.'

'Petra wanted her to know everything. She was about to tell her.'

'Petra isn't here anymore. It's not her decision

now. And besides, she never told me anything like that,' Christina lied.

'She told me repeatedly. We talked about it over and over again before she passed.'

'How do I know if you're telling me the truth? How did you reconnect with Petra, anyway?'

'I'll start from the beginning.' Ricardo took a sip of his drink. 'I moved to London a couple of years ago,' he said calmly.+

'Why did you move to London?' Christina didn't feel calm.

'Because of my work and to be closer to my children. My ex-wife is from Scotland and moved back here when we divorced five years ago. We met in the US when I was at university there. You remember, I moved to the US after we all met.'

'I remember well.' Christina looked down and took a deep breath.

'At first, I thought I'd leave it all behind and didn't plan to stir up the past.'

'So why did you? Why are you doing it now? I mean, contacting Marina?'

'I told you. That was what Petra wanted.'

'You haven't answered my question yet. How did you and Petra reconnect?'

'I passed by your gallery one day. I saw a nice artwork, very colourful.'

'The retablos. Peruvian work.'

'Yes, exactly. And then I saw your art. I mean, I didn't know it was your art. As I was about to buy it,

I saw Petra. We recognised each other. We went out for a coffee; we talked about the past...'

'And then you two decided to ignore everything that happened and started dating?' The more Christina heard, the more agitated she got; she felt as if she was talking like a mad woman now.

'It wasn't like that. We felt attracted to each other and continued seeing each other. It happened slowly; we fell in love.'

'And she didn't think of telling me? Her best friend? The one who'd been by her side her entire life? I need another wine, please.'

Ricardo went to the bar, coming back with a bottle of red wine. 'Here you go. I got crisps as well. Not good to drink on an empty stomach, especially not at eleven in the morning.'

'Look Ricardo. I can't tell you not to live in the same city as us or go back in time and advise Petra to stay away from you, but I can ask you to leave Marina alone. Please.'

'I'm sorry, Christina, but no. You can't ask me that. I have the right to talk to her.'

'You have no rights! You can't barge into our lives after decades and decide you have rights.' Christina was almost shouting and people turned to look at them.

'Please, don't raise your voice. I know how hard it is. I know how much you love Marina and how close you were to Petra, but you must understand. I promised her before she died.'

'You promised her? And where were you all these years? Where were you when she died? You didn't even come to her funeral.'

'I was in Brazil, and believe me, I was devastated. We'd made plans, Christina. We were going to tell Marina, and we were planning to move in together.'

'And you were going to do it behind my back? Behind Teresa's back? We raised Marina with Petra. Did you know that? And what about Marcus? '

'We were going to talk to all of you. But then I went to Brazil and when I came back, I went to the gallery and found out that Petra had passed. My world collapsed. Can you imagine how I felt? I loved Petra.'

'No, *I* loved Petra. You barely knew her.' Christina had raised her voice again.

'Look, Christina, I made a mistake in contacting Marina without talking to you and Marcus first. But I won't hold back from telling her the truth.' Ricardo's voice was firm now.

Christina shook her head and covered her mouth with her hands. The world around her seemed to collapse; faces became blurred and sounds faded into a distant hum. Her eyes were glistening with tears about to pour down, reflecting the hurricane of emotions brewing inside her.

'You're going to ruin everything. Marina is coming to terms with the loss of her mother. She's found out that her father's gay, and his marriage to her mother was fake. She left her job and is going to work with me at the gallery. There's too much going on. Please, let things settle down. Let me think. We can find the right time and way to tell her. You owe me this.' Christina realised she wouldn't be able to dissuade Ricardo from his determination to coming clean to Marina, but she could at least gain some time to think.

'I don't think I owe you, or anyone, anything. You don't know my side of the story. But I agree. For Marina's sake, I'll wait. I'll be travelling for work for two and a half months. I'll call you when I'm back.' He finished the wine left on his glass and stood up. 'Bye for now.'

Once Ricardo had left, Christina stayed there, crying, all by herself. She felt sad, betrayed and alone. She'd never felt so alone. Her best friend had hidden all this from her and now she wasn't there anymore, so they could at least talk, so Christina could understand what had been going on inside Petra's head. She needed someone to share this burden. Someone to be in her corner and help persuade Ricardo to change his mind. She picked up her phone. 'Hi Marcus, we need to talk. It's urgent.'

◆ ◆ ◆

Christina met Marcus at his house that same day.

'Hi, what happened?' Marcus asked as he opened the door and noticed Christina's red eyes. It was clear she'd been crying. He led her to the living room, and as she sat down, he grabbed her a glass of water.

'Thank you.' Christina drank the whole glass at once. 'Ricardo, THE RICARDO, from Rio, is here, in London. Did you know that? He's the man Petra was seeing before she died.'

'What?' Marcus was livid. 'How come?'

'Apparently, his family, his ex-wife and children, live here. He bumped into Petra one day and they reconnected and fell in love.'

'Bumped into each other? By chance? How is that even possible? Destiny?'

'I guess yes, destiny. He was attracted to an artwork displayed in our gallery. He came in and surprise, surprise, there was Petra.'

'Wasn't she mad at him after everything? I mean, we all were mad at him.'

'Apparently not. Maybe at first, but then not anymore. They kept seeing each other and she fell for him and he for her, apparently. At least that's what he said. Truth is we'll never know. Whatever happened died with her. We can only know his version. And he said she wanted to tell Marina. Tell her everything.'

Marcus let his body crash down on the sofa. It was Christina's turn to grab a glass of water. As Marcus drank the water, someone put a key through the door and turned the knob. Marcus jumped as he saw Paolo coming in.

'Christina, I've been meaning to tell you, this is…'

'You must be Paolo.' Christina was so unnerved

that she had no time for pleasantries. She looked at Marcus. 'Marina told me everything.'

'Of course she did. Now you know,' said Marcus.

'It's nice to meet you, Christina,' said Paolo. 'Marcus has said amazing things about you.'

'I'm glad he did.' The sudden interruption of Paolo's arrival had brought a pause to the agitated situation and conversation they were having before.

'We can carry on talking. Paolo knows everything.' Marcus held his partner's hand in a gesture as if saying we trust each other. It made Christina feel like the smallest person in the world. She'd never been able to trust her husband with their big secret, and to this day he was oblivious to the facts of hers and her friends' past. That bothered her profoundly. 'At least someone is honest in our big extended family,' she said sarcastically

'Come on, Christina. Don't feel bad,' Marcus said. 'The situation between me and Paolo is different, and you all had your reasons to keep secrets.'

'Well, guess what? Secrets will surface now and destroy our lives, our families, everything. Ricardo wants to tell Marina. He'd be telling her right now if I hadn't found out and interfered with his plans.'

'Ricardo? *The* Ricardo?' Paolo asked.

'Yes, *the* Ricardo. This is bad.' Marcus let his head fall back and brought his hands to his face.

'Maybe not so bad. Sorry, I don't want to interfere, but haven't you all kept secrets for a long time? Isn't it time to come clean? About everything?

I met Marina the other day and I could see how much joy she felt around Marcus, knowing that he'd opened himself to her. And I've never seen Marcus so happy.' Paolo threw a tender look at Marcus.

Christina's eyes narrowed, and she snapped at Paolo. 'You *are* intruding. This is different and none of your business,'

'Please, Christina. You're being rude. Paolo is family, for me at least, and he has a point.' Marcus's words were laced with irritation.

'He's just arrived in this story. I've been in it for thirty-six years.' Christina was crying again.

'I'm sorry.' Paolo approached her. 'I didn't mean to...' He gestured to Marcus to calm down.

Marcus took a deep breath. 'Look, Christina, I'm not saying that Ricardo's right, and I'm not going to call Marina right now. But we must think about this and make the decision together. I'm tired of secrets. I've been miserable for a long portion of my life because I kept things bottled up. I feel so much lighter now. Let's think about it.'

'Petra wanted Marina to know,' Christina said in a low, almost inaudible tone.

'That was what Ricardo said, right?' Marcus asked.

'Yes, he did. But we don't know if it's really true,' Christina lied, omitting Petra's last words to her.

'Let's sleep on it, shall we?' Marcus proposed.

Christina agreed and told him that Ricardo was going to be away for a while and had agreed to wait and talk to her before approaching Marina again. Then she realised how late it was and remembered that she was supposed to take her mother out to talk about Theo. She had no bandwidth for that now. She called her mum and cancelled. Once home, she said she had a migraine and went straight to her room, leaving dinner and everything to Peter, Vanessa and Harry to sort out.

Peter noticed something was off and tried to approach Christina. She lashed out at him. 'I need to be alone, please. I'm sorry I was rude. I've been struggling all day with this headache. I'm not thinking straight.'

Peter decided to leave Christina to her thoughts, but he wasn't happy. Their relationship was in a fragile state. He'd been filled with hope after their romantic evening not long ago, but this attitude from Christina changed his perspective. *And we're back to normal.* Peter felt sad; he was starting to lose hope that their relationship could be mended.

12

Teresa

'My darling, come here.' Teresa said, taking a sobbing Christina in her arms as soon as they met the next morning at Christina's house.

Christina had told Peter and the kids that she wasn't feeling well and she'd stay home. As soon as they'd all left the house, she called Teresa, crying and asking her to come round.

'He's back, Teresa. Ricardo is back, and he wants to tell Marina everything.' Christina's voice cracked between her sobs.

'How come? Where did he come from, after all this time?' Teresa was flabbergasted.

Christina told her everything.

'Here, have a drink.' Teresa handed Christina a glass of water. 'Have you had breakfast? You're so pale; I'll get you something.' Teresa was a couple of years older than Christina and sometimes she felt like the mum of the group.

She went to the kitchen and came back with a slice of lemon drizzle cake. 'This is delicious. Vanessa baked it.'

Christina took a small bite of the cake.

'Let's think rationally. Let's assume Ricardo will come back and there's no possibility of changing his mind. How bad could it be?' Teresa asked.

'How bad? It would be a disaster. Marina would hate me, and you, and all of us who knew everything. And worse, she would suffer. Our beautiful big family would be shattered. Petra's gone, and she'd never be able to talk to her about it. How could she come to terms with that? She'll never understand Petra's side of the story.'

'Yes, she would. We can explain. It will be hard, but she'll understand, eventually. She's strong and her heart is in the right place. Don't you think?' Teresa was trying to be pragmatic.

'Honestly? I don't think so. I've never come to terms with it myself.' Christina's face was flooded by the relentless cascade of tears — each drop filled with heavy emotions that had been suffocating her for a long time.

Teresa succumbed to the sadness of the moment and was overtaken by memories and the heavy weight of all the actions they'd taken in the past, all the secrets they shared. Tears began to well up in her eyes as well as each drop tracing a path down her cheeks.

'If only Petra was here. We could decide this together. I miss her so much.' Christina tried to speak through her sobs.

'I miss her too. But we must be strong, dear. We'll

find an answer. We should have talked about it, all of us, a long time ago when Petra was still here. But who'd have guessed that she'd leave us, so early, so suddenly?' Teresa's voice was breaking with the raw emotions she was feeling as she looked for the right words to say, even though she didn't necessarily believe them herself. She knew how devastating the consequences could be once the secret was out.

Teresa stayed until Christina fell asleep on the sofa; she'd been up all night, after all. As Teresa was about to leave, Christina's phone started to ring. Teresa answered quickly so as not to wake Christina. It was Marina. Teresa took a deep breath, trying to disguise the fact she'd been crying.

'Hello, who is this?' Marina said.

'Hi, Marina. It's me, Teresa.'

'Where's Christina? She was supposed to meet me and the architect who'll do the project to refurbish the gallery's layout.'

'What gallery?'

'Christina's gallery, our gallery. Sorry we didn't tell you; I've quit my job. I'm joining Christina at the gallery. I'll take my mum's place.' Marina sounded enthusiastic.

'That's great! Listen, you get started and I'll make sure Christina gets there as soon as possible. She wasn't feeling well and is having a shower now. I came earlier to check on her.'

'Is it serious? What happened? She was fine yesterday.'

'Nothing serious. She must have eaten something bad. She's better now and will be there soon.' Teresa hung up and reflected for a minute. Christina had convinced Marina to join her at the gallery, and bringing back secrets from the past would muddy the waters, but maybe it was the only way. For now, however, she wanted Christina to simmer down her emotions until she was able to think clearly and make the right decision. Telling Marina was probably inevitable, but it had to be done in the proper manner. *Damage control,* she thought.

Teresa managed to wake up Christina, who looked recharged after her nap. She reminded her about the architect and once Christina had managed to have a shower and felt more composed, Teresa dropped her off at the gallery. Christina was feeling better and they agreed to think about the next steps in relation to Ricardo's and Marina's situation.

'Thank you. I was desperate this morning. I think I needed someone to cry with me,' Christina said as she was about to go inside the gallery.

'Of course you did. It was good for me too, it's good to share tears from time to time. It cleanses our souls.' Teresa blew her friend a kiss and left.

◆ ◆ ◆

When Teresa got back home, she had a massive surprise. 'Mum? When did you get here? You never told me you were coming.'

Teresa's mother, Ines, was standing in the kitchen with Alex and Daniel. 'I decided to surprise you. It's been a while since I've been to the UK.' Ines hugged her daughter.

'I'm so happy to see you. It's like you've read my mind. I needed to talk to you today but having you here, in the flesh, is so much better.'

Teresa and Ines started talking Portuguese and went together to the garden.

'That's it, now I can't understand you anymore... *obrigado*.' Daniel said jokingly.

Alex laughed. He could speak a bit of Portuguese. Daniel on the other hand knew three words: *obrigado* meaning thank you, *bom dia*, good morning, and the name of his favourite cocktail, *caipirinha*.

Mother and daughter spent the afternoon in the garden chatting away. Teresa had given in her notice the week before and was enjoying being free in the middle of the week. She told Ines about everything that had been going on — her decision to follow Daniel on a world tour with a famous singer, and the drama that was unfolding with Christina, Ricardo and Marina.

'I feel guilty, too. I'm part of that secret. I was there.' Ines reminded Teresa. 'I've never told you, darling, but I've always felt guilty about the way I handled things at the time. You were all staying with me, my responsibility.'

'What could you have done? We were legally adults.'

'Legally, yes. But you were children. And I acted with my heart, not with reason.' Ines's face expressed the regret and even shame she was feeling. With downcast eyes, she continued. 'I've carried it all my life and I feel bad about it. Not for what you've done, I see the love in that, but by allowing you to keep it secret. We could have been honest from the beginning.'

'You shouldn't feel bad. It was our decision to do things the way we did. It wouldn't have been the same, especially for Petra and Marcus, if we'd been open about everything from the beginning. At that time, the lie seemed like the best way, the only way. Please, Mum, don't worry about it and don't blame yourself. Christina and I'll find a way. Let me tell you something else you haven't heard.'

'There's more?'

'Oh yes… Christina has a brother. George had a second family. And brace yourself – Karishma's in love with him and Christina doesn't know. And one more thing, this will be a big surprise for you, a good one. After the tour, Valerie's tour, Daniel and I'll move to Brazil for a while.' Teresa had saved the best news for last.

Ines became visibly emotional at the good news. She'd respected Teresa's decision to move back to the UK after her gap year, but at the same time a day hadn't passed when Ines hadn't missed her daughter. 'Is that true? Why? Do you think I'm dying? I'm not. I'm just old.'

'You're not old, Mum. Age is only a number; you head is all there, thank God.'

Ines was seventy-eight but didn't look a day past sixty-five. She'd re-married twenty years ago, but had no other children. Her second husband had died a couple of years ago and Ines's only sister had moved in with her. They had a good group of friends and kept each other company. But Ines did feel lonely. She missed Teresa and had always felt saddened by the fact that Teresa had moved to the UK and she hadn't been physically present for most of her daughter's life. She missed all those years that didn't happen, the ones where she'd have helped raise her grandchildren and see them growing up. She spent a couple of months in the UK with Teresa every year and Teresa went back for holidays, but it wasn't the same. 'Teresa, this is the best news I've ever had. Is Alex coming too?'

'I haven't told him yet, but maybe. He's welcome to come, and I'm sure that with me and Daniel in Rio, Hugo and Alan will come to visit.'

'That would be fantastic. Have you decided where to live yet? You can stay with me for a while. My place is huge.'

'We will. We'll stay for a couple of months at your place, if that's OK, and then we'll find our own place.'

'By the way, I've started looking for accommodation for December. You're all still coming for the holidays, right?'

Teresa didn't want to mention that maybe she wasn't coming to spend that Christmas and New

Year's Eve with her as planned, as Daniel had other plans for them, so she lied. 'Of course we're all coming. What did you find?'

Ines told about two apartments in her building that were for temporary rent, and that she'd reserved them. 'You, Daniel and Karishma can stay with me. Hugo and his fiancée, Alan, Alex, Vanessa and Louisa can stay in one apartment. Are they all still close?' Ines was doing the math.

'They're very close, and Alex has a boyfriend now, Ollie. He might come with us.'

'That would be OK. We can still fit in one apartment and the last apartment can accommodate Christina and Peter, Samantha and Harry, Marina, Anthony and their little ones. It's perfect.' Ines had it all planned.

Talking about the plans and knowing that Teresa would move close to her, albeit temporarily, made Ines forget the whole Marina, Marcus, Christina and Ricardo drama.

'Dad and Purnima may come as well, Mum. I need to find a place for them. But we still have time for that.'

'They're welcome to join us for the festivities, but it would be best if they stayed in a hotel. What about Declan, Ellie and Margaret? Are they coming too?'

'Maybe. I'll book hotels for them, just in case, for now. They're not that young anymore and they're not as fit as you, Mum. But maybe they'll come. Let's see.'

Making the plans for the upcoming holiday and the prospect of all of them being together in Rio after all those years filled Teresa with happiness, so much so that she thought maybe she could postpone her Hawaiian dream holiday with Daniel. She'd have to think about that.

'Can I have some time with the most gorgeous grandma in the world?' Hugo had appeared at the top of the stairs with Patricia behind him.

'Oh my God, don't you look handsome? Come here, my oldest grandchild and his beautiful fiancée.'

Ines hugged and kissed Hugo as if he were a little boy. That was the Brazilian way, tactile and warm-hearted. Hugo loved that, and even Patricia got a big hug.

They sat down for dinner all together. Alan also came, and Alex invited Ollie to meet his boyfriend's grandma for the first time. It was a happy evening that made Teresa feel joyous in a way she hadn't felt in a while. Seeing her mum's happiness was all she needed to feel reassured that moving to Brazil for a while after the tour was a good decision. Part of her regretted moving away and depriving her mum of being a constant part of her life and now she had an opportunity to give some of that lost time back to Ines. Even if it was only for a few years, it was better than nothing.

13

Karishma

Karishma opened her eyes and quickly turned off the alarm so as not to wake up Theo. It was five o'clock and she had a surgery to attend. She looked at his naked body wrapped in her bedsheets. Theo lay gracefully on his side, revealing a sculpted back with well-defined and toned muscles. Their age gap was still a lingering concern for Karishma; she couldn't help but think that her body was aging faster, she was perimenopausal and felt big changes within herself, mood swings, constant tiredness and even hot flashes. In her head, she pictured Theo in ten years, still looking hot and probably even more sexy than now, while she looked like an old lady. *Nature can be so unfair to women,* she thought.

The alarm went off again. She hadn't stopped it but snoozed by mistake, and this time it did wake Theo. 'Hey. Morning.' Theo looked at her with a big smile.

Theo's big green eyes staring at her were enough to make Karishma forget all about menopause, age gap and old ladies for a moment. All she could think about was how much she wanted to get back into bed with him. 'Sorry, I didn't mean to wake you. Go back to sleep. It's way too early.' Karishma kissed him softly on the tip of his nose.

'I don't want to sleep. I want you.'

Theo pulled her closer and started kissing her neck, moving slowly down to her chest and her belly button. She felt numb and any thoughts she might have disappeared; she surrendered her body, mind and soul to that moment. Karishma felt whole and free in a way she hadn't for so long. The desire to be with Theo was stronger than any self-sabotage kind-of thought she could have, for a few minutes at least.

'I don't want you to go,' Theo said after they'd made love.

'I don't want to go either, but I have to.' Karishma gently moved Theo away and got off the bed.

'What time are you back? We can go for brunch. David's mum's in town, and she has him for a few days.'

'She's in town? For how long?' Karishma tried to sound casual in a bid not to show she felt a bit jealous.

'Two weeks, I think. Does that bother you?'

'Maybe. Maybe a bit. I know you were mad about her. You even mentioned it to Christina.' Karishma spoke faster than she'd intended and immediately regretted saying anything.

'I told you I was in love with her, yes. But that was a long time ago, I promise. There are absolutely no romantic feelings between us, nothing at all.'

'I'm sorry. I have no right to act like that, being jealous of you. It's just the thought of this gorgeous young woman that has a past with you, a son with you. I lost it for a second,' Karishma said.

'You have nothing to be sorry for. I understand. I'd be jealous if you were meeting your ex, too. You told me how you were crazy about him,' Theo confessed.

Yes, but my ex is dead and buried, Karishma thought, but she didn't say anything. 'You're right. Let's forget about what I said, please.' Karishma didn't want to think about Iain, not now.

'So, is it yes? For brunch, later?' Theo asked hopefully.

'Yes. It's a yes. Do you have anywhere in mind?' Karishma asked as she moved closer to him. 'You can wait here for me; Otto and Star would love that.' She looked at the two dogs staring at her from the floor next to the bed.

'Sounds like a perfect plan. Come back here and we'll go from there. I have something in mind. I'll walk the dogs for you.'

'Oh, they'd love that, for sure.' Karishma was about to let the dogs out for a few minutes in the back garden — having someone walk them was a big plus.

'What time are you back?'

'I'm hoping to be back by eleven. Is that too late?'

'Not at all. Eleven is perfect. See you then.'

The surgery was a success and Karishma couldn't wait to get back to Theo. She had a quick shower at the hospital and rushed back home, getting there fifteen minutes earlier than planned. As she opened the door, a scent of flowers and food invaded her nostrils. A massive bouquet of roses and chrysanthemums adorned her dining table where brunch was served.

'You're early! I haven't finished.' Theo jumped as he saw her.

'You haven't finished? How many people are coming?' Karishma pointed at all the food on the table. Sourdough, croissants, Danish pastries, a cheese board, charcuterie, avocado, juices and a pot with freshly brewed coffee.

'I'm making eggs benedict and the cherry on the cake, mimosas. And there's also cake.' Theo looked so sexy with an apron over his tracksuit.

'We can't eat all this for brunch. You're insane.' Karishma laughed and kissed Theo passionately.

'We can't have it for brunch, you're right. But… we can dip into it all day, if you'll allow me to stay over.' Theo kissed her back.

Karishma thought about the meeting she'd set up with a potential surrogate for her embryo. But the idea of spending all day, all weekend, with Theo was stronger than anything, and once again, she surrendered.

The weekend was perfect, like a dream, something Karishma had wanted ferociously, but had convinced herself would never happen for her. Together they walked the dogs, watched movies, talked about their lives, and made love again and again.

On Sunday night, Theo left.

'This was probably one of the best weekends of my life. I'm in love with you, Karishma,' Theo turned back to say before she closed the door behind him..

She didn't say a word but kissed him with passion and tenderness. She saw on his face the disappointment of not hearing a similar statement from her, but he was clearly happy with the kiss.

Karishma didn't know what to say. She was madly in love with Theo, but couldn't shake the feeling that she'd let it go way too far. *What am I thinking? I'm having a baby. Iain's baby.* In her head, Theo had already made up his mind about her baby plans, even though he didn't know anything about them yet. *He'll freak out and leave as fast as he came into my life and both our hearts will be shattered.*

They'd gone too far, too fast. And there was Christina. Karishma was sure that Christina wouldn't accept her friend dating her much younger brother. A brother Christina hadn't yet had the time to get to know. Karishma couldn't steal her thunder. That wasn't fair.

The wondrous feeling of happiness suddenly turned into melancholy thanks to Jiminy Cricket's evil twin — he was back in Karishma's mind.

All she could think now was that she had to put an end to their relationship and go on to have her baby. It was the right thing to do, and the sooner the better. The more involved they got, the bigger the pain and sorrow would be. She didn't want that. *I'll have to nip the evil in the bud.*

◆ ◆ ◆

That same week, Karishma met with the surrogate candidate to discuss the details of their agreement.

Karishma had spent weeks researching IVF, surrogacy, options and risks and talking to doctor colleagues about the details of the process. It was going to be a host surrogacy where there's no genetic connection between the baby and the surrogate. The embryos were to be from Karishma's eggs and Iain's sperm. They'd been frozen for a long time but were healthy enough to be thawed and implanted.

The meeting went well. The surrogate was a single young woman who seemed intelligent and pragmatic. The main thing for Karishma was to make sure she was healthy and would be clear about her role in the process so there was less risk of issues. The surrogate would be the legal parent at birth and a parental order would be needed to transfer the baby to the biological parent.

Karishma was using a non-profit organisation that helped people through surrogacy. They offered guidance and support throughout the entire process.

She and the surrogate discussed the terms and conditions of their agreement. Karishma would provide all the medical support through private medical cover; she'd be in touch and have regular meetings with the surrogate during the gestational phase and would be present at birth. She'd also cover all additional expenses. The surrogate was going to do all the required medical tests that same week and, all being well, the embryo transfer would take place in less than a month.

Theo had been texting Karishma every day, but she'd been evasive in her responses. Not that she didn't want to answer. Part of her was desperate to call him, tell him about her desire to be a mother, about the dream she'd once shared with Iain that had led them to freeze their embryos. That part of Karishma, the dauntless one, wanted to share the excitement she felt in learning that the embryos were healthy and that she'd found the perfect surrogate. The dauntless portion of her wasn't scared of how Theo would react to the fact that she was about to have a dead man's baby. That same side of her wouldn't keep dreading the fact that soon enough, when the honeymoon period of their new love was over, he'd leave her for a younger, more attractive, fertile woman who would give him the big family he dreamt of.

But unfortunately, that part of her was powerless compared to the broken Karishma. The part of her whose dreams and hopes of love and a family of her own had been lost on the summit of the Matterhorn the day Iain died. The Karishma who had been abandoned by her father as a young girl wasn't an audacious person. She knew better than to take risks and knew that the higher you climb, the harder you fall.

Broken Karishma had already decided her fate. She knew that Theo would leave her as fast as he'd entered her life, that he'd go the minute he learned about the crazy idea she was putting in motion.

Not to mention that she was forty-six — he'd think she was too old to be a mum. Even if he accepted all that, as soon as the hardships of parenting a young child kicked in and the collagen ran out, and that would be soon, Theo would get tired of her, of all that, and leave.

And the final challenge — her best friend would be mad at her for dating her newly found younger brother. Karishma had imagined over and over in her head Christina's reaction when she found out about them. *He's young and has a whole life ahead of him. What were you thinking? I haven't even had the chance to get to know him and you're all over Theo.*

Of course, that Christina, the one in Karishma's mind, was an entirely different person from her friend of a lifetime.

Karishma's traumas had been so deeply rooted in her soul that she'd stopped noticing they were there, very much alive and dealing all the cards in her life.

After the meeting with the surrogate, Karishma went back home, determined to put an end to her relationship, or whatever it was, with Theo.

Theo was waiting outside her door. 'Hey. Are you all right? You haven't replied to any of my messages. I'm sorry to show up like this, but I was worried.'

Karishma hadn't expected to see him. She'd already elaborated in her head the text she'd write or words she'd pronounce over the phone, but seeing Theo there in the flesh changed things. She wasn't sure she was strong enough. 'Hi. I'm — I mean, I don't know what to say.' As soon as she said those meaningless words, she burst into tears.

'Karishma, what's happened? Come here.' Theo wrapped his arms around her and kissed the top of her head.

For a moment, Karishma felt safe, protected from her own thoughts inside that embrace. For a split a second, she felt inebriated by the now familiar scent of his skin and forgot about all the red flags, all the fear inside her head. But that was only for a second.

Karishma gently pushed Theo away and recovered the strength to say the words she'd rehearsed over and over in her mind. 'I'm sorry, Theo. This was fun, it really was, but I can't do it anymore. It's not the right time. There's so much going on in my life. Please, leave me.'

There she was, defeated Karishma begging hope and joy to leave her alone, to forget about her. *How could I self-sabotage like that?* But that was just a thought, a brief thought.

Theo was the one with tears in his eyes now. 'I don't understand. I honestly thought the last few months were real. That last weekend was real. What changed? What happened?'

'Nothing changed. I'm not in the best place right now.'

'Oh, I see. You were simply having fun. Of course. How stupid of me. Are the tears fake as well? Did you rehearse that?'

Theo's body was arched as if he was experiencing physical pain, and his words were full of resentment and despair.

But Karishma's pain was even more intense. She wanted him to disappear from sight so she could crumble alone in her home and avoid any chance of changing her mind. The risk of failure was too high. 'Please go. I have nothing else to say. I don't owe you an explanation. Sorry if I've caused you pain, but please go.'

'You fooled me. I thought we had something. How stupid was I?' Theo was looking up and talking to himself. It had started to rain, and his face was covered in tiny droplets of water. 'You needn't worry. I'll go and I won't bother you anymore. You should be an actress, not a doctor, Karishma. You're a great pretender. I thought more of you. Bye.'

Karishma stood in the rain, sobbing as Theo walked away from her until his silhouette was out of her sight. She went home and curled up in bed with her two dogs, like a snail. She'd experienced this feeling before. The feeling of abandonment, of losing hope and being completely alone.

But she knew all the pain was of her own doing, at least at that stage, since she hadn't even given Theo the option to be part of her decision making.

Karishma transferred her scheduled surgeries to a colleague and called work to say she needed time off to deal with some private matters. She also cancelled her two upcoming appointments with Mia, her therapist, and told a big fat lie to Teresa and Christina, and to her mother and stepfather. She said there was a medical conference abroad that she was attending for the next ten days. She didn't want to see or talk to anyone.

'How come? You haven't mentioned anything before.' Teresa was suspicious.

'I'd missed the deadline, but a colleague managed to pull strings for me,' was her lousy explanation.

Karishma packed up and went north. She rented a small cottage in the Lake District, in an idyllic location by a lake, and decided to stay there alone as she tried to forget Theo and regain her senses.

The transfer of the embryos to the surrogate was going to happen soon, and she wanted to be emotionally prepared. The decision was made, and she wanted to dedicate her mind to that child from now on. Even though she wasn't going to be carrying the baby herself, she'd be pregnant in a way, and she wanted to experience all stages of that miracle, prepare the nursery, choose the clothes, the cot, the pram.

Being away from everybody, everything, helped

her. Karishma spent the next ten days wandering around beautiful scenery, visiting manicured gardens and enjoying the quiet and peace of the Lake District. It was way too early, of course, as the upcoming procedure with the surrogate had a chance of not working, but Karishma couldn't stop herself from buying a cute plush toy, a bunny for her child. *Your first toy, my love.*

Being a doctor, Karishma was aware of the chances of the embryo transfer procedure being a success, around fifty per cent. But she had a strong instinct that it would work out fine. She wasn't a religious or spiritual person, but when in contact with nature, Karishma felt connected to herself in a way that she could almost hear her instincts. And her instinct was telling her that she was going to be a mother, the mother of Iain's baby, at last.

Her certainty grew even stronger when the doctors who were overseeing the pre-procedure tests with the surrogate called to say all was well and she could have the embryo transferred.

After ten days, she felt recharged. There was still a lingering sadness for all that had happened between her and Theo, sadness and guilt, but Karishma managed to bury those feelings deep inside and focus solely on the pregnancy.

A few days after she returned, Karishma, Teresa, Christina and Marina met at their local wine bar.

'So, how was the conference?' Teresa asked with suspicion. She hadn't bought her stepsister's story and suspected that something was off with her.

'The conference? Oh yes. Boring. You know, these things are always boring,' Karishma said firmly, hoping she sounded convincing.

'Where did you go? Where was it?' Marina asked.

'In Spain. Yes, that part of it was fun. How are you all?' Karishma tried to change the subject.

'Wait. Tell us more. Did you meet any interesting single doctors?' asked Marina.

'No. Nobody interesting. To be honest, being in a relationship is the last thing on my mind right now.' Karishma looked at Teresa, who picked up the hint that something had gone wrong with Theo.

'Who's talking about a relationship? What happened to good passionate sexual encounters?' Marina was pushing it.

'I don't think Karishma is interested in that right now, Marina.' Christina had noticed that the conversation was making Karishma uncomfortable.

'I'm sorry, Karishma. It was a joke.' Marina looked uncomfortable.

'I know. I get it, I'm just tired, as usual. But tell me about the gallery. I've heard you two are now working together.' Karishma pointed at Marina and Christina.

'Not yet, but we will be. We're refurbishing the gallery, and it's going to look fantastic. I'm still finishing up with Alberta. I can't leave her hanging after all the time I've worked for her,' Marina explained. 'But I'm excited about it.'

'It makes me happy that you are, Marina. I'm excited about it too. I believe we'll do great things for the gallery together.' Christina looked at Marina with affection.

'By the way, that client I was going to meet, Ricardo. Should I invite him to the opening day after the gallery refurbishment is done? I'm putting a list together,' Marina asked Christina.

'No. Please don't. I mean, I'm not sure who he is, and I prefer to keep it more *petit committee*, with our old and trusted clients only.' Christina realised that she'd been too abrupt in the manner she'd responded and added. 'Don't you think? What do you think?'

'Well... I agree. It makes sense. Are you sure you don't know him? You seemed startled when I mentioned him.' Marina had picked up on Christina's reaction.

'I don't know him, but your mum mentioned a couple of weeks before she died that she was having trouble with a client trying to return some art and being unreasonable. It could be him. I didn't want to say anything before, but let me figure it out. Let's focus on getting ready and then we can invite him over one day.'

Marina bought it. Teresa watched, ready to jump in, if needed, to corroborate Christina's made-up story.

'Fine for me, sounds like a plan,' Marina agreed, and she picked up the menu. 'Are you all hungry? I'm starving. Do you want to share some nibbles?'

'Yes, please! I'm starving too.' Teresa grabbed a menu as well.

They ordered six small plates to share between them.

'Christina, tell me. Have you told your mum about your brother? What's his name again? Theo, isn't it?' Marina asked.

'I was going to but I've been busy with the gallery and to be honest I've been trying to figure out the best way to tell Mum. I honestly don't know how she'll react. But I'll have lunch with her tomorrow and will try to tell her then,' Christina explained.

'Have you seen him lately?' Karishma asked as Teresa stared at her, almost as if asking how she was holding up.

'Not really. I was supposed to meet him last weekend, but he cancelled on me. He said he wasn't well and to be honest, he didn't sound well on the phone.'

'How do you mean, unwell? Is he sick?' Karishma asked abruptly.

'No, he sounded sad maybe, pensive, I guess,' said Christina. 'But hey, I don't know him well, so maybe I'm mistaken. Why are you so interested?'

'There's a bug going round. A lot of colleagues are off at the hospital and I wondered if maybe he's got it too.' Karishma took a long sip of her wine.

'Is it serious? Another pandemic? Do you know something we don't?' Marina asked.

'No, nothing serious. I mean a new strand of flu

that can leave you in bed for a few days, but not pandemic level, rest reassured,' lied Karishma.

They stayed for another hour at the bar, chatting about trivialities, and then said their goodbyes. They all could walk home except for Marina who lived a short bus ride away. Teresa, Karishma and Christina walked home together. Christina's home was first. She said goodbye and the other two continued walking.

'What happened between you and Theo? You didn't go to a conference, did you?' Teresa said, calling out Karishma's lie.

'No. I didn't. I was on a retreat. Organising my thoughts and my heart, I guess.'

'And Theo?'

'I ended things with him, for good. Better this way.'

'Better for who?'

'For me. I don't want to complicate things. The more involved we get, the harder it'll be.'

'What will be harder, Karishma? Do you hear yourself?'

'I've found a surrogate, Teresa. The embryo will be transferred soon. I'm going to be a mother, and I'm happy about that,' Karishma announced.

'And I'm so happy for you. But why not share that with Theo — at least hear his opinion. You seemed so smitten with him.'

'I was, but I decided to be realistic. Theo is much younger than me. He already has a lot of drama in his life with his son and ex-partner, his newfound sister, who happens to be my best friend, and I don't want to have to navigate all that now. I want to focus and dedicate myself to my baby.'

'Realistic or scared of trying? Of failing?' Teresa continued to push.

'Terrified, to be honest. But my decision's made. Please understand. I don't want to discuss this anymore and I don't want to tell anyone. I'm not sharing about the baby either. Not until the procedure is a success and the twelve weeks have passed.'

'That bit I understand. And I can only accept your decision regarding Theo. However, I think you're missing a great opportunity here.'

'Please, let's not talk about it again. I've made my mind.'

'Fine, I won't, but I want you to be sure that I'm here for you. Whatever you need. And I'm so excited to be an auntie. You can't imagine.'

'Not auntie, godmother.'

'Really? Do you want me to be the baby's godmother?'

'Yes, I do.' Karishma hugged her stepsister and rested her head against her.

Part of her was still broken-hearted about the situation with Theo, but sharing her news with Teresa and being sure of her support meant a lot to Karishma. She was happier and feeling strong enough to bear the weight of her decision.

She went home and as she was going to bed, she looked at the bunny she'd purchased in the Lake District. *You're all that matters now*, she thought as she hugged the plush toy.

14

Christina

The following day, Christina picked up her mother for lunch promptly at twelve noon.

'Hi, Mum. How are you?' Christina gave her mum a hug.

'I'm fine, darling. Thank you. How are you? You have powder in your hair.'

There was a fine layer of dust on top of Christina's head.

'Oh, thank you, Mum.' Christina gave her hair a good shake with her hands. 'I was at the gallery; it's getting beautiful, but there's dust everywhere. They're sanding the walls.'

'I'm glad to see you this happy. Is Marina happy too?'

'I think she is, Mum. I hope she doesn't regret leaving her old job.'

'I see.' Margaret had a cryptic look on her face. 'She did love the gallery she worked on with Alberta, right?'

'Yes, she did. But she'll love working with me as

well. Why not?'

'Of course she will. It's not always easy to mix family and friends with business. Just keep things clear.'

'I know, Mum. Even with Petra, sometimes we had disagreements, but we always found a way to mend things, align our views. I guess we'll have to see.'

'Sure. I wish all the best for you two, working together. And I can't wait to see how the gallery will look.' Margaret spoke from the heart. 'By the way, where are we going? I'm curious. You said it was somewhere special.'

'It is, Mum. You'll love it. If we make it on time for our booking...'

The traffic was horrible. Christina wouldn't usually drive through London, she'd take the tube, but Margaret's mobility wasn't so great these days and besides, Christina had no idea how her mother would react on hearing that her dead husband had cheated on her, that he had a whole secret family and that it had all happened while Margaret was mourning her dead son, so she decided to avoid public transport and drive. Christina had reserved a table for afternoon tea at the top of the Shard, the tallest building in London with breath-taking views of the city. Margaret had never been there and had mentioned on a couple of occasions that she'd love to.

'Here we are. Only ten minutes late. Hope they've held our table.' Christina looked at her wristwatch as she helped her mother out of the car and handed the key to the valet.

'Oh my God, are we going to the Shard?' Margaret was in awe.

'You said you wanted to come here. I hadn't forgotten. Here we are.'

'Darling, it must be expensive. And with all the money you've been spending at the gallery...' Margaret had always been frugal.

'Don't worry, Mum. I won't go broke because I'm taking my lovely mum for a nice afternoon tea. Enjoy.'

'Afternoon tea? That is what we're having? Can't wait, let's go.' Margaret linked her arm with Christina's, and they walked towards the lift.

At the top they were greeted by the hostess and an amazing view of London. Their table was by the window — Christina had specifically made that request when booking.

'I'm so happy to be here.' Margaret said as a glass of champagne was placed in front of her. 'Oh, I shouldn't drink, darling.'

'Just for today, Mum. Only one glass. We rarely have time alone, the two of us.'

'Are we celebrating something? What did I miss?'

'We're not celebrating anything in particular, but why not? Let's celebrate the fact that we're alive and healthy, the fact that we have a beautiful family and friends.' Christina raised her glass.

As the delicious mini sandwiches, tiny pies,

heavenly scones and mini desserts perfectly distributed on cake stands were placed at their table, Christina started to feel anxious. It was all very well toasting and celebrating life, but the fact was that she had a delicate conversation coming and no idea how to start. She decided to get straight to the point. 'Mum, I must tell you something and I'm not sure how.' Christina's lips slightly trembled with the heavy weight of what she was about to say. 'Recently, I learnt something about Dad.'

As Christina started to talk, she noticed her mother looked tense; she could see sweat forming on her forehead. She wondered if Margaret knew what she was about to say as she continued to speak as calmly as she could.

'Mum, during Petra's funeral — life celebration party — someone came looking for me. His name was Theo.' Christina paused, analysing her mum's face to ensure she wasn't panicking and it was safe to continue. Christina could have been mistaken, but the expression on Margaret's face wasn't one of concern but of relief.

'So you've met Theo?'

Christina froze. 'Do you know about… him?'

'Yes, Christina — I know about Theo and his mother. You father told me everything a long time ago.'

A wave of shock went through Christina's body. She'd imagined several ways the conversation could go, but not that way. Margaret knew, all this time, she knew. And she didn't seem to be upset or angry at all.

'Oh! I have so many questions, Mum! You knew all this time that your husband had a second family? And you didn't mention it? Did you accept him? How?' Christina was trying to process the fact that she was the only one who'd been kept in the dark.

'Don't be upset, please. I'll tell you my side of the story and you'll understand. At least, I hope you will.'

'Well, I'm a little upset, yes. You've known for the last what? You've known for thirty years that I had a brother, and you never told me? You knew my father had another family and you accepted him? How could you keep it from me?' Christina had prepared herself to deal with her mother bursting into tears, but instead she wanted to cry. She felt cheated on. Her mother wasn't a victim, but an accomplice in the lie. And that made Christina think about how Marina would feel when she found out the truth. A much bigger secret had been kept from her, and Christina was part of that. She had no right to judge her mum.

'I expect you to be upset, to hate me even, but please hear me out,' Margaret asked.

'I don't hate you, Mum. I never will, but I'm disappointed. I'm disappointed with you and at you. For lying to me and for being so subservient, for accepting Dad's cheating.'

'I understand you are, but things aren't always so black and white. There's always a context for everything, and that context makes all the difference.'

Christina thought about the context behind the secrets that she'd kept herself. The reason behind the lies she'd told. She decided to listen first, listen before she judged her mother.

'That wasn't the first time your father had been unfaithful to me. When we were young, before you were even born, he was unfaithful. He was a handsome man; he always had women all over him. And he enjoyed that. Your father didn't give that impression, but he was an insecure man. He was always seeking attention and looking for reassurance.'

'By cheating on you?'

'He didn't see it that way. He did love me. But he couldn't be exclusive with me. He couldn't give himself whole to someone because he didn't feel whole himself.'

'That should have been his problem, not yours, right?' Christina was struggling to understand her mother's perspective of her father.

'I'm not perfect myself. I've made my share of mistakes. And when I married your father, I was very young. Times were different.' Margaret ate one of her savoury delights and gently cleaned the side of her mouth before continuing. 'You're lucky, and Vanessa's generation is even luckier in a way. Assuming a bunch of bigots with retrograde views won't succeed in revoking rights that my generation and some before me fought so hard to conquer. Sorry, I'm going off on a tangent. It's been devastating to see the turn the world is taking these days, but that's talk for another time.'

'Look, Mum, I understand times were different and harder for a woman, but you came from a well-educated family. You should know better than to accept a cheat for a husband.'

'Should I? Were you there?' Margaret's tone roughened.

'Sorry, I'm trying to get my head round this. Carry on.'

'My generation changed many things. But expectations at that time were different for a woman than they are today. We were expected to have a good husband, children, to be polite and reserved. Divorce was still taboo. And I had my own insecurities. The idea of getting a divorce was a showstopper for me. I wasn't confident enough to face society, to endure the stigma and the possibility of being alone, not having a family of my own.'

Margaret ate a small sandwich and continued. 'My parents were great, but that doesn't mean they were necessarily avant garde. They had high expectations for me, and they were so proud of me for marrying your father, a good man from a good family. I'd disappoint them as well. They'd be embarrassed in front of their friends.'

'Who cares? It's hard to understand.' Christina shook her head.

'I bet it is. You always had much more freedom than I did, than my generation did. You're allowed to dream to aspire to something big. You can be anything. My generation couldn't, not easily. There were professions for men and professions for women, and ours usually involved carrying for people or somehow serving people, usually men.'

'It must have been hard, and I'm grateful for the changes your generation made for mine and we continued to make for my daughters, but still, you could have told me.'

'I could. I should have. Of course. But as they say, easier said than done.'

Christina thought about her own decisions and Petra's last request to her. She thought about Ricardo's threat to approach Marina and decided to be more understanding of her mother's reasons. *Easier said than done indeed,* she thought.

'You said Dad had been unfaithful before Theo's mother. When was that?'

'Before you were born. We'd moved to the cul-de-sac — we'd been married for just over a year. I was trying to get pregnant and it was taking a while. One day, your father said he was working late. I was already suspicious of him; he'd been distant, and I'd found lipstick marks on his collar.'

'How clichéd. I thought that was only in movies.' Christina smiled.

'Very clichéd, yes, but devastating for me. So I went to the building where he worked and hid behind a tree until he came out. My world crashed down as he came out holding hands with his secretary. Another cliché. They got in a cab. I stood there crying for a while. Then I went home and cried a lot more. But I decided I'd endure that. I wouldn't let that ruin my marriage, my life. I decided I'd take revenge instead. So I had an affair of my own.'

'Wow! Did you?'

'It was only a one-night stand, but I did. He was a friend also going through marriage trouble.'

'Mum, I don't know what to say. I'm sorry. Did you at least think about leaving Dad?'

'Yes, but I decided to stay. I felt better after I'd cheated on him — as if I'd levelled the playing field. I ignored his infidelity, moved on and had the family I wanted.'

'Were you happy?'

'For a while. The secretary moved to another country. I got pregnant with you and then Ralph. I was happy for a while until…'

'Until Ralph died, right?'

'Yes, until I lost my son. You were too young and probably don't remember, but I was very depressed.'

'I remember flashes of it, to be honest. I think I've erased a big part of my memories from when Ralph died. Defence mechanism, maybe, to cope with the trauma. I think I was more traumatised by Ralph's death than I liked to admit. I don't remember the most part of the two years that followed his death.'

'You never told me. I'm sorry I wasn't there for you. I was so overwhelmed by my own loss that I forgot it was your loss, too. I should have been a better mother.' Margaret's eyes welled up with tears.

'You're a great mother; you always have been. I'd have never been as good as you if, God forbid, I was ever to lose one of my children, I'd die with them. I only remember flashes of those two years, but most of my memories were of you, with me, trying hard to be present. I remember when we travelled together to Brighton, just the two of us. Do you remember?' Christina grabbed her mother's hand and squeezed it firmly.

'I do. It was around the time your father started travelling for work. It was hard on him too, you know? He lost his ground when Ralph died on his watch. And I wasn't there for him, either. I was drowning in my own sorrow, suffocating in my grief. I couldn't help but hate your father at that time, and I made that clear to him. He felt guilty and alone. I believe he must have met Theo's mum around that time.'

'And you kept faking it, pretending to be happy?' Christina thought about her own marriage to Peter. It was nothing as hard as what her mother had endured, but she'd also been living a marriage that wasn't necessarily real. There were a lot of unspoken issues between Christina and Peter and some of them were making their married life tough.

'It wasn't faking. I know this will be hard to grasp, but your father and I, we did love each other. And we loved you. You'd been through so much; the last thing you needed was divorced and unhappy parents.'

'Maybe you would have been happier if you had gone your separate ways.'

'Maybe you're right. But maybe not. We'll never know. We make decisions every day, and each of them leads to other decisions and so on. Like branches on a tree, we can end up in many different places, but we can only choose one path at a time. All we can do is try our best to live with the ramifications. Somehow, I think there's beauty in it.'

'Maybe. But it's tough. I've made bad decisions, too. Some decisions that may cause pain to others if they come to light.' Christina thought for a moment about discussing her past with her mother.

'Is there anything you want to share with me? I can see you've been struggling with something.'

'No, Mum, not now. When the time is right, yes. But for now, I want you to continue your story.' Christina drank some of her tea.

'Well, there's not much more to tell you. One day, when you must have been around your mid-twenties, your father confessed that he had another family. He told me everything about Theo and his mother and asked me to forgive him. We found our way back to each other as the years passed and we became grandparents.'

'And you did forgive him.'

'Yes, I forgave him. He left Theo's mother for good but told me he couldn't leave Theo. So he continued to see him, and I agreed, I understood.'

'That was noble of you.'

'The boy wasn't to blame; he was a victim of the situation himself. And after losing Ralph, having Theo had brought a new light to your father's life. I loved your father enough to accept that. To want to see him happy despite the pain he'd caused me.'

'Did you ever want to meet Theo?'

'Part of me did. But the other part was terrified. Afraid of feeling angry with him, and even angry for him to be there alive when my son wasn't. I know it sounds cruel, but I'm only human.'

'I understand, Mum. It must have been so hard. I wish I'd known. I could have been there for you.'

'You were. You're the reason I was able to overcome it all. And when you had your children, oh boy, how happy you made me. Being a grandmother made me softer, made me accept better the bruises from the many stones life had thrown at me.'

'I love you so much, Mum.' Tears were rolling down Christina's face. 'Did you ever tell Dad about your affair?'

'No, never. For many reasons, to spare you, even to spare him. But mostly for selfish reasons. I wanted that to be mine and mine only story to keep. It made me feel better about being cheated on, less of a victim, made me feel in control of my own decisions and besides, I was afraid your father wouldn't have been as strong as I was and love me as much as I loved him. That he wouldn't love me enough to forgive.'

'It's is a bit twisted, but I understand. You know,

Mum, I think I'm becoming wiser as I'm getting older. I'm more compassionate than I used to be. I'm learning to accept people and their mistakes,' Christina confessed, secretly hoping people would be compassionate with her when the time came for her to come clean.

'The wisest attitude of all is being able to forget your own mistakes. It's being compassionate to yourself. Are you?'

That question shook Christina from the inside. Of course, she wasn't nice to herself. She'd been her biggest critic, her worst enemy when it came to forgiving herself for what she'd done in the past. And as a punishment, she'd never allowed herself to be happy, truly happy. Christina wasn't ready to discuss that.

'Have you met Theo? Face to face?' Margaret asked.

'Yes, a few times now. He has a son — no wife, she left him — and he has custody of the kid. They live with his mother.'

'Have you met the son?'

'Not yet. But I want to. I don't want you to feel betrayed by me, but I'm happy to have met Theo. I'm happy to have a brother and a nephew. Is that wrong?'

'Of course not! I'm glad you're happy. And to be honest, I'd like to meet them too,' Margaret confessed.

'That would bring me a lot of joy. I want them to be a part of my life, of our lives.'

'I accept that. And I'll do my best to try to be supportive. Bear with me. I don't know yet how I'll react.'

'I will. I'm thinking of inviting them to Vanessa's, Alex's and Louisa's joint birthday party. They are, once again, celebrating together. But I'll only invite them if you're comfortable with it.'

'Can I meet them first? I mean, soon?'

'Of course. I'll talk to him.'

Mother and daughter enjoyed the last of their delicious afternoon tea and the fabulous view of the River Thames. They'd been blessed with clear blue skies, not a usual sight in London.

Later that night, Christina called Theo. He still sounded sad. She asked if he was OK. He said he was having some issues in his love life but reassured her he'd be fine soon. They hadn't known each other for long, but they'd developed a mutual affection. Christina told him she'd talked to her mum about him and his mother. She omitted the fact that her mother had known about him for so long, but she'd tell him when they next met face to face. They agreed to meet the next day at Margaret's house. Theo was bringing David along.

Margaret prepared a fish pie, her family recipe, and waited for Christina, Theo and David to arrive for lunch at her place. She was apprehensive about meeting her dead husband's son.

Christina arrived first. 'Hi Mum. How are you feeling? Are you ready for this?'

'I am. I confess I feel a bit apprehensive. But I guess that's only natural.'

'Of course it is, Mum. I am so happy and proud of how you are handling this.' Christina *was* happy that her mother had decided to meet her brother, but she worried that seeing Theo in the flesh would bring back all the pain Margaret had felt when she discovered George's unfaithfulness.

The doorbell rang.

'They're here. I'll go.' As Christina opened the door, David was fast to introduce himself.

'Hello, I am David.'

'Hello, David. I'm Christina.'

'She's erm… she's your auntie, David.' Theo said, looking at Christina and smiling.

'Cool! And who's that?' David briefly hugged Christina and then pointed at Margaret.

'That's my mother. Her name's Margaret.'

'Is she my grandma?' David looked at his dad.

'Come in please,' Margaret invited them as they were all still standing by the door. 'Hi David. I knew your grandfather and I would be happy to be your borrowed grandma if you'd take me,' Margaret said tenderly.

Christina threw a loving look at her mother. *You keep surprising me.*

'And you must be Theo, of course.' Margaret extended her hand to Theo.

'I am indeed. It is a pleasure to meet you.' Theo said politely.

At first, they were all a bit stiff — it was a delicate situation. But as they sat down for lunch, and with David being a sweet cheeky monkey, they relaxed and talked about Theo's work, Christina's gallery refurbishment and Margaret's fish pie secret recipe. They had a pleasant afternoon.

'Again, it was a pleasure to meet you. I'm happy you invited us. And the food was delicious.' Theo said.

'I liked the cake.' David said, licking a chocolate ganache bit that remained at the corner of his mouth.

'Whenever you visit me, I'll bake chocolate cake for you, promise,' Margaret whispered to David as if sharing a secret.

'Yay! I want to come every day,' David said happily.

They said their goodbyes and Theo and David left.

When they left, Margaret felt happy. She and Christina sat down together in her garden. 'Thank you for bringing him into my life. He's a lovely man, and I'm happy you have a brother.'

'I'm content too, Mum.'

'David reminds me a lot of your dad,' Margaret said with nostalgia.

Christina wiped a tear from her mother's face with her fingers.

They sat side by side for a while in silence, enjoying the sunshine. Christina loved the long summer nights. The last couple of days had been full of revelations, but at the same time had been happy. But Christina was uneasy about what was to come. Ricardo had told her he'd be back in two months and the time was almost up. Christina was preparing for the reaction that new revelations from hers, Teresa's and Petra's past would cause.

What would Peter say? Her marriage was in a delicate state. To be fair, she didn't even know what she wanted anymore. She didn't know if she wanted to be married or not. And if she didn't, was it because she no longer loved Peter or was she afraid of his reaction when the truth came out? Would he forgive her for not telling him? If they were no longer together, it wouldn't matter. She even considered separating from him to minimise the confrontation. *No, that would be silly.*

There were so many questions in her head. She thought about her long conversation with her mother. She'd always known her mother was a strong woman, but that was another level of strength. She was disappointed at first to find out her mother had known about her father all that time and stayed with him. But after thinking about it and seeing her mother's attitude towards Theo, she concluded it wasn't weakness or subservience that made her mother stay with her dad, to forgive him and ultimately care for him during his struggle with Parkinson's disease. That was nothing but strength — strength and resilience. Christina was proud of her mother.

'Christina, would you stay over with me tonight?' her mother asked. 'I'm fine, I promise, but I don't want to be alone. Seeing Theo did bring back memories of Ralph…'

'Of course I'll stay with you. Let me call Peter. I'm sure he won't mind.'

'And one more thing, please invite Theo to Vanessa's, Alex's and Louisa's birthday. I don't mind and it will be great for the rest of the family to meet them.'

'I will, Mum. I will.'

Christina slept with her mother that night in her mother's bed, as she used to do as a child. And that felt good.

The next day, she went to the gallery first to check on the work. She had a late lunch with Vanessa and Harry and told them about Theo and David. They were excited to learn about their uncle and cousin and couldn't wait to meet them.

Later, at home, Christina told Peter about her conversation with her mother. She described how her mother had known about her father's affair and how she'd concluded that in the end her mother and father loved each other and their love was stronger than their mistakes. She left out the part where her mother had also had an affair. She didn't have the right to share that.

It felt good to share her life stories, her feelings with her husband. She wished it could continue to be like that, but she knew, deep down, it wouldn't.

15

The Party

Alex, Louisa and Vanessa had decided on the venue and date for their birthday party.

Their local Vietnamese restaurant, a charming and cosy space with a reserved area on the lower ground floor was ideal for private dining. It was the perfect place with amazing food, and the fact Marcus knew the owner made things easier and guaranteed them getting a good discount.

The party was set for the twelfth of July, two weeks after Vanessa's birthday, two days before Louisa's birthday and two weeks before Alex's.

Marcus and Christina were very hands on in helping them organise everything. When the day came, they brought three sets of helium balloons with the number eighteen and many balloons in different colours. Several biodegradable confetti cannons were placed at the tables so people could use them once the dance floor was open.

The lower ground floor of the restaurant was a great space for approximately forty seated people that opened to a rear patio with four sets of tables for two and two lower tables with a set of sofas and comfy chairs around each. Festoon lights adorned the space and there was a nice empty space to be used as the dance floor.

The parents of Ollie, Alex's boyfriend, had a business that rented out serious party stuff, so he brought in a cool photo booth and a box full of props including colourful wigs, neon bracelets, fancy glasses and hats and fancy dress items. They removed a couple of tables from the indoor area to place the booth. A DJ was hired, and although the restaurant was providing the catering, Teresa also ordered cupcakes and sweets from a friend's company, and they made a good deal with the restaurant owner for the drinks.

'It looks amazing! We must hope the weather stays like this.' Marcus pointed at the clear blue sky.

'You never know with British weather,' said Christina.

'Don't jinx it. I'm sure it will be fine.' Marcus said, offering a smile to Paolo who'd just arrived.

'Hello all. How are you, Christina?' Paolo said.

'I'm fine, Paolo, thank you. I hope you're well too.' Christina was relaxed enough and by the tone of her voice, she didn't seem to hold a grudge about Marcus voicing his opinion on the situation involving her, Marcus and Marina.

'I'm a little nervous, to be honest. I'll be meeting your whole family for the first time,' Paolo reminded Christina.

'We'll be fine.' Marcus was confident the family would accept Paolo. Most of their big, made-up family knew by now. Marcus had asked Alex to tell his family, without knowing he had already, and he'd had a conversation with Declan and Ellie before the party.

'I also have something to share with the family. Something big.' Christina announced.

'What is it? Are you telling Marina? Today? When I said we should consider telling her, I didn't mean at the kids' birthday, not today,' Marcus said.

'Relax, Marcus. I'm not telling Marina anything. We've yet to talk about that, but for now, I'm not even thinking about it. Ricardo is still away and will be for a bit longer. He called me the other day, so I have more time to deal with his threats.' Christina looked at the man arriving at the place with a little boy holding his hand.

'Marcus, Paolo, meet my brother Theo and his adorable son, David.' Christina pulled Theo by the hand, taking him to meet her friends.

'A brother? How come?' Marcus was surprised.

'Don't be rude, Marcus. Say hi first,' Paolo said in a joking tone.

'Of course. Hi, Theo. I'm Marcus. I'm Marina's father, Louisa's mum.'

'I've heard about you all. I'm happy to finally meet you.' Theo said politely.

'My father had a second family. It was a surprise for all of us, but it's all good now. My mother knows and so do Peter and my children,' Christina said, noticing the shock on Marcus's face and trying to anticipate his questions.

It was almost party time. Vanessa, Louisa and Alex had arrived and had been introduced to Paolo, Theo and David. They already knew about Paolo and Vanessa had told them about Theo, so no big surprises there, just the anticipation of meeting them all.

The guests started to arrive. Their extended family alone accounted for more than half of the guests, including Ollie's parents and sister. Apart from the family, each of the three birthday people had invited a handful of friends.

Teresa came with Daniel, Hugo, Patricia and her mother, Ines, who was still staying with them. Alan arrived soon after, followed by Bianca. Then arrived Marina, Anthony and their young ones, Gabriel and Archie. Peter and Harry arrived with Margaret, Declan and Ellie and Karishma brought Robert and Purnima.

Mrs Phillips, the gossip neighbour, had also been invited and arrived on time. She could be a pain in the butt sometimes, but she'd been their neighbour forever, and they all had a soft spot for her and were alert to the fact she was lonely.

The whole family was together again. Christina looked around as they gathered and was taken by an immense feeling of happiness and fulfilment. Nice music was being played, drinks and food were flowing, and everyone seemed to be enjoying themselves.

'I know exactly what you're thinking,' Teresa whispered to Christina.

'Do you? I'm thinking so many things right now,' Christina said, raising her glass to Teresa for a toast.

'You're thinking how amazing is the family that was formed by our collagen coven…'

'Tick. Next?' Christina made a gesture with her hands as if ticking an imaginary box.

Teresa continued. 'You're missing Petra, dearly, as I am.'

'Big tick. I wish so much that she was still here.' Christina rested her head on Teresa's shoulder.

'You're also thinking how much you'll miss me when I'm away with Daniel.'

'Oh, God. Don't even mention that. I haven't yet come to terms with the fact you're leaving me for so long.' Christina looked at Teresa in the eyes. 'But I'm not thinking about that right now. I want to enjoy being with you while you're still here. So, buzz, no tick.'

Teresa took a deep breath. 'I'll miss you all too, so much, but I must go. I owe it to myself and to Daniel. But there's one more thing in your head, I bet. You're thinking about what you'll do next about Marina and Marcus.'

'Nope. Not that. I'm trying not to think about that. Not today. Today, I want to enjoy this moment. And let them enjoy it too. Look at how happy they are, all of them.' Christina looked at all the faces one by one and Teresa copied her. 'I'm also thinking that I must introduce my brother, and Marcus has to introduce Paolo,' she said and immediately started to tap a spoon on the side of her glass to attract attention.

Teresa's first reaction was to look for Karishma; she knew it would be hard for her to see Theo. Karishma was sitting on one of the sofas outside, talking to Hugo and Patricia, and probably hadn't seen Theo yet as he was trying to persuade David away from the box of props.

'Hello, everyone.' Christina made a gesture for Marcus to join her, which he did. 'Words can't describe how happy I'm to be here today, celebrating the birthdays of these three amazing people. I love you guys.'

She looked at her daughter and her best friends. Everyone cheered and clapped Vanessa, Alex and Louisa, and Christina continued her speech. 'Marcus and I have some people we'd like to introduce to you. I know some of you already know about them. I'm happy to see you all of you here today and it fills my heart to see how much love is involved in this big family of ours.' Christina looked at Marcus.

'Hi all. Thank you for joining us to celebrate my gorgeous granddaughter and her equally gorgeous best friends' birthdays,' he said. 'By now, most of you know that since my divorce from Petra, years ago, I've found a partner, someone I love and respect dearly. I want to introduce him to you all today. Please meet Paolo.' Marcus pointed at Paolo who was as red as a beetroot as he sat next to Theo. Everyone looked at Paolo and smiled.

'Hello, I'll introduce myself to all of you during the night,' said Paolo.

Mrs Phillips's jaw had dropped, and as soon as she composed herself, she made her way towards Paolo. She had to be the first one to introduce herself, of course. Christina watched her and laughed internally.

'And now, I want to tell you all that recently I learnt that I have a brother,' said Christina. 'From my father, George. His name is Theo, and he's here today with his son, David. Please introduce yourselves to him. I've told him about you all. Enjoy the party.' Teresa pointed to Theo, who together with David made a hello gesture with his hands.

Everyone seemed more shocked by this revelation than by meeting Marcus's partner. Most faces were turned to Margaret. Christina noticed and walked towards her mother. 'How are you feeling, Mum?'

'I'm fine, believe me, I am. I'd pictured this moment in my head a thousand times, and I'd thought about how I'd feel. If I'd feel less of a person when my friends and family found out I'd been cheated on by the same man who I cared for until his last breath.'

'Do you?' Christina asked her mum with her arms wrapped around her shoulder.

'No, not at all. I feel stronger, superior to all that. I can't explain why, but I feel I'm better than your father's flaws.'

'And so you should.' Mrs Phillips appeared out of nowhere, surprising Christina and her mother. 'My husband cheated on me as well. May he rest in peace. I also forgave him. The poor bastard got sick early and spend most of his life battling dementia. Karma got to him. And to yours too.'

'Mrs Phillips, I don't hate my husband.' Margaret spoke politely.

'Neither do I. I don't hate my husband or yours for what it's worth. George seemed like a good man. And they gave us our daughters. I have a daughter too, and though I don't see her often, we're close. She often calls me. Now, if you'd excuse me, I have to say hi to your brother, introduce myself, Theo, isn't it?'

As Mrs Phillips walked away, Christina turned back to her mum. 'Quite a character, Mrs Phillips. She doesn't look as sad and lonely as I thought she might be. I thought her daughter didn't care much for her.'

'Oh no, she does. She's always calling Mrs Phillips and offering to send her a ticket to visit her in Australia, where she lives. But Mrs Phillips refuses to take such a long flight. She told me her daughter will come to visit with her family next Christmas. Maybe that's why she doesn't look so lonely now,' Margaret explained. 'And I'm fine. Let's talk to Theo.'

Margaret introduced Theo to Declan and Ellie and to Robert and Purnima. Theo talked to them all and introduced David from a distance as the boy had now met Gabriel. They were the same age, and were running around playing, each with a colourful wig and some funny glasses from the props box.

They were all asking questions of Theo. Where do you live? What do you do? While trying to respond and engage in conversation, Theo couldn't take his eyes off Karishma, who was clearly trying to pretend not to notice him.

Paolo was also trying to meet all Marcus's family and friends, one by one. Marcus didn't leave his side for a minute. Both men were happy, happy and relieved to be free to be a couple in public after so many years of hiding their relationship.

Marcus was especially happy. He'd been hiding not only Paolo, but himself and now the cat was out of the bag, he felt lighter —but not completely relieved. The more he felt that coming out and introducing Paolo was the right thing to do, the more he was convinced that he had to tell Marina everything and end all the secrets, once and for all. *Maybe Ricardo reappearing from the past was a blessing in disguise*, Marcus thought. He decided to give it a couple of days and then have a serious conversation with Christina.

Karishma was now talking to Daniel and still trying to avoid Theo. She was asking about the upcoming tour with Valerie Evans. 'You must be so excited to travel the world playing with a pop star,' Karishma said as she grabbed a glass of wine.

'I am. You know, I hadn't realised how much I needed something like this until Valerie approached me,' Daniel responded, grabbing a glass of wine himself. 'I've always tried to convince myself I was fulfilled by teaching children and being a stay-at-home dad while Teresa was the breadwinner.'

'And you weren't?'

'Nope. I wasn't. Don't get me wrong, I've enjoyed every minute of raising my boys, seeing them take the first steps, all the firsts, in fact. I took deep satisfaction in teaching them about life, about food, about music. Taking them to and from school and their activities. And I like teaching children how to play the guitar, I really do. But part of me, a big part, as I've come to realise, was missing something. I was missing what I could have been, the adult Daniel my young self had dreamt of. I've always wanted to be a rock star. I even had a band as a teenager. When I met Teresa, the band was still going.'

'She told me that. She also told me she always thought she was going to marry a rock star,' Karishma said without thinking that maybe that would make Daniel feel bad.

His face turned more serious. 'Did she? Well, I didn't even come close. I gave up. At first, I thought I was destined to be famous, to be great. But as it didn't happen easily, I stopped trying. I met Teresa, had the boys and decided it was easier to hide behind family life than face the fact I'd failed as a musician.'

'You didn't fail. You're great. I love to hear you play. Valerie Evans wants you to be in her band for God's sake. Isn't that amazing?'

'I didn't fail because I'm a bad musician, Karishma. I failed because I gave up on myself. And I gave up on myself, not because I didn't want it enough or because I decided to look after the kids while Teresa invested in her career. It was our choice. To be honest, looking back, I realise that for me that was the easiest route, because I was afraid of trying and then failing. I've sabotaged myself my whole life. You miss all the shots you don't take, isn't it what they say? Valerie Evans is my last shot. My last shot at doing something for myself, to achieve some of my dreams, to do what I love.'

'I'm so happy for you.' Karishma said, thinking of all the shots she hadn't taken herself. She thought about the baby and about Theo.

'I can't wait to play in stadiums full of people.' Daniel noticed Teresa approaching. 'And to have my beautiful wife by my side.' He pulled Teresa close to him.

'Are you guys talking about me?' Teresa asked.

'We were, but only good things about you. Karishma can tell you everything.' He blinked at his sister-in-law. 'Now, if you'll excuse me, Marcus is calling. I must go and meet Paolo.'

Daniel left the stepsisters alone.

'How are you doing? Have you talked to him yet?' Teresa said to Karishma, motioning towards Theo.

'Not yet. But I may. I was talking to Daniel, and he's so excited about the tour. I'm glad you're both taking that chance. Maybe I should take all my chances as well.'

'I love to hear you talking like that.' Teresa always thought her sister had been too hard on herself since Iain had died.

'The embryo was implanted. The surrogate is about to do a pregnancy test, and I may hear from her any minute now. I'm so excited.'

'Amazing news. Again, I'm so happy for you. I'm going to be the best godmother-slash-auntie ever. Are you going to tell Christina about the baby and about Theo?'

'I will, for sure I will. I need to make sure it's worked. The baby, I mean. And I need to talk to Theo first.' Karishma noticed Theo approaching her as a song she loved started to play. The same song that had played when she'd had her first date with Theo. *A good sign,* she thought.

The conversation with Daniel had inspired Karishma to be brave enough to tell Theo about her plans. *The worst that can happen is he decides not to be with me, but at least I'll have tried. You miss all the shots you don't take… I'll take the shot.*

'Hi,' said Theo.

'Hello, Theo.' Karishma's heart skipped a beat as he approached her.

'I wasn't sure whether to talk to you. You were avoiding me all evening.' Theo said softly.

Karishma had known Theo was going to be at the party, but she wasn't prepared for the emotions she felt seeing him there, a couple of feet away from her. His voice pierced her stomach, letting all the butterflies out, and an intense feeling took over her body as the memories of the moments they'd shared not long ago seemed more vivid than ever. 'I was avoiding you. But I realised I'm not strong enough to avoid you. I've missed you.'

'I missed you too. You broke my heart, Karishma.'

'What? This lady broke your heart? How?' David approached Theo and grabbed both his legs with his tiny arms.

'You must be David. I'm Karishma. I'm your father's friend, and I was hoping I hadn't broken his heart.' Karishma introduced herself to the boy.

'Hello heartbreaker lady,' David said.

'She didn't break my heart, son. I was joking.' Theo mouthed to Karishma. *Yes, you did.* He then smiled at her.

David started running around again with Gabriel and Karishma, and Theo resumed their conversation.

'I've broken my own heart too, Theo. I'm just going through a tough time. Things are happening in my world and I thought I'd better not share them with you. I assumed if I did, you'd leave, so I decided I should leave anyway, before you left me.'

'That's not smart, or fair, is it?'

'No, it isn't. But I was scared.'

'Are you still scared?'

'Petrified. But I'm convinced I want to share everything with you. But not now, look. They're about to sing happy birthday.'

Theo and Karishma joined the rest of the party around the table with the beautiful cake on top. Teresa's friend, the baker, was incredibly talented and had made a cake with the theme 'adventure' in the shape of a camper van with surfboards on top of it. It was a big cake. Mini desserts and fancy chocolates completed the table's decoration, although some chocolate was already missing from the table as Gabriel and David had got to it.

They all sang happily and as the song finished, Vanessa, Louisa and Alex cut the cake together, giving the first slice to be shared between the two young boys, who were pleading for it.

As everyone gathered to eat cake, Karishma and Theo walked towards the back of the garden and were about to take a seat on one of the comfy chairs when Karishma's phone rang. The surrogate's number appeared on her screen.

Karishma's heart was pounding with anxiety. *Is it good or bad news?* Her mind was racing as fast as the beats from her heart and for a moment she forgot about everything else. She'd been so confident that she was about to have a baby, that the embryo implantation would be a success, that she hadn't considered the alternative. But as she saw the name on her screen, panic started to take over and the bad scenario was all that came to her mind. 'Sorry, Theo. I must take this. I'll be back.' Karishma rushed back upstairs to street level and left the restaurant. 'Hello. Hi, how are you? Did you take the test?' Karishma was speaking so fast she didn't give the woman time to say much.

A few seconds of silence ensued. They were brief seconds but long enough for Karishma's world to crash down. She knew what she was about to hear.

'Karishma, I'm sorry.'

Karishma was leaning against the restaurant wall. She let her body melt until she reached the floor and sat down, staring at the phone in her hands without saying a word.

'Karishma, hello. Are you there?'

'Hi. Teresa here. I'm Karishma's sister, you can talk to me.' Teresa had seen Karishma rushing up the stairs and followed her. She'd assumed it was the phone call Karishma had been expecting.

'Hi. I'm Maya, the surrogate; I'm sure your sister told you. I took a pregnancy test today and the result is negative. The procedure didn't work. The chances were around fifty-fifty. I told your sister I'd be up to trying again, if it didn't work the first time. I need to wait a few weeks. Please tell her.'

'I will. Thank you for everything. She'll call you later. She needs to digest this.'

Theo had followed Karishma and Teresa and

was standing there, confused by seeing Karishma in tears, sitting on the floor with Teresa leaning over her and talking.

'Please talk to me. I'm here for you. You can try again. You knew this could happen. Please tell me what you need.' Teresa was worried as Karishma was sobbing and staring at the floor without saying a word. She noticed Theo standing next to them.

'Would you help me bring her up, please?' Teresa asked.

'What's happening? Karishma, please tell me.' Theo looked concerned as he helped her stand up together with Teresa.

'I need to go home, please.' Those were the only words Karishma managed to say.

With Theo's help, Teresa got a taxi and left together with Karishma, asking a confused Theo to explain to Christina they had to leave and that she'd explain everything later. She promised to explain to Theo too. But the priority now was to make sure Karishma recovered from the news she'd received.

'Trust me, she'll be fine. And she'll tell you everything. She needs space now. Please understand,' Teresa asked him before the taxi took off.

Theo didn't understand a thing. He had no clue what was happening, but he had a feeling that whatever was going on with Karishma, it had nothing to do with him. He worried she was ill, and that thought terrified him. He was going to give her time, for sure, but whatever it was that was keeping her away from him, he would face it. Before that night, he hadn't been sure. Karishma had been rude, almost aggressive, with him after they'd had a great time together and following that, he thought he'd better stay away. But seeing her at the party changed everything. He recognised the woman he'd fallen for. Her voice, her smile, had lit a fire again inside him. He was deeply in love with Karishma, and as he watched the taxi leave the restaurant, he decided he'd fight for her. He'd give her time and space, but he wouldn't give up.

Theo told Christina that Karishma wasn't feeling well, and Teresa had taken her home. He also told Daniel. Both Christina and Daniel were so involved with the music, the dancing and the celebrations that they felt sorry Karishma had to leave but didn't think much of it.

Theo left soon after. The party continued for a couple more hours. The weather was warm, the sky clear and the days longer because of it being summer.

Vanessa, Louisa and Alex happily danced and celebrated until the last minute with their family and friends.

Christina had a fantastic night and managed to block any thoughts that could stop her being present in that special moment. But as the guests left and the party ended, her thoughts came back to haunt her. She couldn't help but think that this lovely evening had been the calm before the storm.

Teresa had taken Karishma home, made her a cup of tea and stayed with her the whole night. Karishma picked up the bunny she'd bought for her baby.

'I was so sure it would work,' she said, sobbing. 'Could you please get rid of this for me? I can't look at it.' Teresa promptly put the bunny in her bag.

The sisters slept together like when they were younger. Although they weren't blood related, they loved each other as if they were. More than most sisters do.

16

The Storm

During the weeks after the party, the time rushed by, for Christina at least.

She was under pressure from Ricardo to decide how she was going to tell Marina about the secrets she'd shared with her friends. He'd been sending her text messages almost daily since he'd returned from his work trip, and he made it clear she had no choice but to tell the truth. Also, Marcus was trying to convince Christina that Marina and the rest of the family had the right to know everything. That pushed Christina to the limit, resulting in her having a big argument with him. To make things worse, the date for the gallery re-opening was set, and the invitations had been sent to clients and selected family members, but work was delayed due to a contractor who was falling behind on the delivery of his agreed work.

For Karishma, time had been dragging since she'd found out that the embryo transferring to the surrogate hadn't resulted in a pregnancy. Since the trio's birthday party, she'd been isolating herself from the world. Work had become an obsession, and she was doing all the shifts and overtime she could get. Teresa had been calling to check on her every day and she answered with monosyllabic words and refuse to allow her sister, or anyone else, to visit.

Theo had called a few times, but she refused to speak to him. All Karishma did was send him a text saying:

> I'm not ready to have the conversation I know I owe you. Please, give me some time and I'll call you back. I know I'm not in a position to ask you anything, but I ask you to trust me and give me some space for now.

He sent a simple text back. When you're ready, I'll be here.

A week later, after spending all afternoon at the gallery with Marina doing some of the decoration work herself in an effort to finish the refurbishment in time for the opening, Christina decided she was ready to tell her everything, but she needed a few more days and asked Ricardo to give her until after the opening. He reluctantly agreed.

Two days before the opening at the gallery, most of the work was complete. All that remained to be done was a deep clean and positioning the new furniture and artwork. Marina and Christina had been working insane hours, but Christina had been doing the bulk of the work since Marina had a three-year-old to look after.

"The whole space is looking amazing, isn't it?' Marina said as they arrived at the gallery to open the doors to the professional cleaning crew.

'Better than I'd imagined,' Christina said with joy and a tiny bit of sadness. 'I wish your mother was here to see it.'

'Me too. I was thinking about that. She'd have loved it. I never understood why you didn't use the back patio before.' Marina opened the new bi-folding doors to the renovated patio.

'Me neither. I guess Petra and I never paid much attention to it. This was a fantastic idea, and I wish we'd done it sooner. But hey, now it's done, and this has become the most exquisite art gallery in this city.'

The patio had been converted into an outdoor lounge area with a couple of structures to display art, a stylish water feature, and a pair of interesting sculptures in bronze. Part of the patio was covered by a modern glass roof. The lighting design had been carefully planned to highlight the display areas and create an inviting ambience. A combination of glass, wood, concrete and metal was used on the finished surfaces and on the furniture.

The interior design in the gallery was extraordinary. Christina had a refined taste, and Julio, the architect, a meticulous attention to detail. The result was a sophisticated, captivating space.

Christina was proud of the project and the idea of working side by side with Marina was heartwarming. Since Petra's death, it had been difficult for Christina to be at the gallery. She hoped that with the new space and with Marina by her side, things would be different and she'd find the same motivation to work she'd had before her best friend's death. And more than anything, she hoped that Marina would forgive her and Marcus for keeping secrets for so long.

'I FUCKING LOVE THIS PLACE!' were Patricia's words as she came into the gallery for the first time after the refurbishment started. She'd taken time off to study as she was doing her masters.

'Is this my own desk?' Bianca was right behind Patricia and was ecstatic to find out she no longer had to share a desk with Patricia.

'All thanks to this genius!' Christina pointed at Julio as he arrived to help with the furniture arrangement and final touches to the décor.

'How are you, my darling? I'm so glad you like it.' Julio gave Christina a big hug.

'When Christina said you were amazing, I had no idea how amazing she meant. Thank you so much! You've transformed this place,' Marina said, walking towards Julio.

'You both deserve the best. There was so much potential here, it just needed a closer look. And your idea of using the patio was the cherry on the cake. Now let's go to work.' Julio grabbed a vase and went off to position it in the perfect place on top of a pedestal by the entrance door.

They worked together for the whole day. There was music playing, food and drinks were ordered, and they had fun while finalising the decor. The cleaning crew left the space sparkling, and all the furniture was in place. They just had to display the artwork and they'd be ready for the opening. But that was to be done the following day.

Teresa was busy preparing for the long trip she was about to take, following the music tour with Daniel and the sabbatical she'd planned to take in Brazil after the tour finished. She'd finished her gardening leave at work and was making sure everything else, including bills, the house, and her finances were all well organised. Her mother, Ines, was still staying with her, and had been a great help. They had their disagreements sometimes, but in the end it was great to have her around.

Teresa dropped by the gallery at the end of the day as Christina and Marina were closing. 'Hello! Are you closed or can I have a look inside?' Teresa said, putting her face through a slightly open door.

'Teresa! What a nice surprise! You should have come earlier to help us!' Marina said.

'Darling! I'd have loved to but have been so busy, believe me, preparing for my trip.'

'I bet you have. I was kidding,' said Marina. 'How are you? We haven't had a wine Thursday in ages. Will we have time before you leave?' Marina greeted Teresa with a kiss.

'Next week? I'm free.'

'It's a date,' Marina said. 'I must fly. Anthony is working late tonight, and I've got to pick up the kids at my dad's house. He fetched them from school and nursery for me. Bye Christina. I'm so happy. See you tomorrow. I've arranged for our artworks to be picked up at the storage and delivered here at eleven. See you then. Kisses.' She left, running.

'Come in, Teresa. I'm not in a hurry. Let me show you around.' Christina grabbed her friend by the arm and locked the door behind them.

'I can't recognise this place. What a transformation. Well done, you and Marina! I know Petra would have loved this.'

'Come and see what we've done with the patio.' Christina grabbed two glasses and a bottle of white wine from the fridge at the small bar they'd installed as part of the new layout.

The two friends sat down on the patio that was looking even more incredible with the mood lighting on.

'I'm going to miss this — and you — so much. Do you think I'll survive?' Teresa grabbed her glass and toasted Christina.

'Of course you'll survive. Imagine all the amazing places you'll visit and the hotels you'll stay in. Not to mention the parties and the celebrities. I'm so jealous.'

'No, you're not. I know it will be amazing. But I won't see you, Karishma and Marina for so long. And my children, your children, Marina's children. Oh my God, I'll miss the kids.'

'Some of them are no longer kids. Time has flown. We'll miss you too. What about Hugo and Patricia's wedding?'

'Valerie will have a couple of weeks' break next spring, and the wedding is in that period, so Daniel and I'll come.'

'Great. Problem solved. I've been meaning to ask you — how's Karishma? Since she left the party early the other day, I haven't reached out. I feel bad, but I've been so busy with the gallery. How is she doing? Theo told me she wasn't feeling great.'

'I shouldn't be the one telling you this, but I don't think Karishma will mind.' Teresa told Christina everything that had been going on in her sister's life.

'That explains why Theo has been so down.'

'Have you seen Theo a lot? Are you guys bonding? What about Margaret?'

'I'm happy to have a brother. Theo and I have seen each other a few times. Mum knew about him. But she forgave Dad a long time ago. She was happy to meet Theo and his son David. She's at peace with the situation, and I wouldn't be surprised if she asks to meet Theo's mum. My mother is so amazing.'

'I've always admired Margaret. I looked up to her as a kid.'

'You should tell her. She'd be happy to know that. About Karishma, why didn't she tell me about her and Theo?'

'I don't know. I think she was scared you'd be angry with her. She wondered if you'd judge their age gap, and I think she was concerned that you'd think she was trying to take him away from you before you'd even had the chance to connect with him, or something silly like that.'

'Of course not! Who cares about the age gap? Age is just a number. But I think she should tell Theo about the baby.'

'I think so too, but she's concerned about that, and I can understand. Some men get funny and possessive. In the end, this is Iain's baby.'

'Yes, biologically speaking. But Iain's dead. Look, I don't know Theo that well, but I get a good guy vibe from him. He mentioned he wanted to have more children and if he likes Karishma, the baby could be a plus. Don't you think?'

'I think she should tell him, yes. But I don't know him yet. You should tell her what you think. It will help her. She's been avoiding me, but I'm sure she's not well. The failure of the procedure was a big shock. In her mind, she was having a baby.'

'Are there any embryos left? Can she try again?'

'Two more, I think. And she can try again. The surrogate has agreed to try one more time, but Karishma is too scared to go through it all again.'

'I'll talk to her.' Christina paused and the two friends stared across the patio for a moment. 'I'll miss our conversations so much. Losing you and Petra in the same year is too much.'

'I'm not dying. I'll be back, and you can come to meet me. We've talked about that.'

'I don't know. I have the feeling this is the end of the collagen coven.'

'Why?'

'Ricardo keeps pressuring me to tell Marina everything,' Christina said, 'and I've agreed to do so after the opening. '

'Why is this the end? I have a feeling that once she digests the information, Marina will be fine, though she may need time. And I'll be back. And Karishma is still here.'

'I don't think Marina will forgive me. And after all this.' Christina looked round the gallery. 'I have a feeling we won't get to enjoy this place, our gallery, together.'

'I think she may be sad and disappointed at first, but something tells me she'll come round, though you may have to give her time. When are you telling her?'

'The day after the opening, I think. If I don't, Ricardo will, and the shock will be worse. I don't like the way he came back into our lives and the way he threatened me.'

'To be honest. I never liked him.' Teresa made a face of disgust.

'He said Petra and he were in love before she died. Do you believe that?'

'Maybe. Who knows? She was happier than usual in the months before she passed. She was probably in love with him. But I don't know about him,' said Teresa.

'He told me his wife and daughters moved here years ago. I don't think they have a good relationship. Maybe that's why he decided to look for us. Maybe he needs attention, a family?'

'It could be. But there are ways to do it, and I don't like the way he's done it.' Teresa looked at her phone. 'I lost track of time. Mum's making dinner for us. She'll be mad at me if I'm late.'

'Oh no! You don't want that. Let's go.' Christina turned off the lights and locked up. 'Love you. Thank you for coming by. I needed this.'

'My pleasure. The new space is fantastic. I'm sure it'll be a total success. And I love you too. Shall we walk back together?'

'Sounds like a good idea.'

The two friends walked home arm in arm. It was a beautiful end of summer night. The calm before the storm as Christina had predicted.

◆ ◆ ◆

On the evening of the gallery opening, everything was perfect. The artwork had made it back from storage on time and in perfect condition. Marina hired the same catering company she'd used for a preview at her old job. Their canapés were heavenly and paired perfectly with the flowing champagne.

Julio was receiving a lot of attention; everyone wanted to find out who the architect behind the renovations was. The gallery looked truly exceptional.

Almost all the clients invited had shown up.

Alberta, Marina's old boss, was there too and couldn't disguise her envy. Teresa's family were all there, including her dad and Purnima. Karishma sent her apologies and offered the excuse that she had an emergency surgery to attend.

'Hello my dear. I'm so proud of you for continuing your mum's work here with Christina,' Ellie, Petra's mother said as she arrived and hugged Marina. 'Your grandad has a cold and couldn't make it, but he'll come and visit the new gallery as soon as he recovers.'

Theo came and brought two bouquets of roses — one for Marina and one for Christina. Margaret arrived with Ines.

A photographer had been hired and was capturing every moment. Christina posed for a photo with Margaret, Peter and their children. Even Samantha had managed to come all the way from Bath. Marina did the same, with Anthony and Louisa who were very happy for their partner and mother respectively.

'I want to be in this photo,' said Marcus.

'Of course, Dad. You too Paolo, come, please,' Marina called the two men and they proudly joined her for the camera.

It was a perfect evening and Patricia and Bianca were attentive to the clients and managed to get a few pieces of art reserved. Everything was a success.

By ten o'clock, all the clients and guests had left — only family members remained. As they were preparing to leave, a drunk Ricardo arrived at the door. The bouncer Christina had hired blocked his access while asking his name to verify he was on the list.

Christina saw what was happening and made a gesture to the bouncer to not let him in. Ricardo started shouting, attracting everyone's attention. 'I'm here to see Marina. Marina! Please, I need to talk to you.'

'Please take him out. He's drunk.' Christina moved closer to the bouncer, who was now holding Ricardo by his arm. 'Ricardo, please. You said you'd wait.'

'Wait, *Ricardo*? Is this the Ricardo who was seeing my mum? The client who called me?' Marina was now next to them.

'Marina, please, he's drunk. Let him go. We'll talk about this another time.'

'I'm not drunk. She's lying. She's lied all her life. She lied to you! Tell her! Tell her Christina.' Ricardo was now shouting louder as he tried to push the bouncer away from him.

'Let him go, please.' Marcus had heard the commotion and joined Christina, Marina and Ricardo at the door, followed by Teresa and the rest of the family. Marcus turned to Christina. 'There's no point in avoiding this anymore, Christina. Let him in.'

Christina reluctantly told the bouncer to let Ricardo in.

'Avoiding what, Dad? What are you talking about? Who is he? Why is he saying Christina lied?' shouted Marina.

Ricardo grabbed a glass of champagne and downed it in one. 'Tell her! Tell her who I am.'

Christina was paralysed. This scene was the last thing she wanted. Telling Marina would be traumatic enough, but telling this way, at that moment… Their special moment — that was so unfair of Ricardo. One more unfair, selfish action from the man who'd changed the course of their lives thirty-six years ago. *What a total prick!*

Noticing Christina was frozen, Marcus jumped in. 'He's your father, Marina. Your biological father.'

'What? My biological what? It can't be. You're my father!' Marina shouted. Louisa ran over to her mother and grabbed her hand. Teresa covered her face with her hands and moved closer to Christina.

'I am your father, of course I am. But not biologically. He is. I'm sorry we kept this from you for all this time.' Tears were rolling down Marcus's face. Paolo stood firmly at his side.

'All this time? A lifetime! My entire fucking lifetime! Why did you lie to me? Did you all know? Did you know, Christina?'

'We did. I knew as well, Marina.' Teresa intervened, trying to help the situation as she could see on Christina's face that she was in panic mode as she knew it wasn't over. Not all the secrets were out yet.

'Babe, did you know this? You never told us, me,' Daniel asked Teresa.

'Daniel, please. We'll talk about it later.' Marina was who they had to pay attention to now. 'Marina, please sit down. Can someone please bring her a glass of water?'

Samantha brought the water to Marina and a glass for her own mother. The colour had disappeared from Christina's face. Peter was looking at Christina, also in shock. Christina looked back at him and mouthed, *I'm so sorry*. Peter's face was filled with disappointment and even a bit of anger.

'Marina, I'm sorry to tell you like this,' said Ricardo. 'Me and Petra, we were in love, I swear. I mean, we fell in love. We'd agreed to tell you everything. Then she died. I was away and when I came back, *she* tried to stop me.' Ricardo pointed at Christina, his voice calmer now.

'Why? Why all the lies?' Marina looked at Marcus and then at Christina. 'I'd never expect this from you, Christina. And my mother, why did she lie to me?' Marina could hardly speak between sobs.

'Tell her, Christina. Tell her everything!' Ricardo looked directly at Christina.

Christina's legs were shaking and her heart was pounding. She grabbed a chair and sat down. She looked at all the faces in the room — her children fixedly looking at her without saying a word. Peter was looking down, shaking his head. Christina turned to her mother, then the rest of the extended family, and then Marcus. He stared back at her with red, watery eyes. Her gaze finally met Teresa's, who made a gesture with her head as if saying, *it's time.*

Christina took a deep breath and gently pressed her closed eyes with her fingertips before she started talking in a broken, faint voice. 'This isn't the way I wanted you to find out. I did try to stop him.' She looked at Ricardo. 'I asked for time. I wanted to be ready. He's not entitled to demand anything from me, to make it clear. You'll understand why.' Christina wiped away a tear and held back a sob.

'I'll tell you everything, Marina. I want you to know that everything we did was for you. For you and our family. We wanted the best for you, all of us.' She glanced at Marcus and Teresa and looked deeply at Ines. Teresa's mother was watching and hadn't said a word, but the look on her face indicated that she was well aware of what was about to come.

Christina continued. 'I'll start from the beginning. It was 1987, Petra's, Teresa's and my gap year...'

17

Gap Year

'He said yes! Christina, open the door! My father said yes! We're going to Rio.' Petra was frantically banging at Christina's door.

Margaret opened the door as fast as she could. 'What's going on? Is someone dying?' she joked.

'My father said I can go with Christina to Rio for the gap year. I mean, she's still going, right?' Petra noticed Margaret's serious face and felt a pang of anxiety in her stomach when she realised Christina hadn't yet discussed the trip with her mother.

Christina appeared behind her mum and made a gesture to Petra to shut up.

'Too late. I've spilled the beans.' Petra covered her mouth with her hands and made a funny face.

Margaret sat the girls on the sofa and called her husband. 'You two, wait until George is home. We need to discuss this. You hadn't told me you were planning to go to Rio.' She looked at her daughter's defiant face.

'I'm almost eighteen now and you'd agreed I

could go travelling for a gap year.'

'I did, but I thought you were going to France or Scotland, somewhere nearby.'

'We want the weather, Mum! Sunshine, and music and fun. No disrespect to France or Scotland… but who plans to have fun for a year in Scotland's weather?' asked Christina.

Petra shrugged in agreement.

'I did. I went to Scotland for six months when I finished school, went to stay with my auntie and had a great time,' Margaret said, feeling silly. 'But that's not the point. Brazil is across the ocean. You don't speak the language and it could be dangerous. Two British girls alone in Rio? Why did Declan agree to that?'

It was Petra's turn to respond. 'We won't be alone. We'll be with Teresa and her mother, Ines. They live there, remember? And my friend —' she corrected herself '*our* friend Marcus is going too.'

'Is that boyfriend of yours going?' Margaret and the other parents didn't approve of the boy Petra had been dating.

'God, no. I'm no longer seeing him. He's not my boyfriend, though he was trying to be, trying hard. My dad said he was stalking me. Maybe that's why he agreed I could go,' Petra explained.

'I don't know. It all sounds too dangerous to me.'

The entrance door swung open, and George entered, followed by Robert, Teresa's father, who'd arrived to talk to George and Margaret about the girls' gap year plan. Robert explained it had been Teresa's idea, and Ines had agreed to look after the girls. 'To be honest, I think it's a great idea. It would be good experience for them, and they're eighteen, now. I mean, Teresa and Petra are and Christina will be soon. Technically, we can't stop them.'

'We can't stop them, but if we don't fund them, they can't go.' Margaret wasn't convinced.

'We'll work there! We'll teach English.' Christina jumped in. The girls had it all planned out.

George sent the girls to Christina's room and called Declan. He wanted to discuss it with the other adults before deciding, and not in front of the teenagers. Declan arrived — it was convenient that they were all neighbours — and explained that Petra deserved a change of scenery.

'And besides, Petra never got over the fact that Ellie left us. The girl hasn't seen her mother in years. Maybe I should have discussed it with you all first, but even if Christina doesn't go, Petra will.'

'As if one would go without the other.' George had a point. He turned his gaze to his wife. 'Margaret, I know you're scared, but let's face it, they'll be with Ines and Teresa. They're young adults now and it's a once in a lifetime opportunity. What could go wrong?'

George knew that deep down, Margaret didn't want Christina to go, as she didn't want to be alone. He travelled a lot for work and Margaret would feel lonely without her daughter for a whole year. But he didn't think it was fair for Christina to be deprived of such an opportunity, so she could act like her mother's lady-in-waiting. Margaret had been fragile since the loss of their son, but Christina had also lost her brother, and it wasn't fair to deny her an opportunity to take her mind off that tragedy. After all, Margaret had good friends and there was Purnima next door with little Karishma. They were always around. 'Let's give our girl this opportunity. What do you say?'

'I'll go and meet them for the Christmas holiday. I'll take Purnima and Karishma to visit,' Robert said, trying to reassure Margaret.

After taking herself out of the equation and considering what was best for Christina, Margaret finally agreed, and called the girls to the living room to give them the good news. They were ecstatic.

'We're going to Rio!' The girls whirled around, holding each other with tears of joy pouring from their eyes.

George and Robert went to the fish and chip shop, and they all had dinner together. Purnima and Karishma joined them.

The plan was made. Petra, Christina and Marcus would travel together. The girls were going to stay at Ines's house for the whole year and would work as English teachers at a small English school whose owner was a friend of Ines's. Marcus was going to rent a flat and share with two of his friends from school who were also going. One of them was the son of Portuguese parents. That would come in handy until he learned the language.

The girls got tickets to travel at the end of September. Marcus would go a week later. They couldn't wait.

◆ ◆ ◆

As they approached Rio's airport the girls squeezed their faces, one on top of the other, against the plane's tiny window, and as they saw the beautiful landscape with the sugar loaf mountain surrounding the bay and the Christ the Redeemer statue atop of a mountain in the background, an immense sense of freedom and euphoria overtook them.

Teresa and Ines were waiting for them as they landed. Everything seemed magical. The trip from the airport to Teresa's home was something else. As soon as they came out of a tunnel and saw the big lagoon, they couldn't contain their excitement. It was dawn and the sky was clear from any clouds and exploding with colour from blue to purple with all shades of orange and pink in between. The air smelled like the sea, refreshing and salty and sweet at the same time.

'I'll never go back home. I love it already,' said Petra.

'I can smell the sea. It smells like freedom.' Christina closed her eyes and took a deep breath.

The radio played a Brazilian rock ballad. Petra and Christina couldn't understand a word, but loved the rhythm and started shaking their heads to the music.

Teresa laughed. 'I'll teach you Portuguese and the lyrics, so you can sing along.'

Ines was happy to see the girls. After all, she'd lived next door to them until they were about five years old, but since her divorce from Robert, she'd only seen them on a couple of occasions. Nonetheless, they had a unique place in her heart, especially because she knew how close they were to Teresa, like nail to flesh or *unha e carne* as they say in Portuguese.

Teresa lived a few blocks away from Ipanema beach in a duplex on the top floor of a five-storey brownish coloured building with greenish glass windows and white marble steps into a small reception or lobby. It was a spacious four-bedroomed flat with a large terrace on the top floor. As soon as they entered the flat, they started to explore. They were speechless when they noticed the view from the terrace — the big statue Christ the Redeemer was visible from it, an ethereal sight.

That first night, they stayed awake until the first ray of sunshine appeared in the sky. The excitement was too intense; there was no way they could sleep. Jetlag was also to blame. They spent the whole night on the terrace. It was spring in the southern hemisphere, and the warmth of Rio's weather was enough to make Petra and Christina feel like they were at the peak of summer, though Teresa needed a light blanket. They were enjoying each other's company and talking about their plans for the next years. And boy, there were a lot of plans.

The following day was the best. They woke up at ten and put on their swimsuits with a light summer dress on top, summer sandals on their feet. They had breakfast at a juice bar on the way to the beach, Brazilian cheese bread and a fresh tutti-frutti juice, none of the 'from concentrate' drinks they were used to in the UK.

The beach was amazing. Teresa had fun looking at her two *gringas*, heart sisters, braving the waves. They lay on their beach towels under a parasol and enjoyed the sunshine all day. Man carrying barrels on their backs sold a delicious, iced tea that they enjoyed while munching on tapioca biscuits.

'I can't wait for Marcus to get here,' Petra said.

'You have a thing for him, don't you?' Christina teased her.

'Who's Marcus?' Teresa hadn't met him yet.

'A friend from school. He's coming here for the gap year too. Petra convinced him, didn't you?' Christina continued to tease.

'Stop it! He's my friend, that's all. I enjoy his company and yes, I can't wait for him to arrive,' Petra said in a serious tone.

'I know you like him,' said Christina. 'You don't need to lie to us. No issues there, but I think you should enjoy your time here. Look at these guys. Look at their muscles. I wouldn't bring a guy from home. I want to find one here.' Christina was impressed by the young men with Adonis-style bodies parading around the beach on their speedos.

'They do look good. And look at the women, they're sculpted. I feel bad about my white tummy,' Petra said, pinching a bit of extra flesh on her abdomen.

'I know. We'll never turn that colour — you and me both. The two white gringas,' Christina joked as she sipped water from a straw inserted into a coconut.

'You're both gorgeous! I mean it. I'm sure the boys here will be all over you with your gorgeous pale skin and blue eyes.' Teresa had a point. The two girls were good looking and interestingly exotic for the local standards.

'You're gorgeous, Teresa. And look at your mum. How old is she again?' Petra noticed Ines arriving at the beach with equally good-looking friends.

'Do you have collagen on the tap here?' Christina was impressed with how fit the woman looked no matter their ages; even the ones who were probably in their sixties were comfortable in their small bikinis.

A couple of days after their arrival in Rio, Petra and Christina were introduced to their new boss, Ines's friend, the owner of the English school for children. They started working right after. Three or four hours a day was enough to guarantee them some spending money and left plenty of time for them to enjoy Rio and the beach.

Marcus arrived a week later as planned and called Petra straight away. They met the following day at the beach. By then, Petra and Christina had met several of Teresa's friends, including two girls who were always together and seemed to be making fun of the British girls all the time, Maria and Clara.

'Don't mind them. They can be annoying, but they're harmless,' Teresa reassured them. There were three other girls who were nice and kind. They all spoke reasonably good English, but one of them was fluent as she'd spent a year in England when she was fifteen — she even had a British accent. Her name was Renata; the others were Fabiola and Daniela.

Then there were the boys, Fabio, Miguel, Fernando and Ricardo. They were all nice. Apart from Ricardo, they didn't speak great English. They were all upper-middle-class kids. Clara and Ricardo seemed to be wealthy; they both lived in big luxurious apartments in front of the beach.

When Marcus arrived on the beach for the first time, he and his two friends from the UK met Teresa's friends and they all continued to meet regularly at the same point at the beach.

Petra was undeniably more and more infatuated by Marcus as Christina and Ricardo became closer and closer — sharing a beach towel, feeding each other tapioca biscuits, trying each other's ice cream. Clara seemed jealous and was increasingly rude to Christina.

Life was good. Petra and Christina were having the time of their lives. Teresa never been happier, with her best friends living in the same city as her. Marcus had easily adapted to Rio's lifestyle.

While Petra and Christina worked, Teresa studied for a test that was required to get into university in Brazil. Teresa wanted to be a lawyer.

They went to the beach almost every day and at the weekend they enjoyed *carioca* nights. The options were many. Samba in Lapa neighbourhood, Brazilian rock gigs at a place called *The Flying Circus*, dance parties at the top of the Sugar Loaf Mountain or drinks by the bay at traditional bars in Urca or Gavea, two famous neighbourhoods in the marvellous city. There was nothing like a night out in Rio during the eighties.

At the end of October, Ricardo threw a big party at his place. All the group was invited, including the British girls, Marcus and his friends. His flat was amazing — a triplex penthouse overlooking the ocean. He even had a small swimming pool on the terrace on the top floor. His parents were away, and he had the whole flat to himself. At one point, Marcus and Petra were leaning against the balustrade, looking at the ocean and chatting. That was when they kissed for the first time.

Christina and Ricardo were an item by then, and that night they had sex. It was her first time. Later that night, she told Petra and Teresa. They were both happy and slightly jealous as they were still virgins. Ricardo was a handsome man, and most young women who knew Ricardo had a crush on him. Christina continued to date Ricardo while Marcus and Petra were getting closer to each other.

Petra finally admitted to her friends that she had a crush on Marcus and told them they'd kissed. It was mid-December when Petra and Marcus had sex for the first time — the first time for both of them. They continued dating, but the more they spent time with each other, the more they felt like friends and the less like lovers.

Robert and Purnima arrived with Karishma a couple of days before Christmas. They stayed in a hotel not far from Ines's house. Robert and Ines had separated on good terms and had continued to be friends. Purnima respected and understood their friendship and had never felt jealous. They spent Christmas Eve and Christmas Day with Ines, Teresa, Christina, Petra and Marcus.

Christmas was an entirely new experience for the folks that had come from the UK. Besides the fact it was summer, in Brazil, they celebrate it with a big dinner on Christmas Eve when they also exchange presents. On Christmas Day they reunite and have leftovers for lunch, and after lunch, they go to the beach.

A couple of days before New Year's Eve, Ines was having dinner with the girls when Christina suddenly got up and left the table in a hurry to the toilet.

'Darling, what's happening? Go check on her, Teresa,' Ines said, concerned.

Teresa knocked on the door. 'Christina, open the door.' She heard Christina being sick.

'Come in. Close the door, please,' Christina ordered.

'What happened? Did you eat something bad?'

'I don't think so.' Christina looked at Teresa with teary eyes.

'Oh. No! Do you think you are… Are you pregnant?' Teresa joined the dots.

'I haven't had my period since October. I'm so scared.' Christina was whispering and crying at the same time. 'Please don't tell anyone. Not even Petra or your mum. Tell them I had the shrimp at the beach.' Ines had told the girls, many times, to avoid eating the shrimp on a stick at the beach.

'Fine, I won't tell them. Tomorrow, say you're still unwell. When Mum goes out to buy groceries for the New Year's Eve dinner, I'll suggest Petra go with her to help and we'll do a pharmacy test. Take your time and freshen up. I'll go back now before they suspect anything.'

Teresa went back to the dinner table.

'What happened?' Petra asked.

'She had the shrimp at the beach,' Teresa told them.

'I told you girls so many times. It isn't safe. I had a terrible stomach bug once because of that. Had a fever and everything. She needs to drink a lot of liquids. Coconut water and rest.'

'She will. Let's see how she feels tomorrow.

If she's still not feeling well, I might not come shopping. Maybe Petra could help you? I can stay with Christina,' Teresa suggested.

'Of course I will. Or you can go, and I'll stay with her?' Petra offered. She wasn't buying the shrimp story. The first thing that crossed her mind was that Christina might be pregnant.

'Maybe. We'll see tomorrow,' said Teresa.

The next morning, Ines went shopping and Teresa asked Petra to go with her, saying she had period pain. Petra didn't believe her, but pretended to. She was disappointed that Christina had told Teresa and not her. Immediately after they'd left, Teresa went to the pharmacy and bought two pregnancy tests. The result was positive on both tests.

Christina broke down in tears. All she could think about was that her life was ruined. Her mother and father would never forgive her. She could imagine Margaret saying, 'I knew something was going to happen. I never wanted her to go. It's all your fault, George.'

'I'll never go to university or travel the world,' said Christina. 'That's it, my dreams are doomed, life is over. And what should I say to Ricardo? How do you think he'll react?'

'Don't be silly. You're pregnant, not dying. And as for Ricardo, well, only one way to find out. Let's go and talk to him.'

They walked to Ricardo's house. It was only a few blocks away from Teresa's house. Christina cried all the way there, and her eyes were red and puffy.

When they arrived at the concierge — most buildings have a concierge with a doorman in Rio — they asked for Ricardo, saying they were his friends. The doorman used the intercom to call Ricardo's flat. He was told to let the girls in. Once Teresa and Christina arrived at the apartment, a maid in uniform opened the door and told them to sit down on the impeccable sofa in the spacious living room graced with breathtaking views of Ipanema beach.

Ricardo's mum, Helena, was a classy lady in her mid-forties. She had perfect skin and lush brown hair and a great figure. She entered the living room and greeted the girls. 'You must be Ricardo's friend from England.' She looked at Christina. 'And You're Ricardo's friend from school? Teresa, isn't it?' Helena spoke in perfect English.

'Yes. I'm Teresa and this is Christina.'

'I see. Ricardo is at the beach; he shouldn't be much longer. You can go find him or wait here.' Helena said.

As soon as she said that, Christina, who had red eyes from crying, put her hand on her stomach and asked, 'May I use your toilet, please?'

'Sure, this way. Hope everything is alright?'

'She ate bad shrimp. At the beach.' Teresa spoke before Christina had chance.

When Christina came back, Helena said, 'I was about to go out for a coffee. Why don't you both join me? By the time we finish Ricardo should be back.'

The girls initially refused, but Helena insisted, and they didn't want to be rude. They sat at a nice restaurant, expensive by the look of it. 'It's my favourite spot,' Helena said. She ordered a coffee for herself; Teresa went for orange juice and Christina asked for a coke.

Helena was blunt. 'Look, girls. I think we can be honest with each other. I was a teenager once and I know how these things go. My son has a brilliant future ahead of him. He has a place guaranteed at a renowned university in the US. My husband and I have big plans for him. He'll study economics and work at our company as the CFO once he graduates.'

Teresa and Christina had a feeling of where the conversation was going and listened without saying a word. The bluntness of that elegant and intimidating woman had shocked them both.

'Do you understand what I'm saying?' Helena asked.

'We do. I do,' said Christina. 'I just want to talk to Ricardo. It's nothing. I mean, great that he's going to the US. I need to talk to him, please.'

'That isn't going to happen. He's flying to the US tomorrow. We all are, and he has a lot to do today.'

'But you said he was coming back soon from the beach.' Christina's voice trembled.

'I don't think you understand. You won't talk to Ricardo. Take this number.' She wrote a phone number on a piece of paper. 'This is my gynaecologist; her name's Georgette. I'll call her as soon as I get home. Go home, call her and book an appointment. I'll pay for everything. Georgette will help you get rid of this problem. All expenses on me.'

'Wait. What are you insinuating? You can't do that.' Teresa was about to jump on Helena's neck.

'I'm giving you an opportunity. You're young and you have your whole life ahead of you. Ricardo isn't ready to be a father. What did you expect? That he'd give up his career for you and a baby? This was a mistake. I'm sure he was just having fun with you. He has a lot of women after him. Did you think he was in love? Don't be silly.'

Christina sat in silence. *How could that woman be so mean, so vile? Was she telling the truth? Was Ricardo just having fun?* She was in love, her first love. She thought he'd liked her. Maybe Helena was right. Ricardo was always flirty with the girls who were constantly hitting on him. *Helena was telling the truth.*

'I want to go home, Teresa. Please.' Christina grabbed the piece of paper with the doctor's number and stood up.

Teresa stood up with her and before she left, she turned back and faced Helena. 'You know you can't do that to her. Your son is so unlucky to have a monster for a mother. My mother's a lawyer, a good one. I'll tell her everything; she'll come to talk to you. You can't treat us like that.'

Helena's expression changed slightly when she

heard that Teresa's mother was a lawyer. But that was only for a second. She recomposed herself and said, 'You may think I'm a monster, but you'll thank me in the end, believe me. I know what I'm saying. You don't want to waste your life either.' She looked firmly at Christina.

When Teresa and Christina arrived back home, Ines and Petra were waiting for them, worried. Teresa went in first and Ines immediately started talking to her. 'Where have you girls been? Is Christina feeling better?'

A sobbing Christina appeared behind Teresa. They told Petra and Ines about the pregnancy, the visit to Ricardo and the treatment they'd received from Helena.

'She can't do that. Oh, my dear, come here.' Ines put her arms around Christina and guided her to the sofa, sitting next to her. 'Everything will be fine. You need to rest, rest and eat something. I'll take care of you. I'll also talk to that woman. She can't force you to do anything, you know that, right?'

Petra's face was almost as pale as Christina's. She was shocked and angry at Helena. 'Of course she can't force you. It's your decision. Hey, we're here for you. Whatever you decide, but I think you must think carefully. Who cares about Ricardo or Helena? If you decide to keep the baby, we'll be here for you.'

'I'm so scared. I don't know what I want. I just want to sleep now.' It was only a little after lunchtime, but Christina felt exhausted. The pregnancy itself and the huge emotional distress caused by the confrontation with Helena had taken a toll on her. 'Please don't tell anyone. Don't tell Robert, no one. Please.'

'We won't tell anyone, dear. Only when you want to tell and if you want to tell. Now go and have a rest.' Ines followed her to her bed and made sure she was comfortable. She stayed with her until she stopped crying and fell asleep. Christina slept for the whole afternoon.

Teresa tried to convince her mother to sue Helena or something. Ines was trying to think what she could and should do. Unfortunately, at that time a teenager falling pregnant out of marriage was still a big stigma. And in Brazil, it wasn't uncommon for a mother to try to convince, sometimes even coerce, a daughter to have an abortion or force their son to convince the pregnant girl they'd impregnated to get rid of the baby.

Petra was overwhelmed by all that had happened. She was concerned about Christina, angry at Helena, and unsure about her relationship with Marcus. 'I need some fresh air. I'll go for a walk — back soon.'

She left Teresa and Ines discussing what they'd do about Helena, and went to Marcus hoping he'd be finished at work. He'd been working at a gym, helping with all sorts of tasks, from cleaning mats to organising equipment and doing paperwork. Marcus had an hour to go until the end of his shift, so Petra waited for him. Once he'd finished, they went for a walk on Copacabana beach's boardwalk.

They sat down on the soft sand, each clutching a coconut with a straw on it. The sky was beautiful with the last bit of sunshine of the day.

'Are you in love with me, Marcus?'

'Wow.' Marcus was taken by surprise. 'Why are you asking me that, Petra? We like each other, don't we?'

'We do. We like each other. But is this love? Do you see me like a lover?'

'It doesn't matter. We don't need to discuss this. Let's enjoy each other's company, shall we?'

'When we're together, it feels strange. I don't feel like you enjoy it. And I'm not sure how it makes me feel. I like you a lot, but I can't shake off a feeling that you're with me for pity, as a favour or whatever.'

'Why are you saying this, Petra? Of course I like being with you.' He tried to kiss her.

'You don't need to pretend. Not to me.' Petra moved her face away from him. 'I've seen the way you look at the guys at the beach. And I don't feel you enjoy me, my body.'

'Why are you talking about this now? How long you have been feeling like that?' Marcus asked her, moving a strand of hair that had fallen across her face.

'I don't know. Since we had sex for the first time, I think. Tell me how you feel. How you really feel, please.'

'I'm so sorry, Petra. I like you; I do. I'm attracted to you, in a way. But I'm attracted to boys as well.

Maybe more than girls. I know it isn't fair to you. I didn't mean to hurt you; I'm so confused.' Marcus wrapped his hands around his face and bent his head.

'You don't need to hide from me. We were friends before we became lovers. We're still friends. And we don't need to be lovers.'

'I don't know what I like. I don't know if I'm gay. You're the only person I've been with, sexually, I mean.'

'I've only been with you as well. I'm not comfortable with my body.'

'Why? Your body is perfect. You're beautiful.'

'It's not that.' Petra looked down and then around as if trying to find the right words to speak next.

'What is it? You can tell me anything. I've shared my biggest secret with you. I trust you, and you can trust me too.' Marcus looked deep into her eyes.

'I have an issue. A health issue.' Petra was picking her fingernails nervously. 'I have a congenital defect.'

'Is it serious?'

'I never told anybody. Not Teresa or even Christina. Only my father knows.' Petra took a deep breath and looked back into Marcus's eyes. 'Do you promise that you'll never tell anyone?'

'Of course I do. Hey, you don't need to tell me. Only tell me if it will make you feel better.'

'It will, believe me. Sharing with you may make it a less heavy burden to carry.' She had a small smile on her face. 'I have a condition called primary ovarian insufficiency. I've never had a period, and it's likely that I'll never be able to have a child of my own.'

'That suck. I don't know what to say. I'm sorry. I wish I could help.'

'You have helped. Telling you makes me feel better.' Petra stared at the ocean for a minute in silence. Marcus was also silent, giving her thoughts some space.

'I've always wanted to be a mother. Since I was a tiny girl.'

'If it makes you feel better, I may never have kids as well. I mean, if I'm gay… it makes things difficult.'

'Do you even want to have kids? I thought that would be the last thing on your mind.'

'I'd love to have children. I'd certainly treat them differently to how my parents treat me.'

'You parents aren't bad. What are you talking about?'

'They're not bad. They'd just never accept a gay son. They've made that clear. Whenever the word "gay" comes up my father says, "Better a dead son than a gay son." And my mother thinks being gay is a sin, a serious one.'

'If I could ever have a child, I'd want them to be happy.' She took a long breath. 'Happy and healthy with a perfectly functioning body.'

The two teenagers stayed at the beach, side by side in silence until the last ray of sunshine was gone.

'I'd better go,' said Petra finally. 'Christina hasn't been feeling well, and I told Teresa and Ines I'd be back soon. It was nice talking to you. I feel better now. Thank you, for everything.'

'I feel better too. Thank you for understanding me. For not hating me.'

'I'd never hate you, Marcus. You're one of my favourite people in the whole world.'

Marcus walked Petra home. They didn't talk much. Petra was worried about Christina but at the same time jealous of her.

Back home things were calmer. Teresa and Ines were having dinner and Christina was still sleeping. 'I think Christina will sleep until tomorrow. We'd better let her,' Ines said. 'She needs to recover from the emotional distress she's been through and be rested enough to think and make a decision.'

'Do you think she'll keep the baby?' That was all Petra could think about.

'I don't know. But the boy has the right to know. I'll pay a visit to Helena tomorrow morning. I'll go alone and try to have an adult conversation with her. Ricardo and Christina should have the opportunity to discuss and decide, together.'

'That woman is evil. I hate her. I wish I could punch her in the face. Do you think she told Ricardo?'

'Probably not. She was so quick in figuring out about what you and Christina wanted to talk to Ricardo and even quicker in taking you out of the house before he arrived. I doubt she'd take any chance on him even considering that having a baby is a plausible idea.'

Ines woke early and by nine o'clock she was already at Helena's building, only to be told by the doorman that the whole family had left early with bags on a taxi to the airport. They'd told the man that they'd be away for a month — conveniently.

'Cowards,' said Teresa when her mother came back home and told her the news. 'What can we do now?'

'Nothing. We'll do nothing, for now.' Ines sipped her coffee.

'I've made up my mind.' A well-rested Christina appeared on the terrace where Teresa, Ines and Petra were having a late breakfast.

'Christina. You look better, how are you feeling? Come sit down,' said Ines.

'I feel better. I needed a long sleep. I can think clearer now.'

'What have you decided? What are you going to do?' asked Petra.

'I won't have a baby. Not now, not with the son of that woman. I'm calling the doctor. Do you think she'd see me today? Tomorrow is the last day of the year, and I don't want to be still in this situation.'

'Are you sure? We can help you. We can all chip in and help,' said Petra, hoping to convince Christina to keep the baby.

'I'm sure you would, but please understand. It took me a lot to make my decision. Don't challenge it now.'

Noticing that Petra was about to speak again,

Teresa intervened. 'It's your decision. We understand and respect that.' She threw a look of reprimand at Petra.

'I won't take you to Helena's doctor,' said Ines. 'I have a great doctor who I've been seeing for years. She'll help us, I trust her.' Ines went to make a phone call. She returned to the terrace a few minutes later saying the doctor was able to see Christina in an hour. 'Are you sure? I'm not trying to change your mind. I need you to be sure as it's a big decision — you need to be sure.'

'I'm sure,' Christina said trying to look confident.

'Give me the address and I'll meet you there. I need some time to do a couple of things,' Petra said. Christina didn't question her.

Once they'd left for the clinic, Petra went to look for Marcus at the gym where he worked. 'Marcus, I'm glad you're here. We need to talk.' She almost cried in relief as she saw Marcus organising a shelf with pamphlets next to the reception.

'What's happened? You sound upset.'

'Can you get out, for a bit? I need to talk to you, it's urgent.'

Marcus asked his boss to let him take a break, saying it was an emergency. They sat at a bar near the beach and Marcus ordered soft drinks for them.

'I need to ask you a favour, a huge one. I don't know where to start,' said Petra.

'It sounds like you're going to ask me for a kidney. What's happened?'

'It's Christina. I shouldn't be telling you, but I must. We don't have much time.'

'Time for what? What's happened to Christina?'

'She's pregnant. She's going to have an abortion. She's going to the doctor as we speak.'

'Wait. How? I mean, pregnant? It's Ricardo's, isn't it?'

'Of course it's his. But we don't know if he knows. His mother was rude when she found out. She threatened Christina and told her to get rid of the baby. She then took Ricardo and the whole family and travelled to another country.'

'That sounds horrible. Who would do that?'

'A rich, snobbish and vile woman would. She did that.'

'I'm not sure where I fit into this. Do you want me to talk to Christina?'

'I don't want Christina to have an abortion. I want her to have the baby.'

'I understand how you may be feeling after what you've told me but, it's her decision, isn't it? It's a big life decision.'

'I know. But I've had an idea. A crazy idea. Please hear me out and promise you won't judge me. You can say no, but please don't judge me.'

Back at the clinic, Christina was shaking. *I'm doing it.* In her head she was trying to convince herself that this was the right thing to do, but part of her had already created a bond with the tiny creature growing inside her.

The consulting room was decorated in warm colours, different from most doctor's surgeries that Christina had been to. The doctor, a woman, was nice and softly spoken. Christina felt more relaxed but not less anxious. The doctor asked a few questions regarding her health and asked Christina for a sample to do another test to confirm the pregnancy.

Ines and Teresa were in the room with Christina — Teresa was holding her hand.

'Do you think this is wrong? Am I doing something wrong?' Christina looked at Ines as if begging for an honest opinion.

Ines moved closer to Christina as Teresa moved slightly aside to make space for her mother next to the examination couch. Ines grabbed her hands and started to talk kindly. 'I'm not sure about right or wrong. I don't believe in that. What I do believe in is that no one has the right to make decisions over a women's body but herself.'

Christina squeezed Ines hand. 'I've changed my mind. I'm sorry to waste your time.' She looked at the doctor.

'Don't worry about that. You need to be sure. Take more time to think if you need,' the doctor said.

They heard a commotion outside the room and suddenly the door swung open.

'I told her she couldn't come in,' the doctor's secretary said as a huffing and puffing Petra entered the room. 'Christina, please don't have an abortion.

Give me your baby. I want to raise this child as my own, with Marcus. You're like a sister to me, always been and I feel I'm family, your family.'

Christina's jaw dropped. 'Petra?! What do you mean? You're as young as I am.'

'You know I've always wanted to be a mother. And I have some health issues that mean I may never have the chance to get pregnant.' Petra grabbed Christina's hand. 'Marcus and I are in love. We'd be great parents to this baby, I promise.'

Ines, Teresa and the doctor were astonished by Petra's proposal.

'Petra, dear, this is a big ask and a big responsibility. Not to mention the legal issues. You'd need to formally adopt the baby,' Ines said.

'How do you feel about it, Christina?' Teresa asked.

The first thing that crossed Christina's mind was to refuse, apologise and tell Petra she'd changed her mind. But seeing Petra's expression of vulnerability and her longing for Christina to accept her request stopped her. Petra looked desperate and hopeful at the same time.

The next couple of minutes felt like a lifetime for Christina. She thought about her friendship with Petra. She remembered the Polaroids of them as babies. They'd taken their first steps together and shared their first words. Petra and Christina went to the same school. and having Petra by her side had helped Christina through the hard times after the loss of her brother. They were soul sisters; family ties don't get much stronger than that.

'Yes.' A simple word from Christina changed Petra's world forever. And, of course, Marcus's world as well.

18

Christina

'So you gave me away, like a present?' said Marina with resentment in her voice.

'I didn't give you away. I shared you with one of the most important people in the world to me,' Christina said.

'Bullshit! This is all bullshit!' Marina turned her gaze to Marcus. 'You and Mum lied to me my entire life. I was a convenient solution for you to put on a façade of a happy heterosexual family man while Mum just wanted to feel less bad about herself.'

'Is that really what you think?' Marcus spoke with disappointment. 'You're much more than that for us. We've always loved you.'

'And you.' Marina was now looking at Ricardo. 'What were you expecting out of all this? That I come running to your arms, calling you dad? You're a coward, and you're not my father. You will never be!'

'I never even knew about you until recently. My father told me everything after my mother died, a couple of years ago.' Ricardo sounded less drunk now;

'Do you think that's an excuse? You were in a relationship with Christina, and you left.'

'I was young and stupid. I was going away, anyway; my parents just made it happen faster. I didn't think much of it. Christina and I weren't serious — we were so young.' Ricardo looked at Christina. 'I was going to look for you, Christina, to apologise, but then I met Petra again and I — we — fell for each other. What I felt for her was real. She told me everything, and we decided we were going to tell you, together. But she died and my world turned upside down.'

'You don't have any idea of what upside down means. Leave, please. You're not part of this family or whatever this group of people are.' Marina looked around at the astounded faces of her big made-up family. 'Whatever you had with the woman who pretended to be my mother, if it was true or not, I'll never know, but I never want to see your face again.' She was angry at Petra as well. Christina shivered listening to Marina talking about Petra like that.

Ricardo stayed still.

'Did you hear her? Go, now. You don't belong here,' said Marcus.

Christina watched Ricardo leave. She couldn't read him; she didn't understand what his real intention was. Maybe he was telling the truth about not knowing about the baby for most of his life.

Maybe he did love Petra and maybe he really cared for Marina and wanted to connect with her. Or maybe he was pretending. Maybe he was a miserable narcissist who enjoyed playing with people. Or maybe he was a lost, broken man, raised in a cold, loveless home with a failed marriage and children who were indifferent towards him and was trying to find love and affection elsewhere, desperately trying to hold on to a last chance of happiness.

Whatever it was, it didn't matter. Christina didn't feel sorry for him, she felt nothing. She turned back to Marina. 'Nothing I say will change what you're feeling right now. I hope that with time you'll heal from the wound we've caused you with our life choices. I'll give you space, but please know that when and if you're ready, I'll be there for you.'

'I'm so disappointed in you, in all of you.' Marina looked at Teresa, Ines and Marcus. 'I don't think I can ever look at you again. Anthony, Louisa, please let's go.'

The night was over. Christina didn't want to talk to anyone but her husband and children. During the short trip home, no one said a word until they arrived back at the house.

Samantha was angry at Christina for lying to her and the rest of the family. She didn't say much more and left. Vanessa said it wasn't cool that she'd kept them all in the dark all this time but on the other hand, she was happy to know that Louisa was her niece and Marina her older sister.

Harry was the one who offered Christina the most support, surprisingly, since he was the youngest, not even fifteen yet. 'I understand you, Mum. And I'm not angry with you. I can only imagine how hard it was. So young, far from home and with a dickhead like that Ricardo guy.'

'Language,' Peter said. 'Go to your rooms. I need to talk to your mum.'

Christina hugged Vanessa tightly and Harry even tighter. She knew Sam would eventually come round and forgive her. But she wasn't sure about Peter. As the children went upstairs, it was only her, Peter and all their demons standing in their kitchen area.

'Why? Why couldn't you trust me? We've been together for twenty-five years. Why?' That was all Peter could say.

Christina didn't know why. She tried to find the answer in a corner of her brain, in her heart perhaps, but she couldn't. Maybe she thought he'd leave her. Maybe she feared it would destroy her own chance of having a family. Maybe it was to protect Petra and Marina. Or maybe she didn't say anything because if she did, it would be real for all of them.

From the moment she'd said 'yes' to Petra and agreed to let her raise Marina as her own, she'd viewed Marina as Petra's daughter. Ines and Teresa went along with the secret, and Marcus and Petra were happy. So Christina couldn't give one answer to Peter. There was still love between them, but she wasn't sure it was enough to mend what was broken. They decided to separate, for a while at least.

Christina decided to take a sabbatical. She explained to Vanessa and Harry. They both understood and gave her their support. 'I need a few months away to organise my thoughts,' she said. She asked Patricia to look after the gallery during her absence and wrote a letter to Marina offering to sell her own shares to her. Marina didn't respond.

Christina had reached out to Ines, who agreed to let Christina stay with her in Brazil for a few months. Christina had decided that going back to where it all began would heal her. It wasn't long until Christmas and New Year's Eve and being with Ines was always pleasant. She was trying to keep her mind positive even though her heart was shattered.

Christina had been staying with her mother since she'd agreed to separate from Peter. It was easier for her to move out, since she was going away, anyway.

The night before Christina's trip to Brazil. Margaret cooked dinner and invited Teresa and Karishma as a surprise for Christina. 'They wanted to say goodbye,' Margaret said as Christina opened the door for her two best friends.

The three women hugged each other and came inside the house. They knew it was the last time they'd be together for a while.

They sat down on the sofas in Margaret's living room. 'I'm so happy to see you. It's been hard,' Christina said and then she turned to Karishma.

'Are you mad at us for having kept it from you as well?'

'Not angry,' said Karishma. 'I was jealous at first, as I felt a bit excluded from the collagen coven. But I'm fine now. I was too young, ten at the time, and I can see why it wouldn't make sense to tell me years after when I was older. I really do. Are you upset with me for dating your brother? Teresa told me that she told you everything.'

Although the youngest, Karishma somehow often seemed the wisest. It had always been like that. She and Petra were so mature. They'd always been a step ahead emotionally from Teresa and Christina. Maybe because they both struggled with an absent parent and had to mature to deal with that.

'Of course I'm not upset. I'm happy for you. I'd love you to be together.' Christina's tone changed to a more serious one. 'I think you should try again, with the surrogate, I mean. And this time tell Theo. I'm sure he'll support you. Even if he decides he doesn't want to be a part of it, he'll support you and it would give you closure. It will be better than simply running away.'

'I know. I'll talk to him.' Karishma smiled at Teresa and back at Christina who responded with an even bigger smile. 'I may also try with the surrogate again.'

'And tell me about your trip, Teresa. Is everything ready?' Christina asked. 'You should come to Rio to see me and your mum for New Year's Eve.'

'Daniel would kill me. He's already planning the trip to Hawaii. He has less than two weeks' break off the tour. I'd come if I could convince him, but I doubt I'd be able to.'

'You can try.' Christina made a cheeky face. 'I'm kidding. Go and enjoy Hawaii with your man.'

'I'm happy to see you smiling. After everything, I thought you'd be in a worse shape.'

'I'm sad to see Marina suffer. I miss her. Especially after what we did together with the gallery. But I don't regret what Petra and I did. And I feel lighter now without the heavy load of the secret on my shoulders.' Christina crossed her legs on the sofa and made herself more comfortable. 'I feel clean. I'm relieved not to be hiding or lying. It feels better. Have you seen Marina, Teresa?'

'No. She refuses to talk to me, my mother or Marcus. She only talks to Declan. She doesn't know yet that he always knew.'

'Will he tell her?'

'I think so. I think he will. Whether she'll be angry at him or not, I don't know. She needs time.'

'What about Louisa? Did Alex say anything about how she reacted? Vanessa was happy to know that she's her auntie but she hasn't told me much more.'

'Alex told me that Louisa loves the idea of her best friend being her auntie too, and she's happy to have another grandma, you. But she's too loyal to Marina to come to you. Alex thinks she'll stay away, at least for now.'

'I understand. I'll miss her; I'll miss them all.' Christina threw her head back.

'How long will you be away for?'

'I don't know yet. As long as it takes for me to be at peace.'

'What about Peter?' Karishma asked.

'Peter's upset. He also needs time. Things have soured between us. We've separated.'

'Do you still love him?' Teresa asked.

'I do. But I don't know yet if we'll get back together. If not, we'll stay friends. We have three children; twenty-five years of history doesn't just go away like that.'

'How did the kids react?' Karishma asked.

'Sam is still upset. Vanessa, like I said, is kind of happy and Harry is a sweetheart. He's been very understanding and supportive.'

The three of them talked until late. They wanted to enjoy every minute of each other's company during what they knew was going to be the last time they'd spend together in a long while.

As Christina went to bed that night, Margaret sat down next to her. 'You did the right thing, you know. I'm proud of you.'

'You mean telling Marina?'

'That as well. But I meant having Marina. Sharing her with Petra. People will question and judge, but I can see the noble attitude behind everything. You're amazing, Christina.'

'I was raised by you. Thank you, Mum. It means

so much to me, to hear you understand.' Christina fell asleep with her mother looking over her. She was at peace for the first time since 1987.

Margaret watched her daughter and thought about the secrets she'd kept herself. *There'll be a time and place for those secrets to come out — not now. One secret at a time,* Margaret thought before falling asleep next to Christina.

The next morning, Christina left. Theo took her to the airport. He told her to try to enjoy her time off. He also told her she could call him if she needed anything and he'd look after Margaret during her absence. That made her heart smile.

19

Karishma

Karishma had a busy day at the hospital. Her shift had started early, and she had two long surgeries. Both were successful, but exhausting.

When she got home, Theo was sitting on her doorstep, waiting for her with a smile on his face and a bunny plush toy on his hand. 'I think you'll need another bunny.' He shook the toy playfully.

A thousand thoughts crossed Karishma's mind, but within a second they all disappeared, and she threw herself into Theo's arms and kissed him with passion. 'Who told you about the bunny?' she asked.

'Your sister told my sister, and she told me. You could have told me everything before.'

'I was too scared. I thought you'd judge me for having the baby of a dead man and then leave me. So, I left before you did.'

'I'll never leave you, Karishma. I have the son of another woman. Why would I leave you for having the baby of another man? I love you.'

She kissed him again. 'I love you, too, Theo.

I want to be with you, but I don't want to impose anything on you.'

'Karishma, listen to me.' He held her shoulders and stared deep into her eyes. 'I want to have this baby with you. I'll be their father, if you'll let me.'

'Of course I will. I can't wait.'

They spent the rest of the day together. Karishma called the surrogate the next day and was told she was still available and keen to try one more time.

There was still fear that things wouldn't work out, but this time Karishma was at peace. She looked at the new bunny brought by Theo and her heart was suddenly inundated with joy. She was finally happy and prepared for whatever happened from now on. She had Theo by her side.

20

Marina

Marina continued to go to the gallery as if nothing had happened. She hadn't responded to Christina's offer to buy her shares.

Two months had passed since she'd found out the truth about her mother and father. She hadn't spoken to Marcus or Teresa since. Anthony had been overly attentive to her and had vowed to respect whatever she decided regarding Marcus and Christina. But deep down Marina knew Anthony wanted her to forgive them all, and so did Louisa.

At least Ricardo had disappeared. She wasn't sure about forgiving Christina or Marcus, but she was sure about wanting nothing to do with Ricardo. She had no attachment whatsoever to him.

The other person she avoided was Declan. She'd never asked if he knew the truth — she was afraid of asking. Her grandfather was older now, and she didn't want to be angry with him and do anything that could affect his fragile health.

Three days before Christmas, Declan came to

her house as a surprise. Anthony opened the door. 'Declan, hello. Are you alright? Come in, please.'

'Hello, Anthony. I'm fine, thank you. Is Marina home? I need to have a conversation with her.'

As Declan came in, Archie ran straight into his legs and grabbed at them with his tiny hands. Declan lost his balance for a second and Anthony held him firmly at the same time as grabbing Archie.

'Oi. You must be careful, mate. You almost knocked Grandpa over. You cheeky monster.' He lifted Archie in the air and the boy giggled.

Marina came into the living room. 'Hi Grandpa.' She came to him and gave him a kiss on the cheek.

'Come on boys, let's find out where Louisa is. I think she's hiding,' Anthony said to grab Gabriel's and Archie's attention. Gabriel had joined them minutes earlier and was all over Declan.

'I've been meaning to talk to you, but I had to gather the strength to tell you what I have to say.' Declan spoke softly.

'You knew, didn't you? All this time?' Marina asked, gently.

'Yes, I did. Of course I did. But please hear me out.'

Marina brought her hands to her eyes, covering her face for a second as she took a deep breath. She was already upset, but decided to calm herself and hear what Declan had to say out of respect for his old age.

'Petra had been through a lot as a teenager. Ellie had left us when your mother was still very young.

She was different from the other girls. She knew she'd probably never be a mother.' He paused and asked for a glass of water. Marina brought it to him. He took a long sip and a deep breath before continuing. 'I knew how much she'd been hurting. That is why I sent her to Rio. I'd suspected she liked Marcus, but I thought it would be good for her to have a change of scene, and if being with Marcus made her happy, so be it. I wasn't aware, though, that Marcus had other preferences.'

'That Dad was gay, you mean?'

'Yes, that Marcus was gay. Your mother never told me. I found out with everybody else.' He paused again. 'But after your mother and Christina made their agreement, you mother called me, Petra called me. She told me everything, how she felt. I knew how devastated she was when we found out she couldn't have children. And I knew how much she wanted them. So, I went along with it. You know what? I've never regretted it.'

'Didn't you think about the consequences? Didn't Ines? Christina was going to abort me. And Petra was desperate. Feeling sorry for herself. Don't you see it? It was never about me; it was about them.'

Marina was feeling angry but trying to restrain herself. Her instinct was to scream and tell Declan she was angry at him too, that she never wanted to see him again, like the rest of the liars. She stood up and nervously started walking backward and forward in her living room.

Declan started talking again in a paced and kind way. That in itself calmed her down a bit. 'Do you remember when you found out you were pregnant with Louisa? How did you feel? You were young as well, like Petra and Christina were.'

'I felt scared, ashamed, worried. I thought my life was ended. I felt alone, rejected. I'd always known that Joe wasn't going to stick around.'

'I bet Christina felt the same. And those were different times. She was away from her family in a foreign country. Ricardo wasn't even around. For all she knew, he didn't even know.'

'I understand that, but I didn't give my child away, did I? I've given everything to Louisa. I was always there.'

'You had help. And you weren't alone. Your mother and her friends were always there for you, too. Who was the first person you told?'

'It was Christina. I know. But it doesn't change things. What they did was wrong.'

'Look, I don't have the power to change your mind or make you see things through my lens. You can read into what they've done as much as you want. You can judge their actions, try to figure out their motives. But all I see, all I saw back then was a few scared children. Facing difficult situations, each of them. Three young adults with a lot of love to give that found a way to deal with their problems in the best way they could. And they've stuck together. We all have, because of you. You were the glue that brought all of us together.'

Marina had tears in her eyes, but she didn't want to show them. She wiped her face and spoke as firmly as she could. 'Grandad, I appreciate you trying to help, but I feel the way I feel. I'm not ready to forgive them. Any of them.' She looked at her dining table. 'Are you staying for dinner? Anthony is making his pasta bake.'

'I can't, dear. Ellie has cooked for me. I must go now.'

She gave the old man a hug. For a second, it crossed her mind that had Petra and Christina not done what they had, she wouldn't have known this kind, sweet man as her grandfather. She'd still know him, but it wouldn't have been the same. As soon as he left her house, she broke down in tears. Since the gallery opening, she hadn't cried. She was angry. Her heart had been filled with sorrow and anger. She felt betrayed, cheated on. But after listening to Declan, all she could feel was gratitude. Gratitude and compassion.

Marina thought about Marcus. He could have found other ways of hiding who he was, but he chose to help a friend. He chose to give all his love to her, to raise her as his own. Then she thought about Teresa. She wasn't technically involved in their mess, but stood there by their side. She helped raise Marina, Louisa even. And what about Ines? Imagine having responsibility for kids who weren't your own. She'd been there for them all the way.

Instead of judging, she'd opened her house and her heart to them.

Her mind went back to Declan. He was the most altruistic person she'd ever met; he'd raised Petra mostly by himself. Declan had swallowed his pride and accepted Ellie back, and when his daughter came up with the craziest idea, he didn't belittle, judge or question her. He accepted it and stood firmly by her side. Declan was the best grandfather a little girl could ever ask for. And an amazing great-grandfather for her own children. Some people would say he was weak, a pushover. *I can't think of a stronger man*, Marina thought.

She tried to imagine the pain that Petra had gone through. Turning into a woman without her mother around, having to deal with rejection. And on top of that, finding out she'd never be able to fulfil her dream of being a mother. Marina thought about her own children. She couldn't imagine life without each one of them exactly as they were and having arrived at her life exactly when and as they did.

Finally, she thought about Christina. In the end, she'd decided to keep her. She'd grown her out of her own body — Christina had given her life. Of course she'd considered abortion, especially after how she'd been treated by Ricardo's mother. Marina had considered aborting Louisa, for a minute only, but she had. And she had Christina supporting her, her own mother by her side, and for better or worst Joe was still around. And then she imagined herself in Christina's shoes and realised the magnanimity of her act of giving her own child away to make her best friend happy.

Louisa and Anthony heard her sobs and came to the living room. As Louisa saw her mum sitting on the floor, she sat beside her and laid her head on her lap.

Anthony stood there and waited for Marina to speak first. 'Do you think I'm being too hard on them all?' she finally said.

'This has been hard on you, darling. You're trying to deal with a traumatic situation. Take your time.'

Marina cried all the tears she'd kept inside for the last two months. They then had dinner together. Marina saw Anthony preparing his pasta, Louisa playing with Gabriel and Archie. She thought of Petra — she'd always be her mother.

'I'd do anything to have my mother here, even if it was to be mad at her, scream at her. I want to be able to thank her for everything.'

'She is around, Mum. I can feel she is. She'll always be with us, in our thoughts, in our hearts.' Louisa hugged her mum tightly, followed by Gabriel, Archie and Anthony.

◆ ◆ ◆

It was the first Christmas without Petra. The first where everyone in their big made-up family was apart, different to every year Marina could remember.

Christina was in Rio with Ines, far away from her family. Teresa and Daniel were probably in Hawaii.

Marcus was feeling guilty and miserable, as Marina hadn't spoken to him in a while. Declan and Ellie had decided to stay at home.

'This isn't right. And it's all my fault. I'll fix things, everything. I'll make some phone calls,' Marina announced to Anthony and Louisa as they were having their Christmas dinner. 'Christmas is ruined, but we still have New Year's Eve.'

A couple of days later she went to see Marcus and said she wasn't angry anymore. She paid a visit to Declan and thanked him for helping her see what was in front of her. How love had been the force behind everything, how it had brought all of them together.

She contacted Vanessa and Alex and said she had a plan but needed their help. All the family had to agree.

It was the twenty-ninth of December. After dinner, Louisa was helping her mum tidy up the kitchen and Anthony was putting the two boys to bed when the doorbell rang. Marina ran to the door. 'I'll go. I was waiting for them.'

'Them?' Louisa asked before seeing Alex and Vanessa come through the door.

'Hi niece!' Vanessa teased her.

'What are you guys doing here?' Louisa asked, surprised.

They both ignored her and looked at Marina, saying almost at the same time. 'They're in, all of them. Did you manage to get the tickets?'

'What tickets? What's going on?' Anthony had arrived.

'Louisa, Anthony, pack your bags. We all fly tomorrow night. We're going to Rio.' Marina said with the happiest face anyone had ever seen.

Epilogue

31st *December 1987*

Christina, Petra and Teresa were still trying to come to terms with the decision they'd made and trying to gasp the consequences it would have in their lives.

But they weren't sad or worried; they were happy, hopeful and excited. It was New Year's Eve, and they were going to see the fireworks in Copacabana at midnight. The world-famous event was predicted to be an even greater spectacle with a new attraction that year. A fireworks cascade flowing from the top of a building, a five-star hotel, in front of the beach. Robert, Karishma and Purnima were going to meet them and so were Marcus and his friends.

'Before that, we must go to the beach at sunset while all is still calm. To offer flowers to Iemanjá,' Ines told the girls. 'Robert will drop Karishma here; she wants to come with us. My friends will meet us there and bring the flowers. We should all dress in white.'

'Who's Iemanjá?' asked Christina.

'Iemanjá is the queen of the sea, in the *candomblé*, a religion from Africa. She represents the feminine, protector of mothers and children. We offer flowers and ask for protection, love and other things. It's a beautiful tradition. You'll enjoy it, believe me.'

'I love it already; it sounds like witchcraft, and I've always wanted to be a witch,' Petra said excitedly.

When they arrived at the beach at sunset, the sky was a colourful mixture of blue, pink and orange. The sea was calm, more calm than usual, Teresa said.

Ines's friends were there, all beautifully dressed in white dresses. Petra and Christina were still impressed by how amazing they all looked. The youngest one was in her early forties and the oldest in her late sixties and they all looked incredibly fit.

'I still think your mum's friends drink collagen. Look at how gorgeous they are,' Christina pointed out to Ines.

The women were carrying flowers and each walked into the sea, laying the flowers carefully in the water. Some seemed to be praying with their eyes closed. Others had their arms open with palms turned up as if receiving a blessing. Some went head first into the sea, emerging with an expression on their faces as if they'd been purified, as if all their spiritual bruises had been left out in the sea.

'They look like witches in a coven,' Petra said in awe.

'Yes, they do. A collagen-fuelled coven,' Christina said, smiling.

'That's it! The perfect name for us, our friendship and the family we'll forge,' Teresa said as Ines walked towards them holding little Karishma's hand.

The girl had all colours of flowers in her hands. 'Yellow for prosperity, pink for love, red for passion and white for...' Karishma turned back to Ines.

'For peace. To be at peace with the paths we

choose.' She looked at Petra, Christina and Teresa.

'You've taught her well, Mum.' Teresa said, taking her young stepsister by the hand. 'You're now officially part of our coven.'

'What coven?' Karishma was confused.

'The collagen coven,' Teresa answered proudly as the four of them laid their flowers in the sea. They joined hands and went into the water to receive their blessings.

31st December 2024

'This is the same place, from that New Year's Eve, thirty-seven years ago, isn't it?' Christina asked Ines. 'I remember well. Exactly in front of the building with the green glass on the balconies.'

'Yes, it is. You have a good memory,' said Ines.

'That day is hard to forget. It was then when we named our group the collagen coven. Do you remember?'

'Of course I do. You said we all looked like witches in white, high on collagen or something like that.'

'Yes, something like that.' Christina stared at the horizon. 'Do you mind if I stay on my own for a while?'

'Not at all, dear. Go ahead. I'll meet my friends and bring you some flowers to offer.'

'I'll be here.' Christina walked into the sea, dipping in her toes then her feet until the water was at the middle of her calves.

Christina looked at the beautiful sky, adorned with all shades of colours as she remembered. She felt a spot of sadness in her heart that she was there alone. She missed her family, her children, her friends. She missed Petra, Teresa, Karishma and especially Marina.

But she also felt freer, lighter and more hopeful than she'd ever felt before. The sea wasn't as calm as that day in 1987, but it wasn't too agitated either. It was calm enough for her to stay there or even go further in the water.

Christina felt the presence of someone behind her. She turned back, expecting it would be Ines with the flowers.

It was Marina. Christina brought her hands to her face as her heart was inundated with joy and tears flooded her eyes.

'I'm so sorry.' That was all Christina could say before her voice was lost to her emotion.

'Shh.' Marina approached her and hugged her for the first time knowing that Christina was the woman who had given her life. 'You don't have to apologise for anything.'

'I'm sorry to have lied to you.'

'You did it for love. I can see that clearly now. And to be fair, you've always been there. You never left me. I love you, Christina.'

'I love you too, and I'll never leave you.' Christina hugged Marina as a daughter for the first time.

'I have a surprise for you.' Marina pointed behind Christina. Teresa was there, followed by Karishma with four white flowers in her hand, one for each of them. Christina let out a scream of joy.

'We couldn't leave you alone. Not today. This is our first New Year's Eve without Petra,' said Teresa.

'And by we, she means all of us. The whole coven.' Karishma pointed at a group of people standing in the sand a few metres behind them. All the family was there. Peter, Vanessa, Harry, Margaret. Daniel with Hugo, Patricia, Alan and Alex with Ollie. Robert was holding hands with Purnima. Declan was sitting on a beach chair with Ellie by his side. Anthony and Louisa were playing with Gabriel and Archie as Ines and her friends watched.

Christina noticed that Theo was also there with his mother and David. She looked at Karishma. 'Are you together?'

'Yes. And we're having a baby. It worked this time,' Karishma responded peacefully.

'I've never been so happy.' Christina looked at the family and they waved at her. 'Only one person missing.'

They all lay their flowers in the water, white roses. They were at peace with the paths they'd taken.

'She's here; I can feel her.' Marina held Christina's hand.

Teresa grabbed Karishma's hand and then Marina's with her other hand. 'She is. Pulling her magical invisible strings, as always.'

The four women looked briefly at their family standing by the beach. They looked at each other and smiled before entering the water, feeling blessed.

About the author

The Collagen Coven is the first novel by Ana Paula Vasquez for an adult audience. Ana has published four books for children previously, writing as Paula L. Estrela.

With a background in architecture, Ana has always desired to create, write and publish stories. Self-publishing has been quite a journey but one that brought satisfaction, joy and a great sense of accomplishment. One of Ana's biggest motivations for becoming a writer is to show her children that all dreams can come true with dedication and persistence and that it's never too late to try something new or follow a new path.

Printed in Dunstable, United Kingdom